BENEATH THE SOIL

Recent Titles by Fay Sampson from Severn House

The Suzie Fewings Genealogical Mysteries

IN THE BLOOD
A MALIGNANT HOUSE
THOSE IN PERIL
FATHER UNKNOWN
THE OVERLOOKER
BENEATH THE SOIL

BENEATH THE SOIL

Fay Sampson

This first world edition published 2014
in Great Britain and the USA by
SEVERN HOUSE PUBLISHERS LTD of
19 Cedar Road, Sutton, Surrey, England, SM2 5DA.

British Library Cataloguing in Publication Data

Sampson, Fay author.
  Beneath the soil. – (A Suzie Fewings genealogical mystery; 6)
  1. Fewings, Suzie (Fictitious character)–Fiction.
  2. Murder–Investigation–Fiction. 3. Women
  genealogists–England–Fiction. 4. Detective and mystery
  stories.
  I. Title II. Series
  823.9'14-dc23

ISBN-13: 978-0-7278-8373-5 (cased)

All Severn House titles are printed on acid-free paper.

Severn House Publishers support the Forest Stewardship Council™ [FSC™],
the leading international forest certification organisation. All our titles that
are printed on FSC certified paper carry the FSC logo.

Typeset by Palimpsest Book Production Ltd.,
Falkirk, Stirlingshire, Scotland.
Printed and bound in Great Britain by
TJ International, Padstow, Cornwall.

ONE

'**I** don't believe it!'
Suzie's cry of delighted astonishment burst from the study, where she had settled for an evening's session of family history.

Not long ago, the family history website she subscribed to had added the British Newspaper Archive to its resources. It held huge and potentially exciting possibilities for news of her ancestors, stretching right back to 1710. It would be an enormous job to trawl through it, keying in the names and dates of all her forebears who had lived in the intervening three centuries. So far, she had turned up a few fragments of stories. An ancestor fined for letting his trees overgrow the highway. Obituary notices for another pair of great-great-grandparents. The sad inventory for the sale of a family farm. It all added colour, even if it wasn't sensational.

She hadn't tried it until this evening for her great-great-grandparents Richard and Charlotte Day. Which should she try first? Richard's name? Or Charlotte's? But the latter involved two surnames: her maiden name, Taverner, and her married name, Day.

She took the simpler choice and typed in Richard Day with his birth and death dates.

Two hundred and forty-three entries. He was clearly not the only man with that name. Quickly she scrolled through the abstracts. Most were in the wrong part of the county, or a different occupation.

Suddenly, one name leaped out at her: '*Aggett Cottages*'. Swiftly she checked her files. Yes! St Nectan. That major nineteenth-century move from the country to the edge of the city, after all those centuries of tilling the land: 9 Aggett Cottages.

With growing excitement she struggled to read what came next in the brief extract from the article. The optical character recognition wasn't great. The digitized form of the newsprint came across sadly mangled.

'*Aug 2€, Aggett Cottages. Richard Day, dockqard lakourev, was ^oken by breâfhul cries from the £ouse ne^t door.*'
But the meaning was clear.

She was leaning forward eagerly now. This was better than she had expected. What was the cause of those dreadful cries?

She clicked on VIEW to read the full newspaper entry.

This time, the image of the original newsprint sprang up before her, clearly legible. All she needed to do was to enlarge it. She clicked on the + symbol and watched the highlighted column zoom towards her. Now she could read the whole story.

Richard Day, dockyard labourer, asleep with Charlotte and their children, had been woken by those dreadful cries in the night. Richard had run next door to find his neighbour, Maud Locke, dead on the kitchen floor with her throat cut. There was no sign of her husband.

Suzie sat back, shocked by this unexpected drama.

Hurriedly, she set up a new search for '*Maud Locke*'. Only three hits. First was the article she had already seen. The second reported that Anthony Locke, also a dockyard labourer, had been apprehended at his brother's house and would be sent to the Assizes on trial for murder.

The third recorded his execution by hanging.

Suzie's first instinct was to run into the garden, to share the colourful story with Nick. Her great-great-grandfather, coming across the horrific scene, the woman next door lying in her kitchen in a pool of blood. Gruesome, but the kind of story that was like gold dust to family historians.

Yet now she sat there, imagining the reality. This had happened to real people. To her people. Murderer and victim were a couple like Richard and Charlotte. Living in the same conditions, doing the same work. Subject to the same difficulties and privations. How nearly might what had happened to Anthony and Maud Locke have been the fate of Richard and Charlotte Day? She shivered. Had their children woken in the night? Her great-grandmother Elizabeth Day had been six years old.

She ran off copies, snatched the last sheet from the printer and sped in search of someone to share this with.

Millie had spread her teenage limbs over the flowered cushions of the cane settee in the conservatory. She had been flipping through the pages of a magazine, but let it fall with the amused tolerance that only fifteen-year-old daughters, going on sixteen, can show to their parents.

'Don't tell me. You've discovered that we're descended from Lord Nelson and Emma Hamilton.'

'Well, no. But what would you say to murder?'

Millie swung her feet to the floor. 'Do tell!'

But Suzie stepped past her through the open doors of the conservatory into the summer garden. Nick was mowing the lawn. Suzie knew that this was not a chore, as it would be to her, but a source of satisfaction to his architect's mind to see the stripes of cut grass laid out with geometrical precision.

She waited till he neared the edge of the flower bed and waved the papers at him. She thought how youthful he still looked, with his wavy black hair and shorts, as he switched off the motor and came across the lawn towards her.

Suddenly Suzie felt a little foolish. Was it really right to get so excited over something that had happened a hundred years ago, to someone she was descended from, but whom she had never met?

The smile in Nick's deep blue eyes reassured her. 'Go on, then. What have you found this time?'

'I was searching through the newspaper archives and I found that my great-great-grandparents in St Nectan were living next door to a house where a murder took place. Richard Day heard screams and found the body.'

'Poor man!'

Millie was standing behind Suzie, her face now bright with enthusiasm. 'A real murder! Fantastic!' Then her face stilled. 'Except that it isn't, is it? I mean, like, it *was* real. Great-great-great-granddaddy walking in and finding that. Gross.'

You form a picture of your ancestors in your mind, Suzie thought. And then something else turns up and the picture changes. Richard would never have been the same person after that discovery.

A tiny voice at the edge of her imagination whispered, 'Is there the remotest possibility that Anthony Locke's murdering his wife might have anything to do with Richard living next door?'

She would never know.

'So I suppose we're off to St Nectan today?' Nick looked enquiringly at her over Saturday breakfast. 'See the scene of crime.'

'Well, no, actually.' Suzie stirred honey into her porridge. 'I mean, I *would* like to go back there. Have another look at the house where it happened. But we did that a couple of years ago. Richard and Charlotte's house, I mean. You took some photos. And it's an eighty-mile round trip. I was thinking of something nearer home. Richard Day started out as an agricultural labourer. We've tracked down the farm where he was apprenticed by the Overseers of the Poor when he was eight. We've seen the farm above Moortown where he was working when he met Charlotte. And we know a lot about where her family lived when they moved to the city. But the one place we've never been to is the last farm he was working at, before they took off to St Nectan and he ended up labouring in the city dockyard.'

'Fine. So it's a pub lunch in Moortown. How about the Angel?'

'Great. Then we have to find Saddlers Wood.'

Nick looked up as Tom sauntered into the kitchen. Millie was already pouring herself fruit juice.

'I don't suppose either of you want to come? Fit one more piece into the family jigsaw?'

'No thanks,' Millie sighed. 'Honestly, Mum, can't you think of anything else to do on a Saturday afternoon?'

'Well, actually, yes,' Tom smiled. 'I wouldn't mind a pub lunch and a spot of exploration. Count me in. Is there any more of that porridge?'

Suzie felt a glow of affection as he settled into a place at the table beside her. She couldn't really expect her teenage children to share the same passion for family history. She was lucky that Nick was so willing a companion on these expeditions, driving her to remote villages all over the county, exploring farms and churches where her forebears had worked and worshipped, where they had been baptized, married and buried. But it was a particular joy when one of the children indulged her enthusiasm and came too.

Millie put down the carton of fruit juice. 'Fine. So that's me left on my own.'

'You can usually find plenty to do on a Saturday. Won't you be going into town with Tamara?'

'Not today. She's got to go to a family wedding . . . Oh, all right, then. If Tom's going to go . . .'

'It's not compulsory,' Suzie pointed out.

'Mum, I said, I'm coming.'

They left the Angel after an enjoyable lunch. Millie had said nothing about dieting, and tucked into fish and chips with gusto.

'What now?' Nick asked. 'Is this farm near enough to ditch the car and walk?'

Suzie consulted the map, measuring half miles with her thumb joint. 'Probably not. Saddlers Wood is off the road that goes south out of Moortown. It looks a bit remote. Right at the parish boundary.'

The car took them down the narrow country road. Suzie leaned forward, scanning the fields and woods on the left-hand side.

'There!' she cried. 'You've passed it.'

Nick brought the car to a halt. He reversed to where a cart track led uphill between bramble-grown hedges. A weathered board at the roadside read: Saddlers Wood.

Tom got out of the car. 'I can't see a thing. You say somebody lives up there?'

Some way up the track, the open fields ended. Woods rolled down from the ridge to meet them. The summer foliage was dense with many shades of green.

'Do you want me to drive up the track?' Nick asked.

Suzie hesitated. 'I'm not sure. It's not very welcoming, is it? Not even a surfaced drive. Maybe we'll walk. We'll get more of a feel of the place that way. I'm sure it's the way Richard and Charlotte would have come and gone.'

'Yes, like, I can imagine her having to walk all the way into Moortown to do her shopping,' Millie said. 'And I don't suppose she was much older than me.'

'As a matter of fact,' Suzie said, 'farm girls didn't usually marry young. That was more the upper-class girls, who could afford servants to do the heavy work. Twenty-three was actually a typical age for a young woman to get married. She needed to be fully grown and tough to do her share of the farm work and have half a dozen kids as well.'

They started to walk.

'Lucky there's been no rain for a week,' Nick said, as he negotiated the deep, hard ruts of tractor tyres. 'This will be thick with mud in the winter.'

'If Richard and Charlotte lived here, they'll have been used to walking through mud.'

'They'll have a Land Rover nowadays,' Tom said.

'More importantly, there won't *be* any farm labourers,' Suzie told them as they climbed higher. 'They're a dying breed. It's a big social problem. Farmers these days are working on their own. No one to talk to. Not even the cows and horses there used to be. Their children don't want to stay on the land. And then all the worry of prices not keeping up with costs. There's a real risk of suicide.'

'Cheerful,' said Millie. 'Not exactly your rural idyll.'

As if in answer to their thoughts, a gunshot rang out across the hillside.

TWO

They froze. Tom was the first to laugh.

'As you were. Somebody's shooting pheasants.'

'It's July. It's not the pheasant season,' Suzie said.

'Rabbits, then.'

Suzie relaxed. Tom was right, of course. Shotguns were part of the way of life on a farm. It had just been a startling coincidence that they were talking about the suicide risk for farmers just when that gunshot had shattered the rural peace.

They walked on. They were nearing the edge of the woods. Still there was no sign of human habitation up ahead.

The tree covering closed over them. Their feet sank deeper in the litter of last year's leaves. Suzie began to think she could see a clearing near the brow of the hill.

'How much further?' asked Millie. 'You didn't tell me we were going mountaineering.'

'Nearly there,' Nick said. 'I hope.'

From a narrow path at the side of the track, a man came stumbling hastily. He wore a shapeless green waxed jacket that had seen better days, over muddy brown trousers. His fairish hair looked dishevelled. He was about Nick's age.

But what caught the eyes of the Fewings family was the shotgun clenched in his hand.

He looked startled when he saw them and stopped dead on the path. Though his lean, tightly drawn face was turned towards them, Suzie had the feeling that he hardly saw them.

The Fewings were forced to stop too. They could hardly walk straight past him.

Nick took charge of the situation.

'Hi, there. Are you from Saddlers Wood Barton? I hope we're not trespassing. Just out on a family history quest.'

'My great-great-grandparents,' Suzie supplied. 'Back in the 1850s. They lived here. Well, maybe not at the farm itself. Richard was an agricultural labourer. But we thought maybe there might be a cottage. Somewhere where a farm employee might live?'

The man looked at them blankly. Suzie wondered if he had taken in what they had said.

At last a long shudder ran through him. He seemed to relax a little. He looked down at the shotgun he was holding, almost in surprise. Then he broke it and folded it over his arm.

'Philip Caseley.'

He held out an awkward hand, saw the earth on it and thought better of it. Suzie scolded herself for the start of surprise that there was no blood on it. Farmers were no strangers to dirt and blood.

'Yes, I farm up at Saddlers Wood. For now. My family's been there for generations. And likely as not I'll be the last.'

Suzie wanted to ask him why, but it seemed too intrusive. Nick evidently thought so too.

They stood indecisively. Philip Caseley had made no attempt to answer Suzie's question.

It was Tom who took the initiative. 'Is it OK if we go on?

Take a look around? My mother's a family history nut. Likes to ferret out where they lived, so she can get the whole picture.'

'Yes,' Suzie found her voice. 'Richard Day was a pivotal generation in our family. Before him, they'd been agricultural labourers or husbandmen for centuries, in a fairly small area around here. But he was the one who upped sticks and moved off to the city, or a village on the edge of it. He still worked as a farm labourer at first, but soon he was down at the dockyard, labouring there. Suddenly, we were an urban family. That part of the nineteenth century was a hard time for farming.'

'Like now.' There was bitterness in the brief reply.

'So. It's OK?' Tom turned on his most winning smile.

The man stood back a pace. 'My wife's up at the farm,' he said shortly. 'You can ask her.'

Abruptly, he strode across the track in front of them and disappeared along the path on the other side into the wood.

The Fewings looked at each other.

'Rabbits, did you say?' Millie's voice was high with tension. 'I don't know what he was shooting at, but I don't see why a rabbit should get him that upset.'

'Still.' Tom shrugged. 'We've got the go-ahead. Lead on, Mum.'

Suzie had been right about the clearing. In only a few steps, the view opened out. The farm was sited just under the brow of the hill. Just low enough to be sheltered from the northerly winds, Suzie reflected. The farmhouse and its barns made an L-shape around the yard, with an old covered well in one corner. The cob walls, on their stone base, had been whitewashed, but here and there the raw red earth showed through on the barn. The house was in rather better trim, but the window frames had not been painted for years. The black paint was peeling. Moss grew thick on the battered thatch.

'There's no sign of life,' Suzie said.

No chickens scratched in the yard. There was no contented moan of cows. No one was at work out of doors.

Her words came back to her with an ominous echo she had not intended.

'Oh, come on, then!' Millie stalked up to the front door,

elegantly casual in her jeans and ankle boots. She rapped the heavy knocker.

There was a moment's silence. Then a dog barked frantically. Simultaneously, a door Suzie had not noticed opened at the end of the long building. A woman in a floral wrap-around apron came out, overtaken by a noisy black-and-white collie. She was smaller than Millie. Her pale hair straggled around her shoulders in limp curls, a sad contrast to Millie's white-blonde haircut, yet beneath the apron, her silk shirt and linen skirt looked unexpectedly stylish for this rural setting. Her thin face looked scared.

'Yes?' Her greyish eyes were round with questions.

Suzie felt a sudden desire to protect and comfort her. She stepped forward impulsively. The collie ran forward, barking.

'Mrs Caseley? We met your husband back in the wood.' She could not help but see how the woman started back. 'He said it was all right for us to come on up here and ask you where my great-great-grandparents might have lived in the 1850s. It was in the census that Richard Day was a labourer on the farm here. The address was "Cottage, Saddlers Wood".'

She felt the incongruity of what she was asking. It must seem so remote, so trivial, to whatever this frightened woman in front of her was undergoing. Suzie could not help but think, as she knew all the family must be thinking, of that distraught man who had burst out of the trees clutching a recently fired shotgun in his hand.

The collie quietened under Millie's stroking hand.

Mrs Caseley struggled to get control of herself. She even managed a pale smile.

'You'd better come in, then.'

Suzie met Nick's eyes questioningly.

'If that's all right? We don't want to be a nuisance if it's a bad time.'

But Mrs Caseley had turned her back and was walking towards the half-open door. The Fewings looked at each other and followed.

The kitchen was darker than Suzie had expected. A black Rayburn took up most of one wall. The central table and work surfaces were cluttered with unwashed crockery and pans. Mrs Caseley pushed back her hair from her eyes with a weary hand.

'You'll have to excuse it. I'm behind with things today.'
Why? Suzie wondered.

'Not at all,' she said hastily. 'We should have rung up to ask
if we could come. It wasn't fair to spring ourselves upon you
like this.'

Two steps led up into a living room. Suzie had expected to
find it stuffed with old furniture, handed down through the generations. But it was sparsely furnished, and what there was looked
cheap and modern. With a flash of insight, she wondered how
much of the older stuff might have been sold off to pay bills.
Probably what used to be here would have acquired antique
status, snapped up to furnish the cottages and converted barns
that people with higher incomes bought as second homes.

A sadness came over her as she looked around her. A way of
life was dying. The county where her own ancestors had lived
and worked for so long was being taken over by incomers, who
thought of it only as picture-postcard prettiness, or a series of
quaint photographs in a calendar they would send to relatives
back in the city.

The others had fallen quiet.

'Sit yourselves down,' Mrs Caseley told them, with an effort
at hospitality. 'I'll make you some tea.'

'No, really,' Suzie protested. 'You don't need to bother. We
only wanted to ask you whether there are any cottages on the
farm. Somewhere a married labourer might have lived and brought
up his family.'

But Mrs Caseley was already retreating into the kitchen.

The Fewings sat on the hard-cushioned furniture looking at
each other in some embarrassment.

Suzie whispered to the children, 'If she offers you something
to eat, say no, thank you.'

The picture was running through her mind of Philip Caseley,
agitated, with the gun in his hand. How strained was this marriage,
the two of them all alone up here, with money tight?

She need not have worried. Mrs Caseley came back with a
tray set with flowered cups and saucers of strong tea. Suzie was
relieved to see that she hadn't opened a packet of biscuits in their
honour.

She had thought that the woman hadn't heard her question as

she left the room, but the farmer's wife said as she set down the tray, 'Well, no. I can't say as there are any cottages standing on the farm. If there were, I've no doubt Phil would have had them done up and sold them off. Lord knows we need the money. But there are some broken-down walls back in the woods. Cob needs to keep its hat and boots on. If you don't put a roof on it and keep it out of the wet, it'll sink back into the earth it was got from.'

Suzie felt a thrill of excitement. The ruins of a cottage might not look much now, but she knew if she saw it, her imagination could supply the picture of what it had once been. She would be able to see Richard setting out to work on the farm in the early morning; Charlotte in her apron, feeding the chickens, making butter, scrubbing floors. And the children. How many of them were there? Six, she thought, before they packed up their belongings and took the long journey down to the coast and the dockyard town.

She jerked back to the present.

'Where can we find these ruins?' Nick was saying. 'Is it OK if we go looking in the woods? Your husband had been out shooting when we met him. We wouldn't want to get mistaken for a fox, or whatever it was he was after.'

The spoon rattled against the cup Mrs Caseley was handing to Millie.

'You heard that, did you?' There was a moment of silence. 'No. You've nothing to worry about. Go back down the track until you see a smaller path going off to your left. It'll be a couple of hundred yards down there. I hope you're not wearing your best clothes. Likely as not it'll be grown over with brambles. Phil and me, we've not much call to go down there.'

'Do you come from Moortown yourself?' Suzie asked. 'I've got quite a few ancestors there. We might be related.'

'I was Eileen Taverner before I was married. On my mother's side it was the Hutchings. I can't say as I know much about them before Granddad and Granny Hutchings. They kept a greengrocer's shop. How far back they went, I couldn't tell you.'

'I've got Taverners on my family tree! Charlotte Day's father was a Taverner. He was a stonemason, out near the tollgate on the east road.'

She had hoped Eileen Caseley might react with enthusiasm, and they could have enjoyed speculating about how close their relationship really was. But the woman's pale, tired face showed no reaction. The fear all the Fewings had sensed in the farmyard had faded, leaving a dull apathy. Suzie shivered. How nearly might this have been her own experience?

Yet why was Eileen Caseley dressed so smartly this Saturday afternoon on the farm? And where *had* Philip Caseley been when he fired that gun?

Nick got to his feet. 'You've been really hospitable, considering we just walked in on you off the street. But we ought to let you get back to whatever you were doing when we turned up. So it's back down the track and turn left?'

'You'll see it. There's not many footpaths through those woods.'

She did not try to detain them. Suzie sensed her relief that they were going.

She gave Eileen her warmest smile. 'I'm really glad to have met you. I spend so much time hunting up my ancestors from the past. And now and then I stumble across a relation I didn't know about who's alive today. I'm going to have to get my charts out and see if I can find where we fit together.'

'I wouldn't like to go poking around in the past too much. You never know what you might find.'

Mrs Casely watched them walk through her kitchen. But she did not respond to their thanks and farewells.

'Well!' Millie exploded, when they were safely across the yard. 'Not exactly a bundle of fun, was she?'

'Walk in her shoes,' Tom said unexpectedly. 'How would you like to live out here, with precious little money, and only two of you to run all this?'

'It would give me the creeps. Do you suppose they have any children?'

'Well, I didn't see any Lego on the floor. No homework books on the kitchen table or wacky DVDs in the living room. Guess, if they have, they've grown up and left.'

'If it was me, I couldn't wait to get away from this place. All these trees around it – I'd feel smothered.'

'It occurs to me,' Nick said. 'That path she told us to take. It's the one Philip Caseley went down when he left us.'

'So? We'd better talk amongst ourselves while we walk along it,' Tom laughed. 'Let him know it's humans coming and we're not something for the pot.'

They found the footpath without difficulty. Mrs Caseley had been right about the brambles. Nick pushed them aside where they arched over the path through the trees, but they sprang back behind them.

The way led downhill, becoming softer underfoot. Presently sunlight glinted through the branches.

Suzie stopped and gave a cry of delight. 'This has to be it!'

The mounds of red-brown earth, stippled with grit and straw, had almost melted back into the soil they had been dug from. They were cloaked with ivy. Around them, spears of fireweed flamed with bright pink flowers. Nettles spread a less welcoming blanket. Here and there, young trees were beginning to grow back. A little stream ran through the combe below.

'At least she didn't have far to carry water,' Millie observed. 'Could be worse.'

A sudden snap made them start. Suzie was instantly aware how much her nerves were still on edge. They stood alert, listening.

'Philip Caseley?' Nick asked. He raised his voice to call. 'Hullo, there!'

Nothing answered him out of the darkness of the woods around them.

'Probably just a squirrel landing on a dead branch,' he said.

'Or a deer,' Tom added. 'There must be some in this wood.'

Suzie said nothing. The hairs on her arms prickled. She had an uncomfortable feeling that they were being watched. It was silly. She had not yet recovered from the shock of that sudden gunshot. But if Philip Caseley was here, there was no reason for him not to show himself, as he had before.

Nick let out his breath. Then he got out his camera. 'I expect you want me to do the usual?'

He moved around the ruins. Suzie could tell he was enjoying the play of sunshine on the mellow cob and the colourful fireweed. More photographs to enliven her files on the Day family.

She stroked the rough cob. What a contrast it must have been to move from this rural backwater, labouring on the red soil, working with the cows and other animals at Saddlers Wood Barton, to St Nectan on the edge of the smoke-hung Victorian city, and the industrial work of a dockyard labourer. Had he been happy with a bigger pay packet at the end of the week? Or did his heart ache for the peace of these woods and the fields he had left behind?

Nick had strolled away and was turning his lens on the stream and woods beyond. Tom went to join him, while Millie stretched out on the grass in the sunshine.

'All done.' Nick stowed his camera away at last. 'Have you had enough?'

'I think so.' Suzie looked around regretfully. She had been filing away in her imagination Charlotte's life here with her children. Had she been glad of the less lonely life in a street of terraced houses, with plenty of neighbours to turn to?

How did Eileen Caseley cope on her own?

They made their way on down the track towards the spot at the side of the road where they had left their car.

'Hey up!' Tom cried, as they came in sight of it. 'Looks like we weren't the only ones up here this afternoon.'

A small green car was pulling out from the grass verge some way ahead of their own. It was only a moment before it was hidden by the hedges.

'So,' Millie said, stopping dead on the path. 'It wasn't a squirrel or a deer. There *was* someone else in the woods with us.'

THREE

'Should we phone the police?'

Suzie was looking through the windscreen, but the rich tapestry of summer woods and meadows rolled past her unseen. She was seeing the round, scared eyes of Eileen Caseley in the farmyard; her husband plunging out of the trees with a dazed expression and his shotgun clenched in his hand.

'Come off it, Mum!' Tom exploded from the back seat. 'We heard a shot and saw a farmer with a gun. Big deal!'

'Didn't you see his eyes, though?' Millie protested. 'It was like he wasn't really there.'

'You've been watching too many zombie films.'

'Tom's right,' Nick said. 'We startled him. I don't suppose he gets many visitors, up there in the woods. Once he realized why we were there, he was perfectly civil. He even told us to go on up and talk to his wife. He's hardly likely to have done that if he's just come away from a spot of domestic violence. Besides, she certainly wasn't suffering from gunshot wounds when we saw her.'

'No, I suppose not,' Suzie admitted reluctantly. 'But something had frightened her. What else could it be? Did you know that two women a week are killed by their ex or current partner? How many of those would have been saved if someone had stepped in earlier? I take your point that the police are hardly likely to take this seriously, but at least if we put down a marker and somebody else says the same, they're more likely to pay attention to that next call.'

'I leave that to you,' Nick said. 'Like Tom says, I'd feel a bit of a fool, reporting a farmer for firing a shotgun in his own woods.'

'We don't know it *was* in the woods,' Millie argued. 'The house wasn't that far from where we met him.'

An uneasy silence fell over the car. Suzie found her pleasure in discovering the ruined cottage where her great-great-grandparents very probably lived had faded into the background, replaced by more urgent present-day worries.

Nick was out in the garden, weeding the blaze of colour in the flower beds. Tom and Millie had gone out for the evening with their teenage friends. Suzie, as so often, found herself drawn back into the study to write up her afternoon's foraging into family history, while it was still fresh in her imagination.

She cast a glance at the shoulder bag she had dropped on a chair. Should she take out her phone and call the police? She had been too busy preparing a meal to do it when they got home.

But several hours had passed since then. The alarm she had

felt at Saddlers Wood Barton was fading. It was easier to see it from Tom and Nick's point of view. There was no hope that the police would take her seriously. A farmer with a shotgun; a wife who looked alarmed when unexpected visitors called, but who had rallied round and entertained them with cups of tea? It sounded unconvincing, even to herself.

There was just that sharp unease, gnawing away in the corner of her mind.

She turned away and switched on the computer with an air of resolve.

She updated the file on the Day family with a description of the remains of the cottage and its woodland setting. Had the buildings in Saddlers Wood been so lost amongst its oaks and hazels then? Later, she would add Nick's photographs.

She closed the file. What now? Should she go out and join Nick in the garden? See if there was anything watchable on television?

She flicked through the printed sheets covering Richard and Charlotte's lives. Charlotte had outlived Richard, dying in 1913.

1913. An idea flashed through her mind. She had followed up her great-grandparents in the 1911 census, released only three years ago. But it had not occurred to her until now that her great-great-grandmother would still have been alive. A secret smile started to grow.

Charlotte Day. She set to work.

The eager smile faded. A puzzled frown took its place.

An hour later she was holding out her results to Nick, where he sat enjoying a beer at the patio table.

'Result!'

Millie had just come in from her evening out.

'Go on, Mum. What is it this time?'

'Do you remember Charlotte Day? She was my great-great-grandmother. The one whose husband discovered that murder.'

'Don't tell me. She did it.'

'Well, no. It's a bit less dramatic than that. But still . . . I was remembering the time when Dad and I went looking for the church at St Nectan, on the outskirts of the city, where my great-grandmother grew up. I was searching for family graves in the churchyard, and expecting to find quite humble ones, buried under grass and ivy. But there beside the path was this red granite tombstone, with a railing round it, and on it were the names of my great-great-grandparents, Richard and Charlotte Day, and two of their sons.'

'Yes,' Nick agreed. 'I took a photo of it for you. So?'

'Well, the odd thing was that I've never been able to find a record of Charlotte's death and burial, even though her name was on that grave. I found Richard's, but not hers. I hunted through the St Nectan burial register, and tried the GRO death registrations, and Charlotte Day didn't show up. I've just discovered why.' She paused for dramatic effect.

Millie perched on the edge of a chair and brushed back her blonde hair. Tom had appeared behind her, still spruced up for wherever his evening had taken him.

'Shoot,' he said, with that affectionate smile in his blue eyes, so like his father's.

'I've just checked out the 1911 census. I'd done it for my grandparents and great-grandparents, but I'd forgotten Charlotte would still be alive then. And guess what? She's there, but she's not Charlotte Day.'

Nick frowned. 'You're not making sense, love.'

'She's in that census, but she's down as Charlotte Churchward. She must have remarried in her seventies, after Richard died. Yet her name's still carved on that tombstone as Charlotte Day.'

'Slow down, Mum,' Millie said. 'How do you know it's the same woman, if the other name's on the grave?'

'The census gives her age, which is the same as Charlotte Day's. She's living only a few streets away from where Richard and Charlotte lived in the 1901 census. And she was born in Moortown, just like Charlotte Day. Moortown's only a small place. It's thirty miles away from St Nectan, in the middle of the county. How many Charlottes are there going to be, born in Moortown in the same year and moving to end their days in St Nectan, also in the same year? And once I'd got her new name, I found her marriage record easily. Charlotte Day, widow, to Stanley Churchward, widower.'

'I think I'm with you.' A slow smile spread over Tom's face, ending in a burst of laughter. 'You mean, that grand tombstone was put up by Richard and Charlotte's children, and they disapproved of their mum taking off in her seventies and shacking up with this Churchward guy. So they carve her name on their father's headstone with *his* surname . . . well, *their* surname. They want to cut this Churchward marriage out of the record. I like it!'

Millie swung her long legs. 'So great-great-granny shocked the children by having a last fling with her geriatric boyfriend.'

Suzie coloured. 'Well, something like that. Mind you, it probably wasn't as romantic as all that. I expect Stanley Churchward just wanted someone to cook his dinner and darn his socks.'

Millie tapped her fingers on the patio table. Her grey eyes were thoughtful. 'It just shows. That gravestone. You can't always believe the evidence in front of you, can you?'

Suzie had been glowing with the excitement of an unexpected discovery. But Millie's words placed a cold hand over her heart she could not explain.

She walked slowly back to the study.

That scene in the woods this afternoon had been disturbing, but she knew next to nothing about the people concerned. Did she have the right to meddle with the Caseleys' lives?

She had not understood as much as she thought she did about Charlotte Day when she had stood by her tombstone two years ago.

Then she thought of that murder committed in the house next door to the Days. Could Richard and Charlotte have done anything to prevent it? Could *she* keep silent about what she had seen today, even if she had got it wrong?

In a moment of swift decision, she picked up her shoulder bag, took out her phone and dialled 101, the police non-emergency number.

'It's . . . Look, I know it doesn't sound much. But it's something I think you ought to know. We were up in Saddlers Wood outside Moortown this afternoon. We were on our way to Saddlers Wood Barton when we heard a gunshot. And then the farmer, Philip Caseley, came out of the trees. He was carrying a shotgun, but it wasn't broken over his arm. He must just have fired it. He looked . . . well, distraught. And when we went on up to the farm, his wife came out of the house looking really frightened . . . Yes, I know. It sounds a bit lame . . . Yes, I do realize you couldn't do anything about it without more to go on . . . Well, maybe there is an innocent explanation, but you needed to have been there. *Something* had scared her. I wouldn't want to think – if anything happened – that I hadn't said anything . . . Yes, thank you. Yes, if one of your officers happened to be passing, maybe to talk about farm security? I'd just feel happier.'

She ended the call and put the phone down. She was left with a feeling of anticlimax. The sergeant she had talked to had not been unsympathetic, but she had hardly needed him to tell her that a scared expression on a woman's face was hardly evidence enough to act on. No crime had been committed, or none that they had witnessed.

She turned back to the desk. The three printouts about Maud Locke's murder lay beside the computer. That first excitement of discovery had faded. Soberly, she put them back in her file.

FOUR

The evening sun fell warmly on the garden between the shadows of the trees.

'I was thinking of making this bank into a rock garden with a waterfall. What do you think?' Nick appealed to Suzie.

'You've a better eye for garden design than I have. It sounds lovely.'

'Mum! Dad!' Millie's voice shrilled from the conservatory windows.

Nick and Suzie looked at each other in sudden alarm. Nick went loping across the lawn. Suzie hurried after him.

'Where's the fire?' Nick called.

'It's the telly. Local news.' Millie's usually pale face blazed with excitement. 'He's shot her.'

'Who? Shot whom?'

Millie motioned wordlessly at the screen.

A reporter was talking to camera, in front of a scene that struck Suzie as vaguely familiar, a backdrop of woods climbing the hill behind him. Now police tape barred the track, but beyond it she could glimpse a whitewashed farmhouse and the patchy white and red of a dilapidated barn.

'Saddlers Wood Barton!' she breathed. 'No!'

'. . . The shocking find was discovered by a delivery van driver. The police will only say that a forty-five-year-old man is in custody, helping them with their enquiries. But local people believe it to be the dead woman's husband, Philip Caseley. As you can see, Thelma, this is a remote spot. There are unlikely to be witnesses. But a police forensics team are examining the scene of the killing as I speak. My information, unofficially, is that Mrs Caseley was shot in the chest, but the police have not confirmed that. Inspector Tony Battershill will be making a statement to the press later this evening. This is Roger Thorverton for "Evening Southwest".'

'Dear God! That poor woman!' Suzie whispered.

'It's her, isn't it?' Millie said as the cameras returned to the studio. 'That woman we met. The one who gave us tea – what? – three days ago? And now she's dead. And we met the murderer. He even had the gun.'

'They've taken him in for questioning. We don't even know if they've arrested him, still less charged him with murdering her.'

'Come on, Suzie! You were the one who wanted to report it to the police,' Nick protested.

'I did report it.' Suzie's voice came quietly.

'*What?*'

'Saturday evening. I was thinking about that newspaper report, and my Richard Day finding the woman next door with her throat cut. And suddenly I thought, what if Mrs Caseley really is in danger, and I've done nothing? So I rang them. Of course, it was like you said it would be. They couldn't do anything just because I'd seen a farmer with a gun and a woman who looked upset. I didn't really think they would. Only . . . he was actually more sympathetic than I expected. Said there were all sorts of reasons why the police might call at a farm. Crime prevention against thefts of animals or machinery, that sort of thing. He could ask an officer to look out for anything suspicious.'

'I wonder if they did,' Millie said.

The front door opened and slammed. Tom breezed into the conservatory where the three of them were standing. As usual, he seemed to fill more of the space with his personality than his lean frame warranted.

His deep blue eyes were ablaze as he ran his hand through his unruly black hair.

'Have you heard the news?' he cried. 'Yes, I can see you have. How's that for a turn up for the books? I was over at Dave's and we saw this newsflash on the web. Of course, the moment I saw Saddlers Wood, I knew who they had to be talking about. They've arrested her husband.'

'I'm afraid it was inevitable,' Nick said. 'It's hardly likely to be anyone else.'

'Oh, no? Haven't you forgotten something? I bet the police don't know there was somebody else in those woods on Saturday afternoon. Somebody who didn't want us to see him.'

The three of them stared at him.

'What are you suggesting?' Nick asked. 'That whoever parked that green car along the road from ours, and drove away ahead of us, had something to do with this?'

'I'm not saying it's an open-and-shut case. That Caseley guy was upset about something. And his wife was scared. But that doesn't have to mean it was just between the two of them. Mum, you thought somebody was watching us down by that ruined cottage.'

'We heard a noise. But it could have been anything.' She frowned, trying to remember. 'In the end, the rest of you assumed it must be an animal. Until we saw that car. Then we thought it might have been someone out walking.'

'But if it was some innocent hiker, out for a walk in the woods, why stay hidden?' Tom insisted. 'We had a clear view of the footpath, and there was no one on it.'

'Philip Caseley went down that path after he left us.' Nick was frowning too, as he struggled to piece together the fleeting impressions from three days ago.

'Maybe he was meeting someone,' Millie suggested.

'Or maybe he was the one who made that noise in the wood. The one I felt watching us,' Suzie countered.

'Whatever it was, I reckon someone needs to get on to the

police and tell them there may be someone else in the picture they don't know about.'

The Fewings looked at each other.

'Did you mention that when you rang them?' Nick asked Suzie.

She shook her head.

'I'll do it,' Nick said, and strode off towards the phone.

He returned a few minutes later. 'Stand by your beds. They're sending someone round to question us.'

DC Pauline Godden looked up at them over her notes. Suzie had an uncomfortable feeling that what had seemed to Tom to be a great revelation had sounded rather more thin when put down in black and white. A Saturday afternoon in an attractive stretch of countryside. A footpath through Saddlers Wood. A car whose occupant, or occupants, might or might not have gone for a walk in those woods, and who might or might not have met Philip Caseley. Someone who might or might not have had enough power over the Caseleys to upset them. Who might – and here it sounded even more unlikely – have had a reason to shoot Eileen.

Nick signed the statement.

'Will you follow it up?' Tom asked. 'Look for evidence of who was around that ruined cottage?'

'I'm afraid I can't discuss that.'

DC Godden thanked them and left.

'It probably was her husband, wasn't it?' The flush of excitement had left Millie's cheeks. 'The man we met?'

'It's too early to say,' Suzie said unhappily. 'It still seems the most obvious answer, yes.'

FIVE

On Wednesday, Suzie was tidying away the lunch things. Nick was at work; Millie was out with friends, enjoying the freedom of the summer holiday; Tom had gone upstairs. Suzie had done her stint at the charity office in the morning. She contemplated an afternoon of housework with no great enthusiasm. Perhaps she could go to the Record Office instead and pursue some more family history. But, for the moment, there was nothing she could think of that she needed to look up.

She heard steps on the stairs. Looking along the passage, she saw Tom making for the front door carrying a knapsack. There was nothing unusual about that. Why shouldn't he be off to his mate's in the university vacation? But there was something about the quiet, almost furtive way he moved which aroused her suspicions. Her nineteen-year-old son usually exploded with energy, leaving everyone else rocking in the wake of his passing.

With sudden misgiving, she put down the bread board and hurried to intercept him at the front door.

'Where are you going?'

'Ah!' The smile was a shade too broad. She steeled herself against the beguiling dazzle of his blue eyes. 'Just thought I fancied a trip out into the country. I should be back for tea.'

'A trip into the country.' Suzie repeated his words, her voice heavy with suspicion. 'And how are you planning to get there without a car?'

'Dave thinks he can wangle his mother's car. If not, there's a bus to Moortown . . . every hour.' His voice died. She saw the quick flush which told her he had not meant to give her that piece of information.

'Moortown?' Her question rose in disbelief. 'And what would you two want to be doing in Moortown the day after we hear about that murder?'

'Come on, Mum. You know the Bill aren't going to take us seriously about a branch cracking in the wood. I thought there might be something more. That guy, whoever he was, might have left some evidence.'

'What guy? You mean that car we saw? You don't know anything about him. It might not be a he. It was probably nothing to do with the Caseleys.'

'OK. So we don't find anything. We have a walk in the woods. Fine.'

'What if the police are still there? They won't let you through.'

'I wasn't thinking of charging up to the house. I'm not stupid. It was what was going on around that old cottage that interests

me. Eileen Caseley said no one used that path now. But we saw
Philip heading off down it.'

'He was out shooting. In his own wood.'

'So? Look, Mum, I've got to go.'

'I'm coming with you.'

On a sudden impulse, she ran upstairs. It took her only minutes
to throw on a pair of jeans and ankle boots. As she sped back
down, she feared that Tom would have gone. But he stood waiting
by the front door with an amused expression on his face.

'I rang Dave. The car's not on. We may have to run to get
that bus.'

'I'm with you.'

They dashed down the avenue towards the main road. Dave
was waiting at the bus stop. He was a plumpish, gangling lad
with ginger hair, with a suggestion of apology in the stoop of
his shoulders.

'Hi,' he greeted Tom. His eyes went sideways to Suzie questioningly. 'Hi, Suzie.'

'Change of plan,' Tom said with an air of confidence. 'I brought
her along as cover. If we run into police in the woods or anything,
she'll make it sound more plausible than a couple of teenage
layabouts like us.'

'Oh, sure.' Dave did not sound entirely convinced.

The bus came. Suzie settled into a seat in front of the boys and
watched the scenery roll by. She had hardly had time to think
about what she was doing and now she feared that it was a wild
goose chase. What possible evidence could they find in Saddlers
Wood? Worse still, they might be trampling over subtle signs
which forensics would need if they really did follow up on the
Fewings' report.

She thought of the run-down farmhouse, the sparsely furnished
living room, the absence of farmyard sounds. But surely there
must be animals somewhere? She thought she remembered seeing
sheep in the fields below the woods. Who would be looking after
them now, with Eileen dead and Philip Caseley in prison,
supposing he *was* still in custody?

She recalled a newspaper advertisement she'd found in the
online archives for a farm sale in the nineteenth century. Is that

what would happen to Saddlers Wood Barton? Generations of family tradition would be ended if the farm was put up for auction.

But would it be? The Caseleys had looked about the same age as Nick and Suzie, perhaps younger, though Eileen's careworn face had made it hard to tell. There had been no sign of children in the house, but there might be grown-up sons or daughters. Perhaps one of them might come back to farm at Saddlers Wood.

Suddenly she thought of the awfulness of what those children must be experiencing, if there were any. Their mother shot dead. Their father the prime suspect for the murder.

Too late, she wished she had just stayed at home and prayed for them. What possible good could it do to revisit the scene?

Behind her, Tom and Dave were discussing their plans with all the enthusiasm of healthy teenagers.

The bus rolled to a stop in the market square at Moortown. Suzie rose to get off. Tom reached over the seat back and grabbed her.

'Hang on. Next stop's not far from where we parked the car.'

Of course. Tom would have checked it out on the internet. She subsided into her seat and watched new passengers board the bus.

It stopped again at a crossroads Suzie half recognized. There was a cluster of houses and then the lane that led south past Saddlers Wood. She followed the boys off the bus.

'What are you planning to do?' she asked them.

'Take a recce first. If the coast's clear, we walk up the track like we did on Saturday, and take the path to the cottage. If the Bill are around, we find a back way up through the woods.'

They set off along the lane.

Suzie's sense of misgiving grew. How was she going to explain to Nick that she had not only failed to dissuade Tom from this hare-brained scheme, but had actually taken part in it?

But as she walked, the rhythm of her boots beat out a more defiant message. Eileen Caseley had met a terrible death. If there was the slightest chance that her husband was not responsible, then they owed it to her, and to her children, to find the truth.

There was no one at the foot of the track, where they had left their car at the weekend.

'No police tape,' Tom said. 'Guess we're good to go on up.'

'It may be different at the farmhouse,' said Suzie.

'We weren't planning on making a social call, were we? It's that footpath I'm interested in.'

There had been rain since their last visit. The mud was softer underfoot.

Suzie looked ahead over the hedge banks. She had been right. There were sheep grazing in the fields.

'I wonder who's looking after them? Those sheep.'

'How much looking after do sheep need?' Dave asked.

'I'm not sure. It's summer, so they probably don't want much in the way of extra food, but somebody needs to keep an eye on them. See if there's anything wrong with one of them. Decide when to take them to market. Move them to another field when they've grazed this one.'

'I wonder whose responsibility it is,' Tom said. 'I can't see the Bill knowing much about sheep management.'

'There may be family.'

'If there are, they've already cleared off, haven't they? Didn't want to stay down on the farm. I can't see why they should want to come back, especially after this.'

'Might be different,' volunteered Dave, 'if it's their own now.'

'It would have to go through probate,' said Suzie. 'I'm not sure how long that takes. Meanwhile, there are a couple of dozen sheep here, and who knows how many others elsewhere.'

'And the collie,' Tom said. 'Don't forget the dog.'

Suzie pondered the implications of sudden death as she climbed. She and Nick had made their will, but how much were they really prepared for the consequences of unexpected loss? They'd made provision for Nick's brother to act as guardian to the kids. Of course, that would only apply to Millie now. Tom was an adult, incredible though that seemed. She thought of the possibility that both she and Nick might die in a car crash or a terrorist bomb attack, and shivered.

She hardly noticed the grind of an engine behind them, until Tom cried, 'Hey up! We've got company. Guess the Bill's finally caught up with us.'

But when the three of them turned, it was a green Land

Rover, not a police vehicle, rocking its way over the ruts towards them. They moved aside, but the vehicle drew to a halt beside them.

A woman leaned out of the driver's window. She had a mop of tousled hair and a broad, ruddy face. It must normally have given her a cheerful air, but today its lines were downturned in concern.

'You're not on the way to see Eileen, are you? Mrs Caseley?'

'No. We . . .' Suzie struggled to find a plausible explanation for their presence.

'Only, I don't know if you've heard, but there's been a dreadful . . . I was going to say accident. I hope to God that's what it was. But the police have got it into their heads that Philip killed her. Now why would he want to do a thing like that? I know times are hard – it's the same for all of us – but we have to keep muddling on, don't we?'

'Yes, I heard about the mur— Mrs Caseley's death. It's terrible, isn't it? We were only talking to her on Saturday.'

'You know her? You're friends?' The woman looked curiously from one to the other.

'Not exactly. We just came up here checking out my family history. I had folk who worked on this farm.'

It was true, but it sounded rather thin, put like that.

The woman frowned. 'You're not from the press, are you? Lord knows we've had them swarming all over the place, asking questions they've no business to.'

'No. Certainly not.' Suzie had forgotten that such a violent death would draw journalists and press photographers like wasps around a jam pot. She wondered if they were camped out around the farm ahead, or busy doing the rounds of the neighbouring farms and the people in Moortown, nosing out what they could about the Caseleys.

'You won't get much further,' the woman said. 'The police have cordoned off the farm. Goodness knows what they think they'll find, now they've taken her away. You'll have to excuse me. I need to get on. I've all the Caseleys' stock to see to, never mind my own. No rest for the wicked.'

'Isn't there any family who could come and take over?'

'There's a son in Australia, got thousands of sheep on a ranch there. He's on his way. But I can't see him coming back to live at Saddlers Wood, can you? Farming's a mug's game here these days. No, it'll be up for sale. Do us a favour, love, would you? Nip up and open that gate for me. Save me getting out.'

Suzie assumed she was addressing one of the boys. She looked round. The track behind her was empty.

She tried to hide her surprise as she darted ahead to the gate in the hedge and opened it wide. The Land Rover drove through. As it passed her, she saw sitting in the passenger seat a black-and-white collie dog, very like the one Millie had patted in the farmyard.

She closed the gate and watched the woman and the dog get out. Then she turned back to the cart track. Dave and Tom had gone. She was quite alone.

As she started up the track again, she was startled to see how close she had come to the farm. Ahead of her she could clearly make out the barrier of police tape across the path, and the sentinel figure of a tall policeman.

She stopped, uncertain. It was only a short distance to where the footpath crossed this wider track. If she turned off along it, the officer would certainly see her. Would he challenge her, call her back to account for herself? She wondered if Tom and Dave had gone that way, but, knowing Tom, he had probably melted into the trees lower down and joined the footpath more stealthily.

She felt the tension in her throat. But Tom had seized upon the unexpected offer of her company with a readiness that had surprised her. A middle-aged, middle-class, apparently responsible woman. He had relied on her to provide a plausible cover for their intrusion into these woods at such a time. Suzie would not arouse the instant suspicion that a pair of teenage students might.

She racked her brains to think of a convincing reason why she might be here, without resorting to the sort of conspiracy theory which was beginning to sound hollow even in her own ears.

What had they really seen, anyway? A car driving away.

She walked on, trying to appear more confident than she felt. At the crossing of the ways she paused. It was too far away to read the police officer's expression, but she knew that he was watching her. With swift determination she turned right and began to make her way along the narrower path. No voice cried after her. She wondered what the tall policeman was thinking.

It was a relief to let the summer foliage fold itself about her. She even welcomed the brambles that reached long, thorny arms across the path. Each one was another barrier against anyone following her. She could see the prints of Tom and Dave's passage in the soft earth. There were other, differently booted treads among them. If they were Philip Caseley's, he had come along this apparently neglected path several times recently.

She kept expecting to see the boys ahead of her. The path dipped down the hillside to the brighter clearing where the crumbled cottage stood. She felt that same odd lift of her spirits. To her twenty-first-century eye it was an idyllic spot, bright with sunlit flowers, and musical with the liquid crooning of the little brook just below. A blackbird carolled from a rowan tree.

But the clearing was deserted.

Suzie stopped, puzzled. She had been so sure she would catch up with them here.

Then it struck her. Of course. It was here that they had all been startled by that sudden crack among the trees. Not a gunshot this time. The sound of a branch breaking. She hadn't really believed Nick's idea that it might be a squirrel landing on a rotten bough. They had all thought a piece of wood had snapped under someone's foot. Suzie felt herself grow chillier as she remembered that insistent sense that someone was watching her.

Tom and Dave must have ventured into the thicker tree cover around the clearing to look for signs that someone else had been there.

Why? What would that prove? This wasn't a public footpath, but anyone with a map might have chosen to come for a walk here.

A little nagging voice in her mind objected: but wouldn't they have followed the footpath, or been investigating the ruins, like the Fewings? Why would they be hiding among the denser growth, as if they didn't want to be seen?

Perhaps whoever it was had gone off the path in search of an errant dog. But surely they would have heard him calling for the animal? Or her.

The silence mocked her.

*   *   *

More uneasy now, she decided she had no choice but to follow the path further on.

The way sloped on down the hillside. The trees were starting to thin out now. She was beginning to glimpse green fields between the branches. Even the scuttle of cars along a road.

Then she heard it, and breathed a sigh of relief. The sound of voices. It was too far away to be sure, but it must be Tom and Dave. She hurried forward.

The boys were standing on a slope of grass and bracken. Occasional saplings speared their way up through the peaty soil. Tom and Dave were wandering around, picking their way cautiously. They had their heads down, surveying the ground at their feet.

Suzie came out of the trees and stood watching them for several moments, trying to understand what they were doing. Then Dave lifted his head and saw her.

'Hi, Suzie. Come and look at this.'

She moved forward slowly. She was not sure what she was supposed to be seeing. But as she bent her head to watch the ground she was walking over she stopped dead. When she looked up, Tom was watching her intently. He smiled, not with laughter, but with a grave excitement.

'You can see it, can't you? Don't come too far. We don't want to trample all over the evidence. Somebody's been here. Well, not just somebody. I'd say there were more than one of them. Look.'

She followed his gesturing hand. Tom was right. All around her, over a wide area, the grass had been trampled, the young bracken crushed. A little way away from her, something glinted against the dark soil, half hidden by the bracken fronds. She walked carefully to retrieve it: a thick silvery nail about ten centimetres long with a slightly domed head. She bent to decipher the lettering around it.

Tom was at her side in an instant. 'What have you got there? Let's see it.' He took the nail from her. 'Got it! See what it says? SURVEY POINT. So that's what they've been up to. Someone's been up here surveying this area.'

Suzie snapped out of her mood of absorbed fascination. 'So? What's that supposed to mean? He could be selling the land off for housing. They're obviously hard up.'

Tom shrugged exaggeratedly. His blue eyes were sparkling now. 'Only that Mrs Caseley wasn't being entirely accurate when she said no one came down this path nowadays. Something's certainly been going on here.'

'She may have been right,' Dave called from a little distance away. 'You could probably get here from further along the road. No need to use that path through the woods.'

They looked down the hillside. This rough ground ended at a field of brighter green grass, with another below it. Beyond the lowest hedge, they could see the occasional flash of a car roof passing.

'So,' Tom said thoughtfully. 'Was Philip Caseley coming this way to meet someone? And does it have anything to do with whatever's been going on here?'

Suzie retorted, more sharply than she meant to, 'And what's this supposed to have to do with Eileen Caseley's death?'

SIX

S uzie stood on the sunlit hillside, trying to make sense of what they had discovered. She let the boys wander carefully around the site while she thought. Presumably they were still on the land that belonged to Saddlers Wood Barton. Philip Caseley's land. It was a rough outcrop of moorland, quite common in the farmland around the fringes of the moor itself. This patch, with its thin soil and granite boulders, would not be much good for farming. Sheep or cattle might be turned out on it occasionally. Yet someone else had taken an interest in surveying it. Why?

Housing? It was quite a distance from the utility services and amenities of Moortown. Suzie doubted if planning permission would be granted for a housing estate this far out. Could they have been prospecting for gas, oil or minerals? She didn't know enough of the geology of this area to be sure. You did hear of farmers suddenly striking it rich with the discovery of unexpected deposits under their land.

But why would that lead Philip Caseley to kill his wife, just when they might be expecting an upturn in their strained fortunes.

It might have had nothing to do with money. Perhaps Philip had discovered that Eileen was having an affair with somebody else. Goodness knows it was a common enough occurrence. A jealous husband assuming the right to act as executioner.

'Tom!' Dave's sudden cry startled her. Had he found something else?

But he was pointing to his wristwatch. 'The time! We're going to miss that bus!'

Tom looked at his own watch. Suzie could not hear exactly what he said, but she suspected he swore. He turned to her sharply.

'How fast can you run?'

She turned obediently back towards the overgrown path through the woods.

'Not that way! It's much quicker to the road down the hill.'

Dave was already running. Tom took off after him. They went flying down over the rough ground towards the distantly glimpsed road. She hoped Tom still had the survey nail in his pocket.

Suzie ran too. She was glad of the ankle-hugging boots.

She had assumed they would go through or over the gate into the field ahead and then down through the next one to the road. But suddenly Dave disappeared. Suzie almost tumbled over the edge after Tom. At the last minute, she saw how the bracken-and-grass-grown slope ended abruptly, not with the field hedge just beyond, but on the lip of a bank hiding a stony path deep below.

She scrambled down after the boys. They had turned downhill following this hidden track. The road at the bottom looked much nearer now. On any other day, Suzie would have revelled in this deep-cut way, an old packhorse trail worn down between its banks over centuries of use. Now all she thought about were the uneven stones that littered the bottom and the trickle of water between them, even in this dry summer. She struggled to keep her balance without losing speed or turning an ankle.

There was a glimpse of sunlight ahead beneath overarching trees. Dave was already standing at the roadside, holding out an arm.

She saw the red bus come to a halt. Dave was scrambling aboard. Tom waited by the open door, holding the bus up until she got there. Breathless, she clambered up the steps and showed her ticket.

She collapsed thankfully into a vacant seat. If they had missed this bus, they would have had to wait another hour.

Tom grinned at her from the seat across the aisle. 'Well done, Mum. I didn't know you could run that fast.'

She watched the farmland flow past on the way back to Moortown. Tom and Dave were chatting away, with no thought to keep their voices down.

'What do you think's going on, then?'

'No idea. Do you suppose they've hit on something underground? Coal? Oil?' Dave wondered.

'Out here in the middle of a farm? Is that likely?'

'Search me. Maybe it's the site for an archaeological dig. Plenty of that around here – Bronze Age, Iron Age, medieval.'

'Think about that little car that pulled out from the verge ahead of us,' said Tom, 'It didn't say "archaeologist" to me. I'd have expected something a bit more rugged.'

'And why would he shoot his wife over some Bronze Age village?'

Suzie felt the woman in the seat beside her stiffen.

'Are those your boys?'

'One of them is,' Suzie admitted. 'The black-haired one.'

'They ought not to be speaking ill of Philip Caseley. He's got enough on his lap, poor man.'

'You know him?'

'Most of us round here know Philip. And Eileen, God rest her soul.'

'And what do you think happened?'

'It's not for me to say. You've been on Philip's land then?'

'We . . .' Suzie looked sideways at the woman. About her own age, or a little older. A broad, strong face. She had a clutch of carrier bags on the floor at her feet. She must have been shopping in the bigger market town further south. 'Last Saturday, we were taking a walk in Saddlers Wood. We wanted to see where my ancestors lived. We met the Caseleys. First Philip,

then he sent us up to the farm to see Eileen. So when we heard
. . . Well, there was someone else in the woods that afternoon.
We just thought . . . well, there could be something there that
might help Philip.'

'Another man? I don't see what good that's likely to do him.'

'No. Unless . . . But why should anyone else want to shoot
her?'

'You'd be better off minding your own business. But you can
tell those boys they're wrong if they think Philip would allow those
mining people on to his land. He's like the rest of us. Wouldn't
want anything to do with them. Tearing up the countryside, turning
the place into an eyesore. And all those lorries and the dust. There's
some that will do it for the money, but not Philip.'

'Mining? For what?'

But the bus had drawn up in the square at Moortown. The
woman hurried to gather up her shopping bags. Suzie stepped
out into the aisle to let her pass. Her question was left hanging
in the air, unanswered.

'You did *what*?' Nick exploded.

'Give us a break, Dad.' Tom was flourishing the survey point
nail he had brought back as a trophy from their expedition. 'We
found this, didn't we? Something's going on there. It's not just
the run-down, back-of-beyond place we thought it was. If whoever
was using this is right, Philip Caseley could be sitting on a gold
mine. Well, not literally . . . though, come to think of it, why
not? Who knows what might be lying under that granite? Anyone
here know about geology?'

The rest of the family looked back at him blankly.

'It could just be someone with enough money to pick himself
a site for a one-off house out in the country,' said Nick. 'From
what you say, it was outside the woods. Great views, I should
imagine. One survey nail is hardly proof that he's prospecting
for minerals.'

'You're an architect. You would say that,' Tom retorted.

'I'm a sensible enough bloke to know that building a house
is a far more likely explanation than what you're suggesting. And
just supposing for the sake of argument that you're right, what
would that have to do with Eileen Caseley's murder?'

Tom let the nail fall on to the kitchen table with a sigh. It rolled in a half circle before it came to rest.

'You've got me there. Mum tried to tell the police before that there might be something going on in the woods, but it doesn't look as if they've followed it up. No police tape across the footpath, or round the old cottage. We could just come and go as we pleased. And, of course, she was telling them to look in the woods nearer the farm. We didn't know then that the really interesting stuff was further on.'

'And further away from the farmhouse where Eileen Caseley was shot.'

'You think it was just domestic violence, don't you, Dad?' Millie spoke up from the door of the conservatory. 'You think she was having it off with somebody and he took a gun to her.'

Nick paused before he spoke. Suzie saw how he was struggling to envisage this.

'It's hard to say. I only saw him for a few minutes, and Eileen Caseley for – what? – half an hour. I wouldn't say either of them was behaving normally. We've no way of knowing whether they were upset because of something that had happened between them, or whether the fact that there was someone else on their land besides us had anything to do with it.'

'He might have fired that shot to warn her,' Millie said.

'Whatever it is,' Suzie put in, 'this is evidence. The police can't work out what happened unless they have the whole picture. We need to tell them.'

Nick threw up his hands. 'I know when I'm beaten. If you'd asked me, I'd have told you to stay away from a crime scene and not go muddying the waters. But what's done is done. You've trampled all over the area around the cottage, and now that surveying site you found. So, yes, you'd better go ahead and tell the police what you've done.'

'And what we've found,' Suzie argued. 'And if I hadn't been there, that woman on the bus wouldn't have told me about someone wanting to open a mine in the area, and how the locals are up in arms against it. Philip might have stood to gain from it, but from what she said he was dead set against mining too.'

'Do we march round to police headquarters waving this at

them?' Tom asked, brandishing the large nail again. 'Or ring them up first?'

'A phone call would be best,' Suzie suggested. 'Make sure we get to talk to the right person.'

She realized they were all looking at her. She coloured.

'I don't know why I let myself get dragged into this. I tried to tell Tom not to go. But then I thought, well, maybe there ought to be someone there with their head screwed on.'

'Thanks, Mum,' Tom grinned, 'for that ringing vote of confidence in your offspring.'

'It's *because* you're my offspring,' she said darkly. 'I know you too well. All right then. I suppose it'll have to be me.'

She picked up the telephone in the hall with reluctance. 'Could I speak to someone about the Eileen Caseley case? The murder at Moortown? . . .'

She came back to the kitchen to report.

'They're still over at the incident room in Moortown. We must have passed it on the bus. But she'll see us at the police headquarters here at nine tomorrow morning.'

'She?' asked Millie.

'Detective Chief Inspector Brewer.'

SEVEN

Tom and Suzie marched up the steps of the police headquarters; Tom juggled the large survey nail in his hand. Halfway up he stopped. He looked back. Suzie turned as well.

Dave stood at the foot of the steps. His face, below the ginger hair, was pale. Suzie saw the scared expression in his eyes as he looked up at the police station entrance.

Tom was at his side in a few strides. 'It's OK, man. You're on their side now. Queen's evidence. No one's going to hold the past against you. It never was your fault, anyway.'

Dave gulped. Suzie's heart ached with sudden realization. Two years ago, a teenage girl had died. Tom had fallen under suspicion

of her murder, and Dave had concealed vital facts that could have
cleared him. In the end, the verdict had been accidental death.
Dave had received a suspended sentence for withholding evidence.

Suzie could see him now reliving that nightmare as the police
station loomed above him.

Slowly, reluctantly, he let Tom lead him up the steps.

'Can't you see, it will work in your favour?' Tom was saying.
'Another murder . . . Idiot! I mean another violent death, and
you're bang on the nail with evidence. They can't criticize you
this time, can they? Don't worry. I'll do the talking.'

Tom has this sunny confidence, Suzie thought, that he has only
to flash those bright blue eyes at anyone and throw them that
engaging smile and they'll fall at his feet. To be honest, people
usually did.

Chief Detective Inspector Alice Brewer was intimidatingly tall.
The impression was heightened by her long, thin face and the
even longer, fairish hair which fell straight to her collarbones.
She was beanpole slim.

She looked at the three of them, seated before her. Her eyes
settled on Suzie. 'I'm told you have information concerning the
death of Eileen Caseley. Do you want to tell me about it?'

Suzie had half expected this, whatever Tom's assertion that he
would speak for them. She had been the one who made the phone
call to book this appointment. For all Tom's ready confidence,
she was his mother, a generation older.

'I suppose I ought to start with last Saturday. We . . . that is,
my husband and I and my son and daughter, were out in Saddlers
Wood . . .'

'Your husband has already signed a statement about that,' DCI
Brewer said crisply. 'Shall we get to the point?'

Suzie was beginning to feel not so much a mature adult as a
chastened schoolgirl.

'Tom, my son, and Dave thought there might be more to the
incident in the woods. They wanted to have another look. I tried
to dissuade him at first, but when I saw he was set on going I
decided it might be better if I went too.'

'So. You tried to dissuade him. You obviously thought it was
a bad idea.'

Suzie felt herself colouring. 'Nobody seemed very interested in what we said about someone else being there in the woods, possibly hiding from us. But I couldn't be sure that you weren't taking it more seriously than you let us know.'

The chief inspector's fingertips drummed on the table.

'But then,' Suzie went on, 'when we got near the farm, we could see that there was no police tape across the footpath that led to that clearing. And there was none when we got to the ruined cottage. It didn't look as though you were treating it as part of the crime scene. But Tom and Dave went on further than we did on Saturday. They found this area outside the wood, like a small piece of moorland. And somebody, probably more than one person, had certainly been there, trampling all over the place.'

'So you thought you would trample all over it too? How did you know it wasn't the police who had been there?'

'I found this!' Tom exclaimed, lifting up the long, broad nail he had been holding under the table. 'Doesn't look as though there'd been a police search, does it? You could hardly have missed this.'

DCI Brewer took a tissue from a box on the table. She reached across and took the nail from Tom, holding it carefully in the paper. She examined the raised lettering on the head, then laid it on the table in front of her. When she leaned her long thin neck towards Tom her eyes were steely.

'I *see*. You thought you'd play detective in a murder case. You decided the police weren't up to the job. So all three of you trample in with your footprints all over the scene. You pick up what, by your own admission, you believed to be vital evidence. With your grubby hands. You make no attempt to preserve any fingerprints that might be on it. A single phone call was all it needed. I was only two miles away in Moortown. I could have had a squad of officers over there in minutes. We could have done a *professional* search.' The adjective was loaded with scorn. 'But no, you knew better.'

Suzie saw Tom blush fiercely as her words hit home.

'It was my fault,' she protested. 'I found it first.'

Tom ignored her. 'You didn't seem to be taking our first report seriously,' he countered.

'How did you know what we might or might not have done

yesterday morning? The police are not obliged to report to the Fewings family on how they are handling this case.'

Suzie felt herself growing smaller in her chair.

She tried to defend Tom – all of them. 'It could be significant, couldn't it? You've arrested Philip Caseley. I've no idea what went on between him and Eileen. But I talked to a woman on the bus back to Moortown. There *is* someone interested in opening up mining in this area, and the local people are dead against it, including Philip. It may have nothing to do with his wife's death, but it suggests evidence that there was some hostility, doesn't it? We saw Philip going down that path on Saturday. And we're pretty sure there was someone else in the woods.'

'Yes. I have your report in front of me. And why, precisely, would that be a motive for that person to kill Eileen Caseley?'

Her voice was icy. She went on relentlessly.

'And if there *was* any evidence of value in this area you're talking about, you seem to have done your best to ensure that there will be nothing left for the police to find. One phone call. That was all it needed. You didn't even have to *touch* this nail. I'll get an officer to take your statements.'

They were dismissed like naughty children.

'I told you I didn't want to come!' Dave burst out at the foot of the steps.

'Stay cool, man. She hardly spoke to you. It was me she was gunning for. Well, and Mum. Sorry.' Tom turned to Suzie. 'I got you into this.'

'Not entirely. I walked into it with my eyes open. I could have let you go back to Saddlers Wood on your own.'

'But you guessed we were heading into trouble and you wanted to be there to stop a diplomatic incident. That's over and above the call of duty, Mum.' He gave her that bewitching smile.

'Well, partly. But I have to admit I was curious myself. I know we didn't have much to go on, but I couldn't bear the thought that they might pin it on an innocent man because we hadn't said anything.'

'You're forgetting something,' Dave said morosely. 'Ballistics. They must know by now whether she was killed with Philip Caseley's gun.'

Tom and Suzie stopped dead in the middle of the police station car park. A cold hand closed over Suzie's heart. How could she not have thought of that? She had an instant vivid picture of Philip Caseley emerging from the footpath at the side of the track, gripping his shotgun. Of the shot that had echoed through the still country air only moments earlier. What, or whom, had the farmer been firing at then? Had Eileen Caseley been killed with that same gun, with the sort of lead shot you would use on a pheasant or rabbit? Or could a shotgun fire a single bullet? Did Philip Caseley have another weapon – a rifle, perhaps? And could she honestly tell the difference?

She knew an intense frustration that these were questions she could not ask the police.

It was, DCI Brewer had made abundantly clear, nothing to do with her.

And yet she felt that it was. She had met a frightened woman in that farmyard. Instead of trying harder to find out what was wrong, she had asked her trivial questions about family history. She had encroached on the hospitality of a woman who clearly had little time or money to spare. Her thoughts had been in the past, and she had allowed herself to close her mind to what was happening in the present, to tell herself precisely what Chief Inspector Brewer thought: that it was none of her business.

And yet . . . Was it only that feeling of instinctive alarm for her personal safety that had changed her mind? That crack of dead wood from the trees around the clearing? That sense of someone watching her unseen?

Still, when she had made that first phone call to the police on Saturday evening, it had certainly been domestic violence she had been afraid of – the apparently obvious conclusion that Eileen Caseley had been threatened by her husband.

A tiny voice reminded her of that old newspaper report about Richard Day finding his neighbour's wife dead on the kitchen floor. Her fleeting thought that he might have been in some way involved. She pushed the thought away.

If Philip Caseley had been opposing someone who was prospecting for minerals, that might make him a target. But that was very far-fetched. And why should it put Eileen in danger? Dave was right; if the police were still holding Philip Caseley, it must be because they knew she had been shot with his gun.

She shook herself back to the present.

'Sorry, folks. I've got to fly. I'm an hour late for work already.'

EIGHT

Three weeks later, Millie looked up from leafing through the local paper.

'Here, Mum, this'll interest you. There's an announcement of the funeral of that woman who was shot.'

She passed the paper over, pointing to the place on the page.

Suzie read the brief details. Two p.m. at the church of St Michael in Moortown. No flowers. Donations to the Royal Agricultural Benevolent Institution. There was no mention of the dramatic way Eileen Caseley had met her death.

There was a sad finality about it. It was as though all the phone calls and the statements to the police, that search in Saddlers Wood, had been an attempt to stave off the reality of what had happened. As though they could discover something that would reverse the terrible truth.

But holding the paper in her hand, looking at the black-and-white notice of the funeral, brought it home in all its inevitability. Eileen Caseley was dead. Murdered. They would never again see that careworn woman who had given them cups of tea and tried her best to cover up the agitation she had clearly been feeling. Whatever they might have done to help her, it was too late now.

Millie's voice seemed to come to her from a great distance.

'Do you suppose they'll let her husband out to go to the funeral?'

The church of St Michael the Archangel was set back, in a large churchyard, from the square in Moortown. As she stepped off the bus, Suzie was struck by its size. It seemed out of proportion to the little town on the fringes of the moor.

Her historian's mind provided the instant answer. Wool. In

centuries gone by, the sheep of the West Country had provided the woollen cloth for which it was famous. Woolmasters had grown rich on the trade and expressed their gratitude through the endowment of large churches. A branch of her own family had been among them. Their names were inscribed on grave slabs set in the floor of the aisle.

The dwindling population of modern times could surely not provide a regular congregation to fill such a building.

But today the square was thick with people in sober dress, making their way towards the church.

Suzie wondered if they were all friends of Eileen Caseley. Did that woman on the bus speak for many others who protested Philip's innocence? Or were they simply drawn to the funeral by the notoriety of the murder?

As she joined the flow of people through the churchyard gate, Suzie felt that had been an unworthy thought. Most faces had a solemn look, in keeping with their black clothes. It was not sensationalism that had drawn them here, but rather, a strong sense of community.

What had brought *her* here – a single meeting with the dead woman?

She found it hard to explain, even to herself, what had made her come. She hadn't told Nick or the children. She had not asked Nick if she could use the car this afternoon. Nick had a successful architectural practice and Suzie a small independent income from running the office of a charity. The Fewings could have afforded a second car, but there was a good bus service in the cathedral city. Suzie only needed to go beyond the reach of public transport on family history expeditions to rural parishes, or on country walks, and then Nick was always happy to drive her.

So today she had dressed in a white shirt and grey skirt, with a mauve jacket, and taken the bus. Looking at the sea of black around her she felt a surprised strangeness. At her Methodist church it was more common to have a small family funeral service at the cemetery or crematorium, and then a big service at the church to celebrate that person's life.

Here, the setting was more traditional. Except . . . she caught a sharp breath of indignation. Television cameras were set up, filming the mourners as they approached the church door. Other photographers jostled among the gravestones, vying with each other for the best shots. As the bulbs flashed, she had a startled mental image of herself on tonight's TV or in the next edition of the local paper. She would need to explain to the family what she was doing here. She was still not sure that she could.

But no, she wasn't important. Editors would want a more dramatic photograph. The husband? Just for a moment Suzie checked her step on the cobbled path. Would they let Philip Caseley out of prison to attend his wife's funeral. Would he appear in handcuffs? Then it occurred to her that the son from Australia must be here. What would that meeting of father and son be like?

She carried on walking, more soberly now. She had fallen into the obvious way of thinking that Philip must be guilty. But what if he were not? She tried to think of the torment he must be going through, with everyone he knew suspecting him, perhaps even his son.

'I didn't expect to see you here. I thought you said you'd only seen her the once.'

Suzie looked up with a guilty start. It took a moment for her to place the rosy-faced woman in a black coat and skirt, who had just spoken to her reprovingly. Then she remembered. The neighbouring farmer who had been driving her Land Rover to see to the Caseleys' sheep.

She coloured. 'Yes. I really don't know why I'm here. But she was kind to us. Even though . . . well, we probably caught her at a bad time. But she gave us tea and told us where we could find the cottage where my family lived. Coming here was . . . well, a way of saying thank you.'

The dark eyes regarded her suspiciously. 'Looks like the world and his wife have turned out. Just because they've seen it on the telly. There's people here I've never seen before.'

So these were not all local people.

Suzie looked round her with renewed curiosity. Would Detective Chief Inspector Brewer be here? Wasn't that what the police did? Hovered on the edge of the victim's funeral, in the likelihood that the murderer would be there among the crowd, unable to resist the temptation to see their crime through to the end?

She was suddenly at the church door, being carried in by the slowly moving press of mourners. The farmer who had spoken to her marched up the aisle to sit near the front. Suzie looked around for somewhere less conspicuous. She slipped into a pew in a side aisle, near the back. Between the pillars she could see the church filling up.

She craned her neck to get a better view of the front pews. There was a tall, broad-shouldered man she did not recognize, sitting alone. Eileen's Caseley's son? But the figure she had half expected and feared to see was not there. Philip Caseley hadn't come. Unless the police intended to smuggle him in at the last moment.

She thought with a sudden ache of what it must be like to sit in a cell, knowing his wife's funeral was taking place, and not be there. Picturing the church filled with all his farming friends, and wondering what they were thinking. She wondered whether his son had been to visit him in prison, and what would happen to the farm when Eileen Caseley was put to rest.

Suddenly she was aware of a commotion in the churchyard outside. The congregation's heads were turning in alarm. Suzie turned with them. From her pew, she could see little through the door, but she had the impression of flash bulbs lighting up the dark yews.

There was a hiss of indrawn breath. A current of murmurs ran through the pews. Suzie started as two men entered the church. The nearest to her was a burly prison warder in uniform. Handcuffed to him was a lean man in a black suit and tie. His fairish hair was slicked back today, unlike his dishevelled appearance when he had burst from the path in Saddlers Wood carrying a shotgun. But there was no mistaking that this was Philip Caseley.

He had come.

The murmurs stilled. The congregation watched in silence as the widower made his way up the aisle to take his seat with his escort in the front pew opposite his son.

In the long hush that followed, Matthew Caseley did not turn his head to look at his father.

The congregation was standing. That could only mean one thing. Suzie turned her head. Eileen Caseley's coffin was being carried solemnly up the aisle.

As the procession passed behind a pillar, Suzie found herself looking straight across the nave. In the side aisle opposite her stood a tall woman with long fair hair. Her heart jumped with something that was not quite surprise. She had been right. Chief Inspector Brewer was here to watch proceedings.

A more uncomfortable thought struck her as their eyes met across the church. What would DCI Brewer make of Suzie's presence here?

The service was over. The large congregation, protective or curious, was edging its way out of the church door. Suzie wondered as she waited her turn whether they would all be making their way to the top end of the churchyard, where an extension had been opened beyond the old stone wall for newer graves. Or was the committal at the graveside only for close family and friends?

The thinning crowd ahead of her made different decisions. Most headed straight down the path between the yews to the church gate which opened on to the town square. A smaller number, especially those who had sat near the front of the church, were steadily climbing the narrower path behind the church. Philip Caseley and his warder were there too, leaving a conspicuous gap between them and the others.

Suzie hesitated, then followed them. She didn't know why. In no way could she count herself a friend of Eileen Caseley. She had only met her once.

By the time she reached the gate in the wall which led to the new intake, she realised that she was almost the last of those who had chosen to follow the coffin to its burial. The chief mourners were already gathered around the open grave. A sheet of artificial grass covered the mound of newly dug earth at the side. Two floral wreaths had been laid upon it. One, she was sure, must be from the son from Australia who had returned alone for his mother's funeral. Was the other from Philip, her husband and, in the eyes of the world, her murderer?

Would it have been better if he had stayed in prison? The idea haunted Suzie. She tried to imagine Nick dead, and herself prevented from attending his funeral.

She shuddered violently. What a horrible thing to think. Awful enough to imagine that Nick might die in his forties and leave

her alone. But that she who loved him might be in prison awaiting
trial for his murder . . . What black thoughts was she allowing
herself to think?

But someone had killed Eileen Caseley. It happened all the
time. Two women a week killed by their spouse or partner, present
or ex. It was a terrifying statistic. Why should she think that
Philip Caseley was not one of those men? What did she know
about him, or the tensions between him and Eileen?

The rough stone surface of the wall was digging into her hand.
She hadn't realised she was gripping it so hard until she gathered
her wandering thoughts.

Too late now to join the group around the grave. She could
hear the priest intoning the words of the committal. '*Dust to dust.
Ashes to ashes.*' It would have been inappropriate for her to be
there, anyway. She was a stranger to them. She remembered the
inquisitive, almost hostile stare of the neighbour who had been
minding the Caseley sheep. What further questions would she be
asking if she noticed that Suzie had followed them?

She looked around, wondering if it was time for her to make
a quick withdrawal, before the group around the grave broke up
and came this way. This extension to the graveyard was barer
than the older churchyard. It lacked the tall dark yew trees, the
grand monuments and large crosses of the more ostentatious
memorials of the past. Across the wall, in the modern plot, there
were only three rows of graves as yet. The rest was green grass
on an open hilltop overlooking the town. The few gravestones
already there were modest, not more than a foot or two high. It
felt exposed.

She was not the only one to watch from a distance. Two people,
a man and a woman, stood respectfully back among the new
graves. Police? She remembered her conjecture that detectives
might want to see who came to watch the burial of their victim.
Yes. She recognised the beanpole figure of Detective Chief
Inspector Brewer. The shorter, bearded man beside her was
unfamiliar to her.

A prickling on her neck made her turn her head. Her heart
gave a sudden start. There was someone else behind her, on the
older side of the churchyard wall. He wore a dark raincoat
buttoned up to the neck. His balding head was bare. He was half

hidden by the tall shaft of a Celtic stone cross, but through its wheel-head she could see that he was staring, not at the closing moments of the burial, but at her.

With sudden panic, she turned and sped down the path towards the crowded square, at a walk so fast it was almost a run.

NINE

The burial was over. There were still knots of people about in the square, conspicuous in their black funeral clothes. Philip and his warder had been driven back to prison. But most mourners were drifting away, back to everyday reality. At Suzie's Methodist church, there would have been an invitation for anyone at the service to stay and join the family afterwards for refreshments. No such general invitation had been given here. She suspected that the family's friends would have been invited to a funeral tea in some hotel function room.

The press photographers and television crews had packed up and gone, Suzie was relieved to see.

Her heartbeat was quietening, but she was still tense. Should she risk turning her head to see if that man in the black raincoat was following her? Why was she of interest to him? Why had he scared her?

A hand grasped her wrist. She gasped.

'I'm sorry. I didn't mean to startle you.'

It was a woman's voice. Suzie brought her panic under control and turned.

The woman was dressed in a black suit with a crisp white shirt. She wore her funeral clothes with an understated elegance, almost like an habitual uniform. A coil of dark hair fell forward over one shoulder. She was, Suzie guessed, about her own age, with a diamond-shaped face slanting from pronounced cheekbones.

She smiled now, though she was watching Suzie keenly. Her narrow fingers still held Suzie's wrist, like a bird's claw.

Behind her, Suzie saw the party of chief mourners coming

slowly down the path from the grave. The rector's white surplice
flapped in the breeze. Her hurried eyes thought they saw the
watcher in the raincoat following them. A broad-brimmed leather
hat hid his bare head now. The summer day was overcast, but
his shielding clothes looked out of place for this time of year.

She tore her eyes away and made herself speak with a
semblance of naturalness to the woman partly blocking her view.

'It's all right. I think I'm just a bit strung up.'

The woman's dark eyes narrowed. She let go of Suzie's arm
and held out a small hand.

'Frances Nosworthy. I'm Philip Caseley's solicitor.'

The image jumped into place. It was easy to imagine this smart
but soberly dressed woman in a law court, as well as at a funeral.
It was a few seconds before the oddness of the introduction
caught up with Suzie.

'His solicitor?' The unspoken question was, *What do you
want with me?* She had only come because of a moment of
unsatisfied curiosity, and a sadness for the woman so briefly met.

'I hope you won't think me intrusive, but I wondered who you
were. We're a fairly close-knit community here. I think I know
most people in Moortown. But you obviously knew Eileen well
enough to want to follow her to her grave.' A thought seemed
to strike her. 'You're not a reporter, are you?'

'No! No.' Suzie found herself blushing. 'I probably shouldn't
be here. It's just . . .' She heard herself repeating the story of
their expedition to Saddlers Wood, the gunshot, Eileen's evident
distress, but then her gallant attempt at hospitality to the Fewings.

'I felt – I don't know – that I owed her something.'

'Yes, Eileen had a warm heart. You wouldn't have got away
from her without a cup of tea, no matter what was happening.'

'But you're representing Philip.'

Frances Nosworthy made a face of distaste. 'It's a tricky situation. The Nosworthys are the family's solicitors, have been for
generations. My grandfather and old Michael Caseley. My cousin
John is representing Eileen's side, and the son, of course. But
my father branched out into his own law firm, so I'm representing
Philip. It's a bad business. We're trying to avoid a conflict of
interest.'

'You don't really think Philip killed her?'

The solicitor's hand was suddenly back on her arm, drawing her away from the gate. The rest of the mourning party were coming through into the square. Suzie fell silent as they passed. The tall, suntanned man she thought must be the Caseleys' son passed her. His mouth was set in a grim line. He nodded curtly to Frances.

She spoke in a low voice. 'Matthew. I'm so sorry.'

He walked on without answering. The black-clad party turned away along the pavement.

The two detectives, who had watched the burial from a distance, left a tactful space before they followed. As they passed Suzie and Frances, the tall chief inspector let her eyes dwell on Suzie for an electrifying moment. Suzie read all too clearly her surprise and condemnation at seeing her here.

It took a moment for Suzie to recover.

When she did, she was relieved to see that the man in the raincoat and the broad-brimmed hat had gone.

'Sorry about that,' Frances said, letting her go. 'Matthew's not speaking to me. Of course I'm defending Philip. That's my job, but I'd do it anyway. Though at the moment, I'm searching for crumbs.'

Words hovered on the tip of Suzie's tongue. 'Only . . .'

'Yes?' Again that narrowing of the eyes. The sense of a sharp intelligence leaping into action.

'There was more than I told you. That afternoon, and again later.'

The dark eyes summed her up. 'Do you have time for a cup of tea? I've been invited to the official tea at the Tor Hotel, but it might be a bit delicate, under the circumstances. A bit like Banquo's ghost at the feast. And if you have any information that might help Philip . . .'

'We told the police, but I'm not sure it made much of an impression.'

'Well, tell me.'

Suzie let herself be steered to a tea shop, with chintz-covered cushions on the wheel-backed chairs. She would miss the bus she had intended to catch, but there would be another one in an hour.

'Now,' said Frances Nosworthy, setting down her patent-leather

handbag. 'This one's on me. Could you manage a cream tea? I
don't know about you, but I feel in need of something to cheer
me up.'

Suzie looked at the other woman's enviably slender figure.
But the lure of scones with clotted cream and strawberry jam
was too much. 'Yes, please. Me too.'

Frances placed the order. 'Now,' she said, getting out a notepad
from her handbag. 'Let's take it from the top, shall we? You went
to Saddlers Wood on . . .?'

'Saturday, the thirteenth of July.'

She told it all. The path Eileen Caseley said was infrequently
used, down which they had seen Philip stride with his gun. The
crack of wood snapping as they explored the ruined cottage. The
sense of being watched. And then her joining Tom and Dave's
hare-brained adventure to discover more. The evidence of
surveying in the patch of moorland just beyond the wood.

'It makes sense,' Frances said, laying her pen down among
the crumbs of scone on the tablecloth. 'I can't reveal the family
business, of course, but I'm not actually surprised.'

'What I don't understand,' Suzie said, 'is, if Philip was
opposing the exploitation of mineral rights, why anyone should
want to kill Eileen, and not him.'

'Hmm.'

Frances's narrow fingers tapped on the table top. 'I can't
discuss the family's affairs. But you've just said enough to make
me sense it's not an open and shut case of domestic violence. I
was never convinced that it was, but what do I know? I sit in
my snug little solicitor's office; business goes on – wills mort-
gages, land sales, drink driving charges. The recession doesn't
really hit us. Perhaps a few more DIY divorces, instead of paying
people like us who know what we're doing. But out there on the
farms, it's a different picture. It's a hard row to plough – low
prices, high costs. The sort of loneliness there used not to be
when every other man was an ag. lab. And now climate change
on top of everything else. It's either drought or floods these days,
and another season's crop lost. It can drive a man to suicide, or
worse.'

She played with her teaspoon, her eyes bent downwards.

She recovered herself with a visible effort.

'I'm sorry. I shouldn't be loading all this on you. You've been really helpful. And goodness knows Philip needs all the help he can get. Look, take my card. If you can think of anything else that might be relevant, ring me.'

Suzie looked over her shoulder. A single-decker bus was pulling into the square. She yelped with dismay. 'My bus! Sorry, I've got to go. Thanks for the tea – I haven't had scones and cream in ages. Look, if you need me again you can find my number on the website for the Age of Silver charity. I must fly.'

'Of course. And thank you again.' Frances moved her chair aside as Suzie fled for the door and raced to the bus stop on the other side of the square.

Suzie leaned back in her seat, recovering her breath. The bus rolled forwards, past the now empty churchyard.

Only then did she remember that she hadn't told Frances Nosworthy about the man lurking among the graves.

TEN

She should not have felt guilty about attending a funeral. But as the bus rolled homewards, she felt a peculiar reluctance to tell her family where she had been. The lashing tongue of DCI Brewer still smarted. Just for a moment, as the two detectives had passed her at the church gate, she had met the taller woman's cold blue eyes. The police officer had said nothing to her, but Suzie had felt her disbelief and scorn. She knew the chief inspector was angered by her determination not to let the matter go and leave it to the professionals.

It wasn't like that, Suzie argued with herself. I didn't go to Moortown because I thought I might discover something. I went to the funeral because . . . oh, because Eileen Caseley had been so troubled, yet so generous. She could just have sent us away. But she took us into her home and gave us what help she could.

She thought of the woman's attempt at smartness, the silk blouse and the linen skirt, incongruous in the dilapidated farmhouse.

And now she's dead. Violently. I wanted to do what little I could to pray her to her rest.

She was afraid that the rest of the Fewings would see it as the chief inspector did.

And, after all, she *had* found something. She shivered as the summer landscape sped past her. That strange man in the leather hat. She had not imagined that his eyes had been directed at her, rather than at the people round Eileen Caseley's grave. It was unsettling that a silent stare should be so frightening.

At least Frances Nosworthy was an ally. She had seemed genuinely grateful for Suzie's information. It was somehow reassuring to know that the solicitor's business card was tucked into her shoulder bag.

She was later back than she had intended to be. She fended off Tom and Millie's questions with the excuse that she must hurry to get the meal ready.

Millie, untypically, joined her in chopping vegetables. When Tom was out of earshot, she threw her mother a conspiratorial grin.

'So you went, then? To the funeral.'

Suzie paused in the act of stirring flour into the sauce. 'How . . .?'

'Give me credit for some intelligence, Mum. Look at you. Dark grey skirt, white blouse, in the middle of summer. Why aren't you wearing slacks and a tee-shirt? Or a summer dress?'

Suzie looked down at herself. She had hung up the mauve jacket in the wardrobe. What was left was not obviously funereal, just more sober than the clothes she normally wore.

She sighed. 'There's no getting past you, is there? I'd be grateful if you didn't mention it to the others.'

Millie's eyebrows climbed. 'You think Dad would be cross with you?'

Suzie hesitated. She felt again how scared she had been by the stare of the man in the raincoat. She badly wanted to feel Nick's arms around her. Should she tell him after all?

But the moment passed. She heard his key in the door. Something told her he would think she had been foolish. Exaggerated her own importance in a murder case. Failed to heed the warnings of the police. He had been less than sympathetic when Tom had stormed at him about their chilly reception at the police station. He had seemed less enthusiastic than Tom was about the evidence that more had been going on at Saddlers Wood than domestic tension between a couple on an isolated farm.

Now Nick came striding down the hall and kissed her warmly. He said nothing about what she was wearing. Trust Millie to be the only one to notice.

She could not sleep. The night was warm and muggy, the threat of summer rain in the air. She lay awake in the darkness. Even the presence of Nick sleeping beside her could not shut out the remembered menace of this afternoon. She felt again the prickle on her neck that had made her turn even before she saw him. The glimpse of eyes fixed on her through gaps in the wheel-head of a Celtic cross. *Why?* Who was he, and why was Suzie of such interest to him, out of all the people in that graveyard? She had not imagined it, had she? It had been her the man was watching.

She wished now she had asked Frances Nosworthy about him. Here, at least, was somebody who appeared to be on her side. Or on Philip's side, she corrected herself. Suzie only mattered to Frances as a possible lead to strengthen her case for Philip's innocence.

She turned restlessly on her pillow and tried again to sleep. The minutes ticked by on the digital clock at her bedside.

Another face swam into her mind. Skin tanned, hair bleached by a southern sun. Matthew Caseley, the only son of Philip and the dead Eileen. His face had been set grimly as he passed Suzie and Frances. She wondered if he was convinced of his father's guilt? Did he blame Frances for trying to defend Philip?

Suzie had been nothing to him. He wouldn't know of her existence, unless the police had briefed him on what DCI Brewer obviously thought were the overexcited attempts of the Fewings family to find themselves a place in a local murder.

But still the hard lines of that face haunted her. It was wrong. She ought to be feeling sorry for the bereaved son. She should be praying for him. For Philip too. What must the relationship between father and son be like now?

She swung her feet to the floor, carefully, so as not to disturb Nick.

She padded barefoot downstairs to the kitchen and poured herself a glass of cold milk and took it into the conservatory to drink.

Down here, with the windows uncurtained, the night was not fully dark. She could see the ghostly outlines of the garden Nick lavished so much love on.

A sudden cry made her jolt, spilling the milk over her hand. It took agitated moments before she remembered the barn owl she sometimes saw sitting solemnly on a bough of the beech tree in the daytime.

She really must find a way to put all these fears out of her mind. Eileen Caseley's death was a terrible tragedy, but it was really none of her business. She had done her citizen's duty and reported what little she knew to the police. Even to Philip's solicitor. It was up to them what use they made of it. For herself now, she must get back to normality. Eileen was dead and buried. Philip was in the hands of the law.

But she still found herself unaccountably shrinking from the exposure of the French windows to the shadowy garden and the owl-haunted night.

Why was she so important to the man in the raincoat?

She went upstairs quietly, hoping the treads would not creak.

The bedroom was still and dark, the curtains shutting out the starlight. Only the luminous green numerals on the clock winked at her.

She climbed into bed as carefully as she could.

Nick stirred. A hand reached out. 'Having trouble sleeping?' His voice was drowsy.

For a moment, Suzie wondered whether she should fob him off with an excuse that she had just needed to go to the bathroom. Then the memory of that shudder that had come over her in front of the uncurtained French windows gripped her. She was still afraid. It did not help that she could not explain her fear.

She half sat up against the pillows. 'I went to the funeral today. Eileen Caseley's.'

At once Nick was alert, propping himself up on one elbow. 'In Moortown? Why ever didn't you say so?'

'I don't know. I felt . . . Well, I wasn't sure whether you'd think it was the right thing to do.'

'I don't think it was *necessary*, if that's what you mean. We hardly knew the woman, God rest her. But we seem to have got more tangled up with her than we meant to . . . than we *needed* to,' he added with emphasis. 'If you wanted to put a closure on it by attending her funeral, that's fine.'

'Only it didn't,' she said in a small voice.

She was longing for him to fill the silence with words of concern. But he was settling down on his pillow again, letting sleep reclaim him.

'How do you mean?' he asked. But not as if he was really interested.

'After the service in church I followed the coffin up through the churchyard to where they were burying her. And while I was watching I . . . felt something. I turned round, and there was this man watching me.'

'Who?'

'I don't know. I've never seen him before. Fiftyish, I should think, balding head. And buttoned up in a long raincoat, even though it wasn't raining. He'd taken off his hat for the burial, but when he put it on again it was one of those leather ones with a broad brim. You could hardly see his face under it. He was . . . I don't know . . . spooky. And the worst thing was, he wasn't watching the burial, or not when I looked round at him. It was me he was staring at.'

She had expected him to sit up in bed, put his arms around her. Shut out the nightmare of that steely gaze that had come back to haunt her.

Instead he rolled over and said crossly, 'Suzie! This is getting ridiculous. You put a whole conspiracy together because you hear a twig snapping in the wood. You and Tom go haring off on to someone else's land after a murder that had nothing to do with us. The police tell you to leave it, but you don't. Oh, no. You have to go all the way out to Moortown on your own because you can't let go of it. And once you're there, your imagination is so overheated about all this that you fancy some perfectly innocent friend of the family has sinister designs on you. Really! Just listen to yourself.'

'You weren't *there*. You didn't see him. And it isn't true that it's nothing to do with us. While I was there I met his solicitor, Philip Caseley's. And no, I really wasn't being nosy. She was the one who spoke to me. She certainly *did* want to know what we'd heard and seen in the wood, anything that might mean Philip isn't guilty of killing his wife. If I hadn't gone to the funeral, she wouldn't have known I existed. It's bad enough that the detective inspector was there, looking at me as if I was something the cat brought in.'

Nick turned over to face her again. 'Sorry, love. I didn't mean to snap your head off. But it's the middle of the night. Things always seem out of proportion then. I don't know who your guy in the leather hat was, but there'll be some perfectly sensible explanation. You were only scared that he was looking at you because you had a bit of a conscience about being there at all. You said you didn't think I'd approve.'

She slid down under the duvet. She wished she could believe it was as simple as he made it sound. He put his arms around her and drew her close.

'I know what's bothering you, at the back of your mind. It's that newspaper report, isn't it? The one you found about your great-great-grandfather, who went into the house next door and found the man had murdered his wife. I know what you were thinking, reading between the lines, that your ancestor might have been having an affair with the woman, and she was murdered because of him. And now you've got a real contemporary murder on your hands, and you feel some sort of guilt about it. As though we'd stumbled on something we were partly responsible for. But it isn't true.' He brushed her hair aside and whispered in her ear, 'It's nothing to do with us, Suzie. We happened to meet her two days before she died. A coincidence, that's all.' His arms hugged her. 'It's over. You've given all the information to the police. They've told you to leave it to them. Good advice. Now stop worrying. There's no bogeyman out there in the dark watching you. No sinister crook in a buttoned-up raincoat. You went to the funeral. Fine. Now you can put it out of your head. OK?'

He stroked the hair over her forehead and kissed her.

'Yes,' she said lamely. 'I suppose you're right.'

But even in the circle of his arms, she lay in the darkness and sleep would not come.

ELEVEN

N ext day, she was tired and restless. Nick made no reference to their talk in the middle of the night. Suzie went off to her job at the charity office as usual.

A little part of her mind half expected to see the figure of a balding man in his fifties watching her somewhere along the way. The bus drew to a halt in the city centre. She took a quick look round as she stepped off. There was no one sinister in sight.

Nick was right. She should put it all behind her. Case over. Other people would deal with it from here.

But her normal morning's work still had an air of unreality. Designing a campaigning leaflet. Organising the Young Farmers' sponsored tractor pull across the moor.

At one, she closed down her computer and said goodbye to Margery, who managed the charity shop that fronted her office. It was not until she stepped outside that she realized the enigma of Eileen Caseley's death had never really left her.

Instead of going home, she bought herself a sandwich and ate it in the cathedral close among the clamorous seagulls and attentive pigeons. Then she made her way to the Local Studies Library.

She asked to see the parish file on Moortown.

The young woman went away and returned with a cardboard box. 'I did a degree in history. Then a post-grad qualification as an archivist. And what do I do now? Cut out newspaper articles and file them in boxes. Here you go.' She grinned at Suzie and left her to it.

Suzie opened the box. There was a stack of material. The archivist was right. Much of it was articles clipped from newspapers. They showed their age in varying shades of yellowing. There were also manuscripts, typed or handwritten, where other

researchers had contributed their findings. Suzie settled down to
read some of the more recent entries.

Five minutes later she struck gold – metaphorically speaking.
In fact the mineral was tungsten, a substance Suzie knew nothing
about and could not even picture. She had a feeling it had something to do with light bulbs, but nothing more. The article told
her that a company called Merlin Mines had discovered deposits
of tungsten on a smallholding not far from the town centre and
were seeking planning permission to develop it further.

Planning consent had been refused. The firm were reported to
be offering a substantial royalty to the landowner and sweeteners
of new sports facilities for the primary school and the community.
But there was a photograph of the apparently vocal opposition.
They were waving placards saying, 'TODDLERS NOT
TUNGSTEN. 'PROTECT OUR CHILDREN'.

Suzie read on. It appeared that the fields in question lay a few
hundred metres behind the school. Protesters argued that the
mining activity would raise clouds of toxic dust that would settle
over gardens and playgrounds, making it dangerous to eat local
food or for the children to play out of doors. The mining firm's
lawyers had insisted that this was gross and irresponsible exag-
geration. Similar mines were opened elsewhere with no detri-
mental effects, and the struggling community would prosper as
a result. They would improve local roads to increase the flow of
tourists.

Their statistics and inducements had fallen on deaf ears. The
district council planning committee had turned down the proposal
flat.

Suzie sat back in her seat, wondering where this left her. At
least she had a name. Merlin Mines. There was no guarantee, of
course, that this was the same firm who had been interested in
Philip Caseley's land. But at least it was a possibility. They were
certainly prospecting in the area. And a site at Saddlers Wood,
two miles out of Moortown, with no other habitation nearby
except for the farm, would certainly make for a more realistic
bid to the planning committee a second time.

Had that been it? But if so, why would Philip Caseley turn it
down? He obviously needed the money. Suzie had seen the land
for herself. It was a rough outcrop of moorland, which looked of

little use for farming. He might graze his sheep up there occasionally, but it was not like the rich meadows lower down the hill.

Could it simply be a sentimental attachment to the land of his forebears? Suzie frowned. She had researched enough family history to know that the idea of families working the same farm since Domesday was rarely true. As far as her experience of her own family went, a hundred years was a typical time span for a family to stay on the same farm. But then, how much did Philip know about his own family history? Was he being loyal to an ideal that had never really existed?

She checked with the archivist and moved across to a computer, then accessed the 1911 census. She entered a search for the address: Moortown, Saddlers Wood Barton.

There was a flutter of excitement in her throat as the image of the enumerator's handwritten entry came up in front of her.

William Taverner, his wife Anne, and four children, with two farm servants living in. Taverner. Her great-great-grandmother's maiden name. They were probably related.

So, not the Caseleys, even a century ago.

Something twitched at the corner of her mind.

Did it matter? Might Philip not still be defending his old way of life, however unprofitable it seemed to be? His father and grandfather might have worked the same land. That could be enough.

She tried 'Caseley', location 'Moortown'. This time her search brought her three results. Two on other farms, and one at a house in Church Street. So the Caseleys were a local family even then. Living in the same parish, if not on the same farm. She remembered something Frances Nosworthy had said. *'The Nosworthys are the family's solicitors. Have been for generations. My grandfather and old Michael Caseley.'*

She went back to the parish file. There were earlier reports about the tungsten mining. The general tenor was the same. Right from the start, local people had opposed the scheme.

She returned the file to the reception desk and gathered up her things.

It was only then that the memory fell into place. Hadn't Eileen told Suzie she was a Taverner before her marriage? Saddlers Wood had been, not Philip's, but *her* family home. Suzie was tempted to dash back to the computer and check the marriage records to be sure. But no, that was something she could do at home on her own computer.

On the way home her excitement faded. What, after all, had she discovered that she hadn't known already? The neighbour had told them about local opposition to mining. All she had achieved was a name. Merlin Mines.

For the first time that afternoon she allowed herself to remember the churchyard yesterday. That man in the leather hat. Could he have something to do with Merlin Mines? And would it matter to her if he did?

Suzie made herself a cup of tea and took it out into the garden. Tom was sitting on the wooden bench with his laptop on his knee. Suzie knew better than to think that he was pursuing his degree studies. He snapped the current window shut and threw her a welcoming smile.

'Hi. Good day?'

She cupped her hands round the Snoopy mug. 'Merlin Mines. Tungsten. The planning committee refused them consent to mine on the edge of Moortown.'

He set his laptop down on the table and looked at her with respect. 'So it's not just my great-great-great-granddaddy you chase up in the library.'

'Not this time.'

'You don't think Dad's going to be pissed off with you again for sticking with this, like a dog with a bone?'

Her eyes flew up in alarm. 'I never told you about that!'

The grin stretched wider, like a Cheshire cat. 'Didn't need to. Not after the bollocking he gave me when we went to the police about that surveying stuff. Stands to reason he'd say more to you in private.'

'Yes . . . well. It was more than that. I went to Eileen Caseley's funeral.'

His eyes widened.

She described it all to him. Meeting DCI Brewer's reproving gaze across the church. Following the mourners to the grave. The man lurking behind the Celtic cross and seemingly watching her, not the people at the graveside. That still gave her a shiver of apprehension when she recounted it. Then Frances Nosworthy stopping her to ask who she was and why she was there. The grim look of disapproval from the Caseleys' son Matthew as he passed them. Her talk with Frances over scones and cream.

'In the middle of the night I got scared. I thought that man in the leather hat was out here in the garden watching me. I know it's ridiculous, but I had a really bad feeling.'

'So you told Dad and he warned you to drop it.'

'Yes. That sums it up pretty well.'

'Instead of which, you spend an afternoon looking up applications for mining consent in the Moortown area. Has it ever occurred to you to wonder why this family gets itself involved in more crimes than the average for the population?'

'You're a fine one to talk! Who went dashing off to Saddlers Wood to find out what was going on there?'

'*Touché*. I may look like Dad, but I guess I've got a few of your genes too.' The laughter in those deep blue eyes grew warmer, more conspiratorial.

He reached across and took his laptop again. A few brisk taps and a new screen came up. He read it, then swivelled it so that she could see.

TUNGSTEN. Also known by its German name Wolfram. Chemical symbol W. Atomic number 74. A metal valued for its very high tensile strength and melting point. Used in guns and military projectiles, lightbulb filaments . . .

So her slight memory had been accurate in that at least.

. . . X-ray and television tubes . . .

'So you think that's what someone was prospecting for on Caseley land?'

He shrugged and keyed in another search. He started and leaned forward with sudden enthusiasm. 'Here! Look at this. "Because its density is similar to that of gold, it can be used to replace gold or platinum in jewellery or to counterfeit gold ingots."'

Suzie laughed. 'Did you know that several years ago they discovered deposits of real gold in workable amounts over in the Leigh Valley?' She leaned back. 'I've always associated Moortown with tin mines. Like the trenches you see the remains of when we're out walking on the moor. One of my ancestors in Moortown was a tinner. Well, I don't mean he dug the stuff out with a pick and shovel – he was one of the leading citizens in the town – but he had tinner's rights. He could have sat in the tinners' parliament, the stannary court, sent offenders to the stannary jail.'

'Let's hope whoever is wanting to mine at Saddlers Wood now is playing by the law,' Tom said. 'Which brings us up against the old question. If someone wanted the Caseleys out of the way because they opposed the idea of mining on their land, why kill Eileen and not Philip?'

'I think it's possible the farm may be Eileen's.'

'You *have* been busy. So . . .' Tom's forehead creased as he stared out across the flower-filled garden. 'Eileen's dead. Philip's not going to be doing much farming if he's locked up in prison for murder. And you don't think the son from Australia will take over the farm?'

'Not from what the locals say.'

'Then it goes on the open market. How about this? Laddie from Merlin Mines steps in – not in an official capacity which would alert the competition, but some innocuous sounding agricultural land-holding company. Bingo. He's got what he wants. Mineral deposits at farmland prices. And who except Philip is going to raise a protest about mining that far out of town? Well, somebody will. But they're not going to get hundreds of activists, like the first scheme on the edge of town.'

'Do you think it's really tungsten?'

'More importantly,' Tom shut the lid of his laptop, 'how can we convince the powers that be that it may not have been Philip Caseley who used his gun to shoot his wife?'

TWELVE

S uzie was walking indoors through the French windows when she heard her mobile ring. She dived for the kitchen where she had left her shoulder bag and retrieved the phone. It was a number she didn't recognize.

'Hello? Suzie Fewings.'

She heard the tension in the woman's voice immediately.

'Hi, Suzie. It's Frances. Frances Nosworthy. Look, Matthew . . .'

There was an intake of breath. The sentence was cut off short. Suzie had a feeling there was someone else in the room.

Then Frances's voice resumed, on an even keel, so that Suzie wondered if she had been imagining something was wrong. 'Look, I know we had that conversation yesterday, but circumstances have changed. I've had some new information. Thank you for your trouble, but I really think you can put this behind you now. There's nothing further to discuss.'

'Does that mean you've found something that proves Philip didn't do it? Oh, that's really good news! I don't suppose you can tell me what the evidence is? Do you know who *did* kill her?'

'I'm sorry.' The warmth the other woman had shown in the tea shop was gone. She was the formal solicitor again. 'I really can't discuss my client's confidential circumstances.'

'I know. I'm sorry. I just wondered . . .'

'This call is simply to tell you that you don't need to have any further involvement in this case. More than that. Any subsequent move on your or your family's part might prejudice my client's case. Do you understand?'

There was a little rise of her voice at the end. Just for a moment, Suzie caught something of the woman she had shared confidences with over a cream tea. She hesitated, not sure how to connect that momentary appeal with the formal warning that had gone before.

'Yes,' she said, a second late. 'Yes, I understand.'

She ended the call and put the phone down on the kitchen counter. She stared, unseeing, out of the window. What she was really seeing was the elegantly dressed figure of Frances Nosworthy in her crisp white shirt and black suit, the coil of dark hair falling forward over one shoulder. Those keen brown eyes. Suzie felt unaccountably shaken. After the funeral, Frances had seemed to welcome her information. She had given Suzie her business card, in case she came across any other information which could be of use. And now . . .? Suzie had been formally cut off from the case. Her help was no longer wanted. She had been specifically told to stay out of it.

Why? Suzie's curiosity itched to know just what Frances could have discovered that would mean Philip would go free. She could understand why Frances might want to keep it confidential, as she built the case for her client. But was it really necessary to phone Suzie and tell her to back off? If Philip was really innocent, then anything fresh the Fewings discovered could surely not do his case any harm? It might even help him. Why take the trouble to ring a woman she had only met once and warn her so unmistakably to keep out?

Something else clouded Suzie's mental image of the smart solicitor holding her phone. In her mind, a shadow loomed behind Frances's shoulder. There had been that sudden inexplicable conviction that Frances was not alone. Who then? A partner in the firm? Frances had said her cousin John was taking charge of Eileen's interests, as well as those of the son, Matthew.

Matthew. A flash of memory. Right at the beginning, Frances had said, 'Look, Matthew . . .' and then broken off. Had there been someone else in the room who had not wanted her to mention Matthew Caseley? Could it even have been Matthew himself?

It didn't make sense. Why should Matthew Caseley, or even his solicitor, have wanted Frances to pass this clear warning to Suzie without mentioning his name?

She paced across the kitchen, frowning. Into her mind came again that rising note at the end of Frances's call. *'Do you understand?'* It had sounded like an appeal, not the firmly businesslike tone of what had gone before. Had it been deliberate? Was there something she was trying to tell Suzie that would pass under the radar of whoever else had been listening?

She shivered as she confronted the implication. Was it possible that most of what Frances had said to her in that call had been spoken under duress? Was that final question – *Do you understand?* – the only part that was genuine?

'*Yes, I understand*,' Suzie had replied. But did she?

'Penny for them?'

She was aware of Tom standing in the conservatory, looking at her shrewdly.

She jumped. 'Oh, just daydreaming.'

Tom looked pointedly at the phone on the counter. 'Something disturbing?'

'No . . . no, just a friend,' she said, too quickly.

She plugged in the iron and got out a basket of laundry. She was aware that she wasn't fooling him. He knew she was covering up. But she wasn't ready to tell him yet about the phone call, not until she had worked out for herself more clearly what it meant.

And probably not even then, she thought, as she straightened a shirt sleeve on the ironing board. The last thing I want just now is Tom getting the wrong end of the stick and dashing off on another rash expedition. Not when Frances Nosworthy had asked the Fewings so definitely to stop.

He stood watching her for long moments, then sighed, 'OK. Your call,' and left the room.

For a while, Suzie concentrated on the soothing task of reducing crumpled cloth to a smooth finish. If only she could iron out the wrinkles in her mind so easily. She found herself more shaken by the call than she had realized. She felt increasingly sure that Frances's *Do you understand?* had been a cry for help.

Yet what possible help could she give?

Should she tell the police? Tell them what? That she had sensed the presence of someone else behind Frances as she made the call? She could hear DCI Brewer's contemptuous reply. 'Someone else? In a solicitor's office? How very unusual.' Suzie imagined herself reporting the warning to stay out of the investigation. The very same message DCI Brewer had already given her. Which left what? A change of inflexion in the very last words? Oh, and a reference to Matthew Caseley, cut abruptly short.

It didn't sound a convincing case, even to herself.

She picked up a tee-shirt of Millie's.

There was a prickle in the hairs of her arms. There seemed to be only one thing left. The very thing that she had been alarmed that Tom would do. If someone had really been there behind Frances's shoulder, wanting her to warn the Fewings off, then surely the only course that made sense was for Suzie to go on with what she had started. She would have to find out more.

Suzie's fingers reached for the raspberries half hidden under the leaves, but her mind was elsewhere. The impact of this afternoon's phone call was coming home to her. There had been something reassuring about that slip of cardboard in her shoulder bag, inscribed with Frances Nosworthy's phone number and email address. Frances was not quite the police, but she did represent the law. It had been comforting to think that if anything else disturbing happened, Suzie could report it to the solicitor.

Now the disturbing thing *had* happened – to Frances. Suzie's slender line of security had been snapped.

She pulled herself up short and moved further along the row of canes inside the fruit cage. This was no time to be thinking of herself. Someone had been with Frances, she was sure of it. Someone menacing her.

A less brave part of her mind told her: *Yes, and menacing you.* Why else would he, that shadowy figure behind Frances, have been demanding she phone Suzie? Was it really true that Suzie Fewings, who knew so little of what was going on, was a threat? The one who needed to be silenced?

'I said, "What's wrong?".'

She almost dropped the bowl of raspberries. Nick was standing only a few steps away. He had his hand up, shielding his eyes from the evening sun as he stared at her through the mesh of the fruit cage. At his side, the fork with which he had been digging weeds between the vegetables stood abandoned.

'I'm sorry. I was miles away.'

'More than that. You look as if something's upset you. I asked you three times where you're planning to take me ancestor-hunting on Saturday, and you didn't answer. You're picking raspberries as though your life depended on it, but at the same time you look as if you're in another world.'

She managed a weak smile. 'I can't hide anything from you, can I?'

'Do you want to tell me about it?'

Suzie hesitated. She had been afraid to tell Nick, though for a different reason than the prudence which had made her fob Tom off. It was true that she hadn't initiated the phone call, but Nick had warned her firmly to stay out of the Caseleys' business, and now she seemed to be getting drawn deeper in.

Unless she did what Frances told her and kept out of it. The idea seemed like a kind of betrayal.

She stepped outside the fruit cage and closed the gate.

'Look, I know you told me to let the Caseley thing rest. And truly I have. Well, I looked up a few things in the library about what they might be mining in that area. But that was harmless, surely? And then I got this phone call . . .'

It was hard to convey to someone else the menace she had felt behind Frances Nosworthy's carefully chosen words.

'I know it isn't much,' she ended lamely. 'But I just had this feeling she was speaking under duress.'

'And you haven't reported it to the police this time?'

'I don't think they'd believe me, do you?'

Nick stared down at her. The sun was on his face, making him wrinkle his eyes. He passed an earth-stained hand over his forehead.

'No,' he said. 'Put like that, I don't think they would. Though I'm not sure you shouldn't tell them all the same. Just so it's there in the record in case someone at that end ever feels like taking it seriously.'

She felt a flash of surprise. 'You mean that *you* believe me? You don't think I'm imagining it?'

He put his sun-warmed hands on her arms.

'This is a murder case. Someone out there killed Eileen Caseley. It may have been her husband, it may not. I didn't want to believe what you said about that man in the raincoat watching you yesterday. I didn't see how you could be a threat. I didn't *want* to see. But you talk to Philip's solicitor, she gives you her card, and next thing she's warning you off. It wasn't as if you'd told her you were planning any more investigation. And if we did find out anything else, surely it would only help Philip, if he's innocent? Whether there was somebody leaning over her shoulder or not, something strange is going on.'

'So you think I should report it?'

'I think *I* should. And if I can convince them I'm worried, chances are they'll want to hear it from you.'

His blue eyes were unsmiling. The grip on her arms was firm. Suzie felt an enormous wave of relief.

'I didn't think you'd take me seriously.'

The flicker of a smile then. 'I'm sorry if I didn't respond properly in the middle of the night. I've lived with you long enough to respect your instincts. You've honed your detective skills chasing up all those ancestors of yours, and mine. I wish we could have kept the family out of another crime scene, but like it or not, we seem to have got ourselves involved. Only . . .' the fingers on her arms pressed harder, 'don't go haring off and doing anything by yourself. Take that warning seriously.'

'It's Frances I'm worried about. She may be in real danger.'

But Suzie knew that she was scared for herself as well.

THIRTEEN

Millie drifted downstairs in a tee-shirt that barely covered her small bottom. Tufts of her short blonde hair stuck out at unexpected angles. Her sleepy eyes widened as she entered the kitchen.

'What are you two still doing here at half past nine? I thought I was the one on holiday.'

Suzie and Nick glanced at each other with the almost childish guilt of conspirators. Neither had wanted to tell the children last night how things had moved on, how they seemed to be getting sucked deeper into the darkness surrounding Eileen Caseley's death. They were both dressed in the smart clothes they wore for work: Nick at his architect's practice, Suzie in the office behind the charity shop. But Nick had made the phone call he'd promised. Now they were waiting.

The doorbell rang. Nick was swiftly on his feet. 'We'll do this in the sitting room,' he said to Suzie.

As he went to answer the door, Suzie turned apologetically to Millie.

'Sorry, love. We've got another interview with the police. I had a phone call from Philip Caseley's solicitor yesterday. It could be important.'

The milk sloshed out of Millie's cereal bowl. 'The police! You might have told me! Here's me in just my nightie.'

'He won't need to see you. It's mainly me he wants to talk to.'

'Oh yeah? So why isn't Dad going to work either?'

'Moral support,' Suzie said, getting to her feet. 'Husbands do that sometimes.'

She headed for the hall, closing the kitchen door behind her.

'Detective Sergeant Dudbridge.'

The man waiting with Nick in the sitting room was smaller then Suzie expected for a policeman. He had curly brown hair and a little goatee beard. Suzie thought she recognized him as the man who had stood beside DCI Brewer in Moortown churchyard, watching Eileen Caseley's burial from a discreet distance.

But his expression was neutral. There was none of the disapproval she had clearly sensed in his senior officer's attitude.

'Well, shall we sit down?' he suggested. 'I gather there's something you want to tell me about the Caseley murder case.'

Suzie lowered herself into an armchair as the sergeant and Nick settled themselves on the sofa opposite.

'Would you like a cup of coffee?' she offered belatedly. 'Or tea?'

'No thanks. Shall we get down to business?'

He got out his notebook, pen ready. He turned to Nick and then to Suzie.

'So, which one of you wants to start?'

'I suppose I'd better,' Suzie said. 'Nick rang you because . . . well, because I've spoken to DCI Brewer before and she seems to think I'm pushing my nose in where it's not wanted. But yesterday something new happened . . .'

Once again she told the story of the phone call. It was as difficult as it had been with Nick to describe adequately the changes in Frances's voice. The abrupt halt after she had mentioned Matthew Caseley's name. The formality of her warning Suzie to stay out of it, so at odds with the almost eager listening to Suzie's information in the tea shop. And then that rise in her voice as she asked Suzie, *'Do you understand?'*

'It was almost as if she was appealing to me. Wanting me to understand something different from what she'd actually said. As though she was in trouble and she thought I could help her.'

'How?' The detective's eyebrows rose, but his expression gave little away.

'I don't know!' she said in frustration. 'I've got a really bad feeling that she's in danger. But I don't know what I can do about it. Except tell you.'

'And what sort of danger might that be? As I understand it, Frances Nosworthy is the solicitor for Philip Caseley. She is perfectly within her rights to investigate any line of enquiry which could help her client. You had some . . . shall we say, rather imprecise information about something you thought was going on at Saddlers Wood. Though nothing that would obviously have a bearing on Eileen Caseley's murder.'

'Unless it had to do with a dispute over mineral rights.' Nick unexpectedly came to Suzie's aid.

'Hmm. I see.' The detective's tone was unconvinced.

'So, will you do something about it?' Nick enquired. 'Is there any way you can help Frances Nosworthy?'

The detective twiddled the pen between his fingers. 'I can't discuss operational matters.'

Suzie could contain her impatience no longer. 'So where does that leave us? I'm really scared for her. And I don't know whether you're going to do anything to protect her.'

'It's not for me to say how your information will be used. I'll report back to my superiors. The decision's up to them. Thank you for reporting this. If you would just give me a few moments, I'll get you to sign a statement.'

When the formalities were complete, DS Dudbridge rose. He held out a hand to Nick.

'Thank you again. Let us know if there's anything else.'

He shook hands with Suzie and then he was gone.

She ran her fingers through her hair. 'So, did he believe me? Was he taking it seriously?'

'He didn't slam the door in our faces, did he? He said he wants to know if there's anything else.'

What? Suzie wondered to herself. What else could happen now that Frances had warned Suzie not to contact her?

The detective's car had barely drawn away from the gate when Tom came breezing in. He was dressed in shorts and singlet and was glowing from a morning run.

He threw a copy of the local paper down on the table.

'There! Told you! You said the press were all over the shop at the Caseley funeral. They've given a whole page to it. Photographs and all. Recognize anybody?'

The front page directed Suzie to page five. She thumbed through to it, clumsy in her haste.

The full page spread was a mixture of text and pictures. For a horrid moment, Suzie feared she might see herself entering the church. The most arresting image was of Philip Caseley in his black suit, handcuffed to a warder. There was a picture of the son Matthew, his face expressionless, making his way with other mourners to the church door. A photograph of the farmhouse in Saddlers Wood where the murder had taken place. A longer shot of the sober group around Eileen Caseley's grave as the coffin was lowered.

Suzie started. There was a slim figure in a dark skirt and a paler jacket standing just on the nearer side of the wall which separated the old churchyard from the new. She had her back to the camera, but Suzie knew it was herself. And there, not far away, was a tall, broad-shouldered man in a long dark raincoat, standing beside a Celtic cross.

She shuddered and reached her hand forward till her finger hovered over him.

'That's him. The man who was watching me. I wasn't making it up.'

'What man? Let me see.' Millie pushed forward between Suzie and Tom. She stared at it, uncomprehending. 'So? A man in a black coat at a funeral? What's special about that?'

Suzie sighed. 'It's a long story. I didn't realize we hadn't told you.'

'No one ever tells me anything!'

Nick laid his hand on Millie's shoulder. 'It's just your mother thought this guy was rather more interested in her than in the people at the graveside. It spooked her. But we've no idea who he is. There's probably a perfectly reasonable explanation.'

'Like he fancied her?'

'It's a possibility.'

Suzie looked up warily. Nick's eyes met hers over Millie's head. He winked at her, but not in a playful way. He was telling her that they didn't want to alarm fifteen-year-old Millie. No need to tell her what had happened with Frances, or why the police had been in the house. She breathed more easily. Nick was no longer discounting that instinct of fear she had felt, whatever he said to Millie.

'You said you couldn't see his face properly, because of the cross,' Tom said. 'But you can from this angle.'

'And where's that hat you said he was wearing?' Nick asked.

'He'd taken it off for the committal,' Suzie said. 'He wasn't wearing it when I first saw him. Only afterwards, when we were coming away. And then I couldn't see him properly because he'd pulled the brim down over his face.'

'You won't see much, anyway.' Millie was still indignant at having been shut out from the story. 'He's too far away. Just that he's bald. Or nearly.'

It was true. The photographer had been sufficiently respectful not to show a close-up of the mourners at the grave at such a sensitive moment. They were rather like stick figures in a Lowry painting.

'Tell you what,' said Tom. 'You could go to the newspaper office and get a blow-up of this photo. He's pretty much in the foreground. You might get a proper look at his face then.'

Nick seized the paper. 'I'll do it. It's high time I was off into town, anyway.'

'Hey, you don't have to take the photo with you,' Millie protested. 'You know which one you want. Just tell them . . . Besides,' a thought struck her, 'they might have others of him they didn't publish. Clearer ones. It's worth a try.'

'I'm not sure the photographer would want to hand them over to me. I'm not the police.' Nick looked at Suzie uncertainly. 'Should I show the murder team this? Point out it's our best chance yet of identifying the man?'

She made a doubtful face. 'It's up to you. That detective sergeant seemed more inclined to listen to us than his boss did.'

'Did they tell you whether they'd noticed this man themselves?' Tom asked.

'Chief Inspector Brewer wasn't giving anything away. You've met her. You know what she's like.'

'Point taken. And the DS?'

'We weren't really talking about that. It was . . .' Suzie realized belatedly that she hadn't taken the kids into her confidence, 'about something else entirely. A phone call from Philip's solicitor,' she added lamely.

'You're holding out on us,' Millie accused her.

'Look, sort this out among yourselves,' Nick said. 'I've got to go.'

He breezed out of the house, leaving the newspaper lying on the table.

FOURTEEN

'So, Mum,' Millie insisted.

Suzie gave her a watered down version of Frances Nosworthy's phone call and the sense of menace she had felt.

'Probably just my imagination, but I thought she was holding something back.'

Tom picked up the paper and scrutinized the photograph. 'You think it was this guy, leaning over that solicitor and holding a gun to her head? And you say *I'm* the one who takes off into conspiracy theories?'

'Give me that photo,' Millie demanded.

She took it over to the window and stared at it thoughtfully. The morning sunshine made a halo of her tousled blonde hair.

After a while she said, 'I know you two are fixated on the idea of some mining company murdering the poor woman to get their filthy hands on some minerals under Saddlers Wood, but what if there's a different reason why this guy's standing on the other side of the wall watching them bury her? OK, he's middle-aged and bald, but she wasn't exactly Naomi Campbell herself. What if he was her secret lover? He could hardly push himself in at the graveside with her family and friends, but he'd want to be there, wouldn't he, to say a last goodbye?'

Tom rounded on her, 'But then, why would he kill her?'

'I didn't say he did, half-brain. But he might be the reason someone else did.'

'Philip,' said Suzie. 'You mean you think he did it, after all?' She felt a sense of weary disappointment, for a reason she could not name. She felt her brow furrow. 'But Frances Nosworthy seemed sure he didn't, and she seems to be, not just his solicitor, but a family friend.'

'So? She probably fancies him. Doesn't want to believe he could do anything as bad as that. Come to think of it,' Millie was warming to her subject, blue-grey eyes alight now, 'she might even be an accomplice, so that she could marry Philip once she's got him off the hook and this is all over. Mum, you'd never met her before the funeral. And she sounds keen as mustard to have you spin her a story that would throw suspicion on someone else. It all fits!'

Suzie felt a heavy sense of disbelief. She could see the logic of what Millie was saying. It was an old, old story, far more common than the complicated scenario she and Tom had concocted around a surveying nail found on Caseley land. But then, she argued with herself, money was another standard motive for murder.

'That doesn't explain,' she said more aggressively than she intended, 'why this man you say was Eileen's lover was staring at *me*. What would I have to do with it?'

Millie shrugged. 'Look at it from his point of view. Party round the graveside. Two detectives watching. They could be a problem, so he's hiding behind that cross. And then there's you. Unexplained woman. Also watching from a careful distance. You say he spooked you. But what if you spooked *him*?'

Suzie turned this new idea over in her mind. It had a kind of uncomfortable plausibility. She could not explain why she found it so difficult to accept.

'Should we go to the police with this?' Tom suggested. 'Change of heart?'

'No need,' Millie said. 'Your Detective Chief Inspector Brewer was there. She must have seen him. I'm quite sure she can work it out for herself.'

Suzie sat in her office at the back of the charity shop, trying to keep her mind on her job. Confusing thoughts chased each other through her head. She had been so sure that the truth about Eileen Caseley's murder lay outside the domestic sphere. But why? It had all stemmed from that one sharp crack of a broken branch, the feeling of being watched as she stood by the ruins of her ancestors' cottage in Saddlers Wood. She could see now with increasing clarity why that wasn't enough to convince the police.

Millie's explanation made such perfect sense. A secret lover, a jealous husband. And yet . . . Her mind flew back to Frances Nosworthy's phone call. It had not been possible to convey to the others, or to Detective Sergeant Dudbridge, the contrast between the eagerness with which Frances and Suzie had discussed the case over tea, and the curtly formal telephone communication. The woman who had been sufficiently keen for Suzie to call her with fresh information to give her a business card, then flatly ordered her to stay out of it and make no further contact.

Was it just that Suzie's own pride and self-importance had suffered a slap in the face? She was no longer wanted, of no significance in this case.

Or . . . Her skin crawled as she thought through the rest of Millie's speculation. Was it really possible that Frances herself had been behind Eileen's death? That she and Philip . . .?

Had Frances only latched on to Suzie after the funeral in the hope that the latter's suspicions about a mining company might lead the police away from her?

Suzie thought back to that hour in the tea room. She found it hard to believe that the warmth she had felt towards the other woman had been based on a lie. Or did her pride not want to accept she had been duped?

So had she been conned again by that phone call? Had there been nothing after all in that seeming plea for help at the end: *Do you understand?*

She sighed with frustration and turned her attention to the work in hand. It was only two days now to the sponsored tractor pull on Saturday. Teams from a local Young Farmers Club were taking turns to tow a tractor right across the moor. Suzie had walked the moor enough to know what a challenge that was. Of course, they would be sticking to the road, not climbing the higher tors on either side, and the really steep gradients were not on the moor itself, but in the river gorges around it. Still, it was a formidable undertaking. She hoped the weather would keep fine for them.

She reached for the map. The patron of the old people's charity would be starting them off on the western side, and at the eastern end the MP, Clive Stroud, would be there to meet them in . . . Moortown.

The name leaped out at her from the page. She had known this for weeks, of course. She'd made all the arrangements, invited the MP, organised the WI to lay on the refreshments that would be ready for the triumphant team and the welcoming party. She had even known that she would need to be there to see that everything went off smoothly. But not until this morning had she connected the two strands in her mind. She had wanted to keep away from Moortown after her brush with Chief Inspector Brewer and that warning call from Frances Nosworthy. But now she couldn't help it. There was no one else she could delegate this to. It was a small organization. She was the sole local administrator.

She felt her heart sink as she realized that she would have to go.

Her ears were alert for Nick's key in the front door at the end of the afternoon. Until now she had not realized how much she had been both anticipating and dreading a closer look at the face which had been watching her in the graveyard. If Millie were right, then this man might be guilty of adultery, but not murder. He had come to the funeral torn by a grief he could not express openly.

But she was still left with that feeling of menace as her eyes met his between the interstices of the Celtic cross.

And if Philip had found out about the affair, why not kill this man as well as Eileen?

She was in the hall to greet Nick, her face eager for news.

'Hey, I don't usually get this sort of welcome.'

'Have you got it? The photograph?'

'Should have known it wasn't my bright blue eyes you were pining for. No.' He slapped his car keys down on the hall table in frustration. 'Come back tomorrow, they said. Can't do it any sooner. I'm sorry.'

She did not know whether it was disappointment or relief she felt.

Instead she changed the subject. 'Look, I know you'd rather we kept away from Moortown, under the circumstances. But it had gone clean out of my head that there's this sponsored tractor tow across the moor this weekend. I'm supposed to be there when the MP meets them at the finish in Moortown. I can't really get out of it.'

His eyebrows flicked casually. 'Of course you have to go. Why not? It can't do any harm. There'll be crowds of people around. And you'll be there in your official capacity. It's not as if you'd give them the impression that you were nosing around in the murder case. Do you want me to drive you over?'

'If you wouldn't mind. I still feel a bit shivery about going back there. I'd be glad of the company.'

He put his arms around her lightly. 'Consider yourself escorted. I'll be there to watch your back. And a tractor tow sounds like it could be fun . . . as long as nobody's expecting me to take part. OK?'

'Thanks,' she said, and meant it.

FIFTEEN

Suzie hesitated at the end of their avenue. One branch of the main road led to the Record Office in an industrial estate on the edge of town, the other to the police headquarters. It seemed a symbolic choice. There was nothing new to report

to the police, was there? Even if they were interested. Detective
Chief Inspector Brewer must surely have noticed the man in the
photograph – that was why she was at the funeral, to look for
anyone acting suspiciously.

Including me.

The senior investigating officer was not going to welcome
Suzie teaching her her job.

On the other hand . . . Some of what Millie had proposed was
disturbing. About Frances being personally involved in Eileen's
death.

But there was nothing more she could do about it. She felt a
lift of her spirits she had not experienced for several days. She
could go back to what she enjoyed most: delving into the history
of this area that was not only her own home, but that of count-
less generations of her ancestors.

There was a swing in her step as she walked up the hill and
crested the rise above the industrial estate.

The Record Office nestled in an older house that had been
here long before the car showrooms and DIY centres. More
recently the council had added a new wing with state-of-the-art
conservation facilities for the county's historical documents. It
had become Suzie's playground since its opening.

She stowed her belongings in a locker and put her essential
tools in a clear plastic bag. No chance of smuggling irreplaceable
papers out under the archivist's eye. She had brought her laptop.
Suzie smiled wryly as she realized that her decision to come
here, and not to the police headquarters, had been made the
moment she picked it up.

She wondered where to begin. She knew that her ancestor
Barnabas Avery had been a tinner back in the 1600s. As she had
told Tom, that didn't mean he hacked the tin from the moor with
his own hands. In fact, the Averys had run a tannery in Moortown.
But Barnabas had inherited the historical rights and privileges
of a tinner. He was, in a small way, a mining magnate.

She felt the tension immediately. This was too close to what
they had thought when they made that discovery of the survey
nail. That whoever was in that wood the day they'd met Eileen
Caseley had a stake in a mining company that was eager to get
its hands on what lay under the soil. Had it been Merlin Mines?

She pushed the thought away. It was because she thought she could put that idea behind her that she had come here. Should she just zip her laptop back into its case and go home?

She steeled herself to concentrate on the seventeenth century. It was an era that had known the bitterness of civil war, the beheading of its king, the lurch back from Puritanism to hedonism with the Restoration of the monarchy, and then the flight of the Catholic-leaning James II before the Protestant William of Orange and Queen Mary.

Troubled times.

What century was not?

She took down a history of Moortown from the shelves and scanned the index for *Avery*. Her ancestors had been sufficiently significant in Moortown to warrant five mentions. One in particular stood out. A 'List of Tynners' for 1691.

It contained the names of Moortown men and women 'that are to maintain Armes wthin our pish for the Stannary of Moortown'. 'Pish' was, of course, 'parish'. Clearly these citizens, who included several widows, were not working the tin mines on the moor. They were wealthy landowners, who had inherited or otherwise acquired the statuary rights of tinners, and the consequent responsibilities.

'Barnabas Avery Gent' was listed twice. He was solely responsible for contributing 'one man's Armes' towards the Muster Roll and the same amount jointly with three others. Perhaps the second reference, to a lesser amount, was for his son.

Only some of the men were styled as 'Gentleman'. Barnabas Avery was clearly a leading citizen.

She typed out a transcript on her laptop. She could have used the photocopier, but to do so risked transferring the information from one sheet of paper to another without it passing through her brain. This way, she was forced to concentrate on every word she was copying.

She checked the catalogue and the archivist brought her the next papers she asked for, relating to the tinners' stannary court. These were the originals, not yet digitized or microfilmed. She hoped she would be able to read the old handwriting.

As she made a second transcript a phrase leaped out at her. *'Abraham Hutchings sentenced to three yeres in ye gaol.'*

She sat back and looked at the screen. Barnabas Avery had been among those who sat in the tinners' parliament. Might he also have been a judge in the stannary court? Had he passed sentence of imprisonment on one of their number who had broken the rules of their guild?

The Fewings had visited that stannary jail on the edge of the moor. It was partly ruined now, and in the care of English Heritage. It was a gloomy place. It stood foursquare, like a castle keep, grim-faced, without embellishment. They had been down in the dark depths of the dungeon when a thunderstorm broke. Thunder had shaken the walls and lightning blazed through the darkness. Millie, much younger then, had been terrified.

There was no reason to connect that frightening moment with the man in the raincoat and the dark-brimmed hat.

Perhaps it had been a mistake to come here, to open this particular file.

The whole Fewings family gathered around Nick as he drew the large photograph out of its envelope and laid it down on the table.

Suzie hung back a little, letting Millie and Tom pore over it. She felt an odd reluctance to look. It was Tom who noticed and stepped back for her.

'Hey, Mum, Take a look at him. Does this tell you anything you didn't already know?'

Suzie made herself step forward to the edge of the table. The high-quality print showed its subjects in shockingly clear detail. The photographer had not used his most powerful lens, but it was enough.

In the middle distance, the party around Eileen's grave were figures only, the rector most noticeable in his white surplice and black cassock. At the head of the grave stood her son, Matthew Caseley. Suzie could clearly distinguish his tall, broad-shouldered build. At the foot, separated from the other mourners, Philip Caseley and his warder had their backs to the camera. The undertakers were lowering Eileen's coffin into the grave. It was half hidden by the figures standing around it, but it conveyed the ineffable sadness of the woman Suzie had met only once, and would never see again.

The two detectives were more distant onlookers, on the far side of the grave.

What most grabbed her eye were the two people in the foreground, though they stood on either sides of the composition, facing in towards the central group like the supporters of a coat of arms. One, startlingly, was herself. Unlike the newspaper, the colour print showed her grey skirt and mauve jacket, the slightly untidy fall of her wavy brown hair. Her face was mostly hidden, watching the burial over the old churchyard wall.

She forced herself to move her eyes sideways to the man on the right-hand side of the photo. The same large body she remembered. The long black buttoned-up raincoat. She could see now the broad-brimmed hat in his hands, which she had not noticed until he put it on later. His face was much more clearly visible than her own. She had not imagined it: he had turned from the burial in the field above him to look straight across the picture at her. It gave her a shudder even now.

'Well?' Tom asked eagerly. 'Recognize him?'

'Only from that day. I don't think I'd ever seen him before.'

She stared down at the face in the photo. She no longer knew what she ought to think about him. She had been so sure at the time that he was a danger to her, that he had not expected to see her there. But now she thought of Millie's theory. Was this in fact a man paralysed by grief, watching the burial of the woman he loved?

Was he a mining magnate who had either killed, or ordered the killing of Eileen Caseley to further his own commercial interests? Or had he brought about her death in quite a different way, through an unwise affair with Philip Caseley's wife?

How did he feel as he stood, so near, yet not quite part of the burial party? What had drawn him to expose himself so far? And what inexplicable reason could there be for him to consider Suzie Fewings significant?

'You know,' Tom said, his head on one side, 'I think I *have* seen this guy somewhere before. I just can't remember where.'

SIXTEEN

The centre of Moortown was transformed. Last time Suzie had seen the square it had been fuller than usual, but with people in the dark clothes suitable for a funeral. This Saturday afternoon there was a holiday atmosphere. Townsfolk and summer visitors were out in colourful attire. The weather had been kind to the Young Farmers. The sun shone out of a blue sky flecked with white clouds, but not so fiercely as to make towing a tractor up the inclines of the moorland road any harder than it needed to be.

Suzie had checked the square before she and Nick went off for a pub lunch. Tables had been set up under the open-sided market hall in the centre of the open space. She had met with the volunteers from the Women's Institute who were laying on a welcoming tea when the victorious team arrived. A local pub had donated kegs of beer and soft drinks. Local craftspeople and fund-raisers had set up stalls around the square. The police had been informed well in advance, and orange cones ensured that the entry route into the town would be kept free of cars. She introduced herself to a couple of officers she met on the way, and they nodded politely.

There was nothing more she could do for the moment. The MP Clive Stroud would be arriving mid-afternoon to perform the welcoming ceremony and to receive a giant cheque for the sponsor money the Young Farmers had raised. Everything seemed under control.

Earlier that morning, Suzie had met Tom at the foot of the stairs and asked him if he wanted to come too.

'I thought I'd hang out with the guys this afternoon. You don't need me, do you?'

'No. I just thought you might enjoy it. A bit of fun.'

'My memories of Moortown aren't exactly fun.'

She had felt the rebuke. 'I'm not forgetting there's been a murder,' she snapped. 'I'm just doing my job.'

Millie had smiled at her, bemused, over a bowl of muesli. 'Mum, do I look the Young Farmer type?'

Over lunch Suzie tried to convince herself that this was just another weekend expedition with Nick. She hadn't wanted to come back to Moortown, but the tractor tow had been planned months ago. She couldn't get out of it.

It was a weekend. There was no reason to think that Frances Nosworthy would be here on the streets. Suzie didn't even know whether the solicitor lived in Moortown.

A new worry nibbled away at her mind. Should she have ignored the obvious command to stay out of further involvement and done more to follow up Frances's call? Perhaps she should have responded to her gut instinct that what had really mattered was that final plea for Suzie's understanding. If she had been right about that, what had Frances hoped that Suzie could do?

'I feel bad about Frances,' she said to Nick as she sipped her coffee. 'I feel I'm letting her down, somehow. I can't believe Millie's theory that she was in on the murder.'

'You've done what you could,' Nick said sensibly. 'You reported her call to the police. It's up to them now.'

'Mmm. I suppose so.'

'Look, I thought we'd come here because you're responsible for the arrangements for this jamboree. You've got to put this other thing behind you.'

'I know. I'm probably making a mountain out of a molehill. We never did have any proof that there was somebody else in the woods that Saturday.'

'Gosh, was that only four weeks ago?'

'Yes. It's all happened so fast. The murder, the funeral, everything. I wonder how long Matthew Caseley is staying. Presumably they can't decide about the future of the farm until Philip's sentenced – if he is. And the trial could be months away. Meanwhile, there's no one to run the farm. I can't imagine that neighbour I met will be able to go on looking after their sheep indefinitely. Just being in prison may be enough to make Philip give up the farm.'

'You don't think they'll let him out on remand?'

The thought startled Suzie. 'Would they do that? Release someone accused of murder?'

'If it's what they think it is, a crime passionel, he's not likely
to kill anyone else.'

'What about the other man?'

'Who may or may not be that strange guy in the photograph.
We're guessing, Suzie. Let's face it, we haven't really got a clue
what's going on. Let's leave it, shall we?'

It was a relief to let the business of the afternoon take her over.
She checked her mobile frequently to pick up messages about
the progress of the tow. The Young Farmers had stopped for
lunch at a pub halfway across the moor. With luck, they should
reach Moortown by about three o'clock. Suzie thought of the
long hill from the fringe of the moor down into the town. They
would need ropes on the back of the tractor to stop it plunging
downhill out of control. Like the brake horses on the back of
stage coaches in the past, she thought, remembering yet another
ancestor who had kept the toll gate on the stage coach route into
Moortown. A local diarist had hinted he was pocketing some of
the tolls.

She shook herself back to the urgency of the present. Before
long Clive Stroud would be arriving. She had arranged with his
assistant to meet him at the market hall in the middle of the
square.

'You go ahead,' Nick said. 'You don't need me, do you? I
thought I'd look around some of the craft stalls. You never know,
I might pick up something interesting.'

'Fine,' Suzie said. 'I checked before lunch, and everything
seems to be OK for this afternoon. I'm not expecting any prob-
lems I'd need your help with.' A sudden chill struck her. 'Just
don't go too far away.'

'I'll be around. Have fun, then.' Nick grinned at her and
disappeared into the crowd of holidaymakers.

The helpers from the Women's Institute had been busy. Platters
of savouries and cakes, covered in cling film, were appearing on
a table under the shade of the market hall's slate roof. Cups and
saucers and glasses stood ready on another. The Moortown WI
evidently had considerable expectations of the Young Farmers'
appetites. Suzie thanked the women effusively.

'I hope there's going to be a bit of that luscious-looking coffee cake left over. It looks too good to miss.'

A teenage boy about Tom's age was setting up a microphone for Clive Stroud's speech. I have thought of everything, haven't I? Suzie wondered.

She was aware of a disturbance in the square. It had been closed to traffic, but a sleek black car was inching its way through the crowds, which parted reluctantly to let it pass. It drew up in front of the market hall. Two people got out: a man from the passenger seat and a woman from the driver's side. The man marched confidently up the steps to the shaded area of the market hall. A big man in a tweed jacket, his large head almost bald. Suzie took a step forward to greet him, and stopped dead.

It was the man in the photograph. The man who had stared at her from behind the Celtic cross.

Just for a moment, she saw a flash of something in his eyes. It was gone too quickly to interpret what it was, before it was replaced by a beaming smile. He advanced towards her, his hand held out.

'Mrs Fewings, I believe. How nice to meet you in person at last.'

SEVENTEEN

H is hand grasped hers, strong and firm. Too strong. She felt imprisoned by it. There was a moment when she felt the pressure tighten.

He released her just as suddenly. It left her feeling unbalanced. She hoped she was not going to faint.

The woman with him bustled forward: frizzy hair, tied back in an effort to tame it, horn-rimmed spectacles. She carried a clipboard like a shield before her.

'Where will Clive be speaking from? That microphone over there? Have you tested it?'

She was making for the speaker's table, as if to try it for

herself, when Clive Stroud put out a commanding hand to grasp her arm.

'This is my agent, Gina Alford. My nanny, really.' He beamed at both of them. The woman's face softened in its warmth into an enormous smile. 'She's the one who looks after me, makes sure I'm always where I'm supposed to be, and that I stay out of trouble. Gina, meet . . . Suzie . . . Fewings.' He said her name slowly, as though savouring it. 'I'm sure the two of you have been in touch about all this.'

'Of course,' said Gina Alford, returning to her businesslike crispness. 'These things don't arrange themselves. Good afternoon, Mrs Fewings. What time do you expect the tractor to arrive?'

'Three-fifteen, by the latest reckoning. They should be coming down off the moor by now. That's the trickiest bit. It's quite a hill.'

She marvelled that she could keep talking so calmly. If there was tension in her voice, it was no more than might be expected with so much responsibility in her hands. But while she talked with the MP's agent about the arrangements she was all too conscious of his large presence just behind Gina Alford's shoulder. His face had been grim, expressionless, at the funeral. Today he wore the wide and practised smile of a constituency MP. His weekends must be filled with events like this as he moved around his rural electorate. Why did she find that smile more sinister than the sober face she had seen before?

She decided to seize her courage in her hands and take the initiative. While Gina Alford fussed around the table where her MP would make his speech, Suzie turned to him.

'Didn't I see you at Eileen Caseley's funeral a few days ago?'

The eyes narrowed fractionally. But his mouth did not lose its smile.

'She was my constituent. Bad business.'

'Did you ever meet her?' She was pushing her luck now. For reasons she could not begin to guess, he had not wanted to see her at that funeral. Did she really hope that she could find out more by questioning him? Or was she risking making him angry with her? She was deeply sure that, however much he might be smiling in public, this was a man it would not do to cross. Her fingers still felt the crushing power of his grip before he had let her go.

'My dear, I thought you had invited me here for a celebration. A splendid effort, pulling a tractor all the way across the moor. I only wish I were young enough to join in. I don't think we want to be reminded of something quite as unpleasant as a murder, do we?'

He was challenging her now, ordering her to stay out of his business. She had a sudden image of Frances Nosworthy, unseen at the other end of a telephone. Suzie had had that sense of someone in the room with Frances. Someone powerful enough to bring the force of his personality to bear on her and make her deliver that message to Suzie that she must stay out of this murder case in future.

Why? What was it that Suzie Fewings knew, or he thought she knew, that was so important?

And what would he do if she disobeyed?

She looked round in sudden need. Nick had readily offered to come with her. '*I'll be there to watch your back,*' he had said yesterday. It had been half humorous, half not. But she had been glad of it. Nick had been reluctant to take seriously the full gravity of the situation Suzie thought she was in. Still, he had been persuaded. She was sure of it.

Yet where was he? Now that she was truly afraid, now that she was face to face with the man in the photograph, Nick was nowhere to be seen. He had said he was going to look at the craft stalls. But surely he would have remembered to keep an eye open for what was happening here in the market hall? He must have seen the car forcing the crowd apart as it rolled its way across the square. He must surely have seen Clive Stroud getting out and making his way to this dais under the pillared roof. How could he not have recognized the man whose photograph he had ordered from the newspaper himself?

There was a sound of distant cheering. A far part of Suzie's mind remembered why she was here. The tractor. The Young Farmers must have reached the edge of the town, where the first onlookers would be lining the street to welcome them.

Clive Stroud had caught it too.

'Ah, our young friends are approaching, by the sound of it.

Three-ten. I congratulate you, Mrs Fewings. You seem to have everything planned.'

The professional smile was back. He was very good at the charm. He certainly had Gina Alford under his spell. She was back at his elbow now, eager for him to turn his attention away from Suzie to her.

'Clive, do you need a stand for your notes? I'm sure Mrs Fewings could find you one before they get here.' She looked challengingly at Suzie, evidently wishing her away.

'No, Gina, everything's fine.'

Again, that wide white smile. And again, the abrasive Gina softened visibly.

Under its influence, it would be so easy for Suzie to tell herself that she had been imagining things, that this was not the man in the graveyard, only someone who looked rather like him. She had woven a web of fear around him for no good reason. He was just a well-meaning, even rather attractive, MP, giving up his Saturday afternoon for the sake of her charity and, of course, to show his face to a considerable number of voters.

But she had seen that momentary narrowing of his eyes. Every instinct was telling her that this man was a danger to anyone who stood in his way. And that he saw her, bafflingly, as a threat to him.

There was no time to worry about that now. The noise of cheering was growing. People were crowding forward, eager for a first glimpse of the approaching tractor and its energetic team. Stewards were trying to marshal the throng back to clear the route across the square.

Suzie cast round a harassed eye, wondering if she had remembered everything she needed to in the confusion of what had happened. On the public relations side at least, she need not have worried about Clive Stroud. The broad smile was firmly in place. He tweaked his tweed jacket into place and ran a hand over his balding head. He stood waiting on the top step of the market hall, ready. His agent hovered in the shadows just behind him, clipboard clutched to her. It hardly needed Suzie to pilot the MP towards what he should do. Gina Alford obviously devoted her life to that.

Suzie allowed herself a moment to look behind her. The crowd on the other side of the square was thinning, as people jostled around the sides of the market hall for a better view. She could see the brightly coloured stalls in that direction more clearly now. Her eyes raked the few customers left around them, hoping for a sight of Nick's tall form and wavy black hair. She could not see him.

She fought down an indignation that was tinged with fear. Didn't he realize how badly she needed him at this moment?

Her attention was snatched back as the biggest cheer of all heralded the arrival of the tractor in the square. First came the red-faced and perspiring team of Young Farmers, hauling the ropes over their shoulders. More of them walked alongside, some darting into the crowd with buckets of money rattling. They all wore bright red tee-shirts emblazoned with the words: 'AGE OF SILVER. *Help those who once helped you.*'

The tractor was red too, festooned with flags. A young woman in khaki trousers and the same red tee-shirt stood aloft, punching her fist in the air, while with the other hand she held the tractor's course steady as it rolled across the square.

The tow team stopped at the foot of the market hall steps. They let the ropes fall from their shoulders with whoops of triumph. Eyes were already going longingly to the beer kegs ready on the dais.

Clive Stroud came down the steps and shook them all by the hand. Then he mounted to the table in the shade of the market hall roof and took the microphone.

'Young Farmers, ladies and gentlemen. What can I say? Tremendous effort! I can't tell you what a thrill it is to see the generation of the future putting themselves out so far for the generation that all of us look back to with gratitude and respect . . .'

Suzie felt an obscure sense of disappointment as the words of his speech rolled over her. She had put so much effort into this. It was the biggest fund-raising effort she had been involved in. Because of her, hundreds of people had turned out this afternoon. She could already see the giant cheque being brought forward, reporting the four-figure sum the Young Farmers had miraculously raised by their heroic pull across the moor. And she could see the money was still coming in. She ought to be delighted, revelling in the success. Even the weather had turned out fine for her.

Instead, she felt like a rabbit caught in the glare of a fox's eyes, knowing that she was in entirely the wrong place, but unable to run.

She wanted more than anything to feel Nick beside her.

It was over. The speech had been made, the cheque received. The crowd of ravenous Young Farmers around the refreshment tables was beginning to thin. Suzie was longing for the moment when Clive Stroud and Gina Alford would signal that their business was over and they were ready to go.

Could it really be as simple as that?

She took the agent to one side to ask about expenses.

'Oh, no need for that. Clive's always happy to help. He's marvellous, isn't he?'

Her eyes glowed behind the spectacles. Then the frostiness returned. 'I don't imagine you would normally get someone like him.'

Over Gina Alford's shoulder, Suzie was watching the MP. He was talking animatedly to a group of well-wishers. Obviously he was well known in the town.

There must have been many people at the funeral who recognized him. She hadn't seen Clive Stroud talking to anyone in the churchyard, but then, Frances Nosworthy had distracted her attention. Suzie felt her cheeks grow hot as she thought how they had wondered about showing that photograph to the police. It would have seemed foolish to them that the Fewings hadn't known who he was. The cathedral city where they lived had a different MP.

Now he was in plain sight, pressing the flesh, smoothly affable. MP for Moortown and the surrounding area. He looked untouchable.

She was the one who was vulnerable. She felt that now as he swung round to face her.

Again that large hand reached out and enclosed her unwilling one.

'Ah, Mrs Fewings! May I call you Suzie? Thank you so much for inviting me. A truly splendid occasion, don't you think? It's so wonderful to see the young folks in a positive light. You really have done an admirable job in organizing this. You must be very pleased with the sum they raised. And there'll be a lot more to come from your other activities here this afternoon.'

All the time, his hand was gripping hers. Again, that feeling of imprisonment. His broad face was smiling. She could not read his eyes.

'Yes, thank you,' she said a little breathlessly. 'Yes, they did magnificently.'

She tried to withdraw her hand, but he held on to it. The look in his dark eyes was keener now.

'So sorry your husband couldn't be here.' He dropped her hand abruptly. His voice was clear. 'I don't expect we shall be meeting again. I shouldn't imagine you will have any further business in Moortown when this is over.'

With a peremptory signal to his agent, he turned his back on her and strode down the steps to his waiting car.

Suzie was left with his words of unmistakable warning ringing in her ears.

EIGHTEEN

She had underestimated how long it would take before everything was packed up and she was free to go. She accepted a cup of tea from the Women's Institute but she found she was now too nervous to eat the cake.

Where *was* Nick?

She tried phoning him, but his mobile was switched off. She scanned her own phone for text messages. Nothing.

She felt a growing resentment. The enigmatic encounter with Clive Stroud had shaken her. True, it gave him a reason to be at Eileen Caseley's funeral. A shocking murder in his own constituency. A chance to show himself to a large crowd of mourners as a caring MP.

But there had been something more, something personal about that grip on her hand, the warning behind the smile. It was silly to think that Nick's physical presence could have made any difference, but she felt an aching need for him. Here, drifting around the market hall with a teacup in her hand, or touring the square to chat to the stallholders and thank them, she felt unreasonably exposed. To what? Clive Stroud had put no name to the veiled menace behind his words. What could happen to Suzie Fewings if she refused to let the matter drop? It was surely too melodramatic to imagine that Eileen Caseley's might not be the only death to fear.

Still, she longed for Nick's reassurance, for the common sense that would puncture her wilder flights of imagination. Just for somebody to talk to.

'Great stuff,' she said to the lad packing up the mike and loudspeakers. 'Thanks!' And to the straggle of Young Farmers still left in the square, 'Fantastic result!' Someone had driven the red tractor back to whichever farm had loaned it. But the praise and the thanks were sounding mechanical now. She hoped the volunteers did not hear that in her voice. All she wanted was for the afternoon to be over and to be reunited with Nick.

The stalls and their wares were being dismantled and loaded into the boots of cars or the backs of 4x4s. The crowd of spectators had dispersed. Suzie was left with a giant cardboard cheque and the now inescapable knowledge that Nick was nowhere in the square.

Now that the truth was staring her in the face, Suzie realized that she had known it for a long time. She had persuaded herself that he must have found someone interesting to talk to on a craft stall, or that he had run into a friend and they had taken themselves off for tea and a chat somewhere. At every moment she had been expecting that she would turn round, and there he would be, after all, on the other side of the square.

It was five o'clock. Nick was not here.

She tried her phone again. Nothing.

She faced the stark reality.

All this time she had been fearing for herself. She had wanted to share that fear with Nick, to be comforted. Now, for the first time, the truth struck her, that it was Nick she should be afraid for.

Her mind screamed at the unfairness of it. She was the one

who had been alarmed by that crack of wood near the ruined cottage, her conviction that they were being watched. It was she who had made that last-minute decision to go back to Saddlers Wood with Tom and Dave. And it had been her choice to go to the funeral, to share her fears with Frances Nosworthy. At every step, Nick had tried to hold her back. He had only reluctantly consented to give way to her judgement and trust her instinct. And now he was the one who was inexplicably missing.

She had read of people feeling a cold sweat break out. She experienced the reality now. Even the solitary cup of tea threatened to come back from her knotted stomach.

What could she do? She knew without being told that there would be little to be gained from reporting him missing to the police. How long would their car have to sit in Moortown car park unclaimed before anyone would take her seriously?

One little memory whispered to her that there was a lifeline. A small piece of pasteboard in her shoulder bag. Frances Nosworthy's business card.

As though reaching for a forbidden fruit, she drew it out. The letters and numbers danced before her eyes. An insistent voice was hammering in her head. Frances had warned her not to contact her again. New information had apparently come to light. The case was closed. Suzie's help was no longer needed.

Now she was the one who needed help.

That very afternoon Clive Stroud had repeated that warning. *'I shouldn't imagine you will have any further business in Moortown when this is over.'*

But she hadn't initiated it this time. Whatever mystery lay behind Eileen Caseley's murder and Frances Nosworthy's phone call, Nick had nothing to do with it. He had come here this afternoon in all innocence, to give her moral support. And, yes, to 'watch her back'. Had he only been joking?

'Mrs Fewings!' A voice interrupted her swirling thoughts.

A younger man in a navy-style jumper and jeans was holding a heavy canvas bag out to her. 'There's a sizeable taking here from the afternoon's activities. Stalls and collections. Do you want to take it away with you? Or shall I put it in the safe until Monday and then send you a cheque?'

She fought to bring her mind back to the fund-raising effort. 'What? Oh, I'm sorry. I'm not sure . . . Oh, why don't I leave it with you? If that's all right?'

'Will do. John Nosworthy, by the way.' He shifted the cash bag to the other hand and held out the right one to shake hers.

She stared, confused, at the slip of pasteboard she was holding. The name was sounding in her head. John Nosworthy. Frances's cousin. The solicitor from the other law firm who was representing Eileen Casely's interests.

She looked up in time to see his eyes go to the card still in the hand he was offering to shake. Did she imagine the slightly colder note in his voice?

'I see you've been in touch with Frances.'

'I . . . Yes . . . We bumped into each other after the funeral.'

It was unnecessary to say which funeral. Why did she feel the necessity to apologize?

'A terrible tragedy. We all knew Philip. Times are hard, but we never imagined it would come to this. You weren't thinking of contacting Frances, were you? She's not here.'

'No. I haven't seen her. I did wonder if she'd turn up. Most of the town seems to be here.' She was trying to steady her voice, to sound normal. 'Just now, I seem to have lost my husband, too.'

'Can I help? What does he look like?'

'Tall. Black wavy hair. Vivid blue eyes. Wearing a grey gilet with a short-sleeved check shirt and blue jeans. He said he was going to look at the craft stalls.'

'But they've all packed up and gone. Except the fossil man's.'

'Yes.'

There was an awkward pause. Suzie longed to ask where Frances was. Where did she live? The address on the business card must be the solicitors' office in town.

There was something insistent in John Nosworthy's silence. He offered no further help. She was not sure what she was expected to do. Was he someone she could appeal to for help? Or had the advice that Frances wasn't here been meant to warn her off? Whose side was he on?

*   *   *

The phone in her shoulder bag signalled an incoming message. Suzie made a grab for it, forgetting that John Nosworthy was still standing watching her.

She read the message with a relief so powerful it almost had the force of a shock.

'*Sorry. I'm on my way.*'

'Your husband? Is he all right?' The young solicitor's voice sounded concerned.

'Yes.' Suzie managed a weak smile for him. 'I could kill him. Taking off for three hours without telling me.'

'I'm glad he's safe.'

He sounded as though he meant it. He must have picked up the undercurrent of her fear.

'Look, Suzie,' he said awkwardly. 'Sorry, is it OK if I call you that? If I can ever be of any help . . .'

She looked round from returning the phone to her bag in surprise. 'Help? How?'

He looked embarrassed. There was, she thought, a shadow of doubt – or was it fear? – in his eyes. 'Oh, nothing. Just . . . well, you might as well have my card too.'

He reached as though for a familiar jacket pocket, then realized he was in his casual weekend wear. He looked even more flushed and uneasy than before.

'Sorry. Idiot. My office is next door to Frances's, but the telephone numbers are different, of course.' He seemed to hesitate. He looked over his shoulder, then back at her. 'Do you want to take my mobile number down?'

Suzie was growing more intrigued. Why should Eileen Caseley's solicitor feel the need to give his mobile number to a woman who had apparently been working with his cousin to strengthen the case for Philip's innocence?

Unless, the thought screamed at her, he too believed the police had the wrong man in custody. If not Philip, who else?

She looked at John Nosworthy with renewed interest. She had been so caught up with her concern for Nick that she had regarded his arrival with the money-bag as an intrusion. Even now, her eyes were going past him, looking for Nick to come walking across the square. But she made an effort to concentrate on the man in front of her. Younger than herself, she thought, by a good ten years, Thirtyish. Fair hair. An air of neat orderliness about him, even in his weekend clothes. What was it about solicitors?

But she was becoming increasingly aware of his uneasiness. He was starting to look around him nervously. At the close of the afternoon, the two of them were standing isolated on the dais of the market hall. Suddenly he looked as though he no longer wanted to be there.

She got out her diary. 'The number?'

'Oh . . . yes.' He was startled back into remembering he had offered to give it to her.

He reeled off the digits. 'Look, I've got to go.'

He was already making for the steps when Suzie called after him on a sudden impulse. 'Frances? Is she OK?'

He threw her a brief look over his shoulder, which she was almost sure was scared. 'Frances? Yes, sure. She's as right as rain.'

He sped off across the square, leaving Suzie strangely unconvinced.

'Hey, there! I'm really sorry. The prodigal returns.'

Nick's voice made her spin round. She was torn between a desire to throw herself into his arms and the urge to vent her fury on him.

'Where have you *been*? Three hours! And not even a text message, until five minutes ago.'

'I know.' He held up his hands in mock surrender. In spite of herself, she was captivated by the laughter in his bright blue eyes. So like Tom, with that teasing, *'You're not really angry with me, are you?'* smile. 'But you'll never believe what I've found out. The guy I was talking to was a nutter, though. Paranoid. When he saw me getting my phone out, I was afraid he was going to hit me, or at least clam up tight.'

'Never mind who you met! You were supposed to be looking out for me. Didn't you see who was here in the market hall with me all afternoon?'

'Clive Stroud, wasn't it? The MP for Moortown? I saw his car coming into the square. That was just before I met this guy with the fossil stall.'

'Fossils?' she said incredulously.

'It's a long story. I was just idly looking over his stuff . . .'

'But didn't you *see* him? Clive Stroud?'

'Only from a distance. Big, bald. Why?'

'Just that he's the man in the photograph. The one who was lurking behind a cross in the graveyard at Eileen Caseley's funeral, but staring at *me*.'

Nick blinked, recalled from the beginning of his own story with a shock.

'Clive Stroud? Are you sure?'

'Of course I'm sure. That face is burned on my memory ever since you brought the enlargement home.'

'It was only a profile.'

'It was him, Nick!' She almost stamped her foot.

'OK. Steady on.' He put his hand on her arm. To her dismay she found she was trembling. She wanted nothing more than to bury herself in his embrace. But this was too public a place. She struggled to get control of herself.

'And as if that wasn't enough, he gripped my hand really hard and told me he was sure I'd have no further business in Moortown. He was warning me off, Nick. Why? What have I done? I don't know anything about the murder, but people keep acting as though I do. And then you went off, and I didn't hear a thing for *hours*.'

She was very near tears now. Nick had his arm round her. He was steering her down the market hall steps.

'I think we need to find ourselves somewhere where we can talk this over. You haven't heard my side of the story yet.'

NINETEEN

Nick steered her into the Angel Inn. The pub was almost deserted at the close of the afternoon. They found a booth sheltered by oak partitions. Nick bent his head towards Suzie and spoke softly.

'Look, love, I'm really sorry for leaving you. I had no idea.

You looked perfectly OK up there in the market hall with hundreds of people looking on. I didn't think anything bad could possibly happen to you.

'As I said, I drifted around looking at what the stalls were selling, and I came upon this guy with fossils and amber and stuff like that. I got talking to him and it turned out he's a really keen geologist. Almost too keen.' He gave a rueful smile. 'Once he saw he'd got a captive audience he was away. Told me more than I really wanted to know about the Jurassic Age and the local rock formations. And yes, your tungsten deposit just outside Moortown came up. Seems he was advising the local opposition group about the risks. But at the same time you could see he was fired up about the idea of finding something really valuable on his home patch.

'Well, to cut a long story short, the conversation got round to Saddlers Wood.'

Suzie was startled out of her indignation that Nick seemed more concerned to tell her what had happened to him than with her own scary experience with Clive Stroud.

'Saddlers Wood? So there really is some truth that someone is interested in prospecting there?'

'Yes. This guy – Bernard Summers is his name – he says he's thought so for a long time, but no one would take him seriously. To be honest, he comes across as a bit of a nutter. The Ancient Mariner syndrome. Buttonholing anyone who will listen to him and pouring out his theories. And yet, at the same time, he's a guy who sounds as though he may know what he's talking about. I'm no geologist, but he was reeling off facts and figures like an encyclopaedia.

'I was beginning to think I ought to get away from him when he nobbled a mate of his and asked him to look after the stall while he took me home to show me what he'd found in Saddlers Wood.'

'Oh, yes?' Suzie felt her indignation returning. 'And how far away was "home"?'

'Not that far, really. Down the other end of this street and round the corner. He's got a little shop selling fossils, and a flat over it. Honestly, you looked all right, and I was sure I'd be back before the proceedings in the square were over. Be fair. You and

Tom had got it into your heads that something fishy was going on in Saddlers Wood. And here was a guy who might be able to tell me what it was.'

His voice was rising. Suzie looked up. A group of men had come into the pub and settled themselves at the bar. One of them looked over his shoulder at the Fewings. They were not far away.

'Keep your voice down. I'm not sure this is the right place to be talking about this.'

Nick followed her eyes. Was it just because her nerves were on edge that she thought there was something hostile in the way that more of the men were now looking in their direction?

'If they're local,' Nick said more quietly, 'they may have heard this before. Bernard Summers made out like he was telling me a state secret, but I'm not sure he's the sort of man to keep his ideas to himself. I got the impression that he'd bend the ear of anyone rash enough to get within firing range.'

'But you fell for it.'

'What was I supposed to do? This is all about Saddlers Wood, isn't it? I reckoned you'd want me to find out what I could.'

Suzie was acutely aware that the men at the bar were still observing them.

'Look,' she murmured, 'I really think we should do this somewhere else.'

Nick finished his beer and stood up. 'OK, if it makes you feel better. I think you've got yourself worked up into a bit of a state about this Clive Stroud guy. Now we know he's the MP for Moortown, there's a perfectly good reason why he should have been at that funeral. The Eileen Caseley murder was a pretty explosive case for a small place like this. Lots of public interest, press, TV. He's a politician. He'd have wanted to show his face.'

'That doesn't explain why he was looking at me like that, does it?'

'I'd look at you, if I was him.'

'Nick. I'm being serious. You weren't there.'

'OK, OK. Let's find somewhere quieter to talk.'

She led the way to the door. Outside she hesitated.

'We could go back to the car,' Nick suggested.

But Suzie headed across the street to a narrow lane that led down to the small river which flowed through the town. At the lower end was a water mill, its wooden wheel silent now. There was a bench at the bottom, beside the water.

'Right,' she said, sitting down. 'So you've fallen into the clutches of the local nutcase who wants to tell you his pet theory about the geology of Saddlers Wood. And somehow you think this is going to explain why everybody round here seems to be looking at me as though I've got leprosy.'

His hand closed over hers as he seated himself beside her. There was no one else about on the riverside path. The sound of the rushing water made a screening background to his words.

'I told you this guy is a keen geologist. Well, in his spare time he wanders around the place testing out his theories. He's been up on the Caseley farm dozens of times. And he's convinced Philip Caseley has something worth exploiting on his farm.' He looked at her keenly, as if expecting her to guess what it was.

'Go on, then. Spit it out.' She had still not entirely forgiven him.

His eyes sparkled. 'Not tungsten, though that's pretty valuable . . . Gold.'

Now she did turn to him with her full attention.

'Is that possible? . . . Yes, I suppose it is. Didn't they find gold in the Leigh Valley a couple of years ago? And I seem to remember reading that when Prince Charles married Diana the wedding rings were made of Welsh gold. Though, come to think of it, I haven't heard anything about that Leigh Valley find since. Maybe it turned out not to be in commercial quantities, after all. Or perhaps it wasn't really the Leigh Valley. The press was going wild over this secret location. The name could have been a bluff.'

'Look, do you want to hear about Saddlers Wood or not?'

'Sorry! I was just wondering how important it was, if it's true. I don't know anything about mining. I mean, we talk about "striking gold", but I wouldn't know if finding it is really more valuable than finding tungsten nowadays.'

'I can assure you Bernard Summers thought it was. He's picked up traces of it in a stream running down off Caseley land.'

Suzie had a sudden vivid memory of racing for a bus. She had hared after the two boys over rough ground and nearly fallen into a deep-carved gulley. It had been a packhorse trail leading down to the road, but hadn't there been a stream flowing alongside it over the stones?

'The funny thing is that, although he could talk the hind legs off a donkey, he really doesn't seem to have spread this around. I may have been doing him an injustice about that. At one point I got out my phone to tell you where I was, and suddenly he pulled up short. All of a sudden, the atmosphere turned very nasty. He seemed to think I might be a reporter, or something. Even working for the other side.'

'What other side?'

'What indeed? Anyway, it was a complete turnaround. Instead of bending my ear like the Ancient Mariner, he suddenly became threatening. Made it clear that all sorts of ugly things could happen to me if I told anyone what he'd just said.'

Suzie found herself remembering what had happened only minutes ago. That sense that a group of men at the bar were taking a keener interest in her conversation with Nick than was really healthy.

'You said this Bernard Summers was a nutcase who rammed his theories down the throat of anyone within earshot. And he really hadn't told anyone else about this? Why you?'

Nick grinned ruefully. 'Guess I'm just a sympathetic listener, though it was the Saddlers Wood thing that got me hooked. He's obviously not used to finding a victim who genuinely wants to know what he thinks. And he *did* tell someone else, of course. Philip Caseley.'

'And Philip was dead set against any mining in this area. That's what that woman on the bus told me. Though presumably she didn't know what he'd got beneath his own soil. She certainly didn't mention gold. I suppose we all assumed any other find would be tungsten, like that other one.'

'That's just the point. Philip *wasn't* against exploiting this. Just the opposite. He saw it as the end to all his troubles.'

Suzie frowned. 'Then why does everybody think he wouldn't allow it?'

'Eileen.'

The name drifted away, as if he had dropped it into the water and the river had swept it past them out of reach. Something he could not call back.

'*Eileen* was against it?'

'So Bernard Summers says.'

'And it's her land.' Suzie's thoughts were going past him to the research she had done about the surnames at Saddlers Wood in the old censuses.

'You were right about that.'

'I only knew that the Caseleys have been at Saddlers Wood less than a century. Maybe just this one generation. Before that it was the Taverners. And Eileen had told us that was her maiden name. I guessed the rest.'

'Well, you were spot on. It was Eileen who was standing in the way of Philip and a potentially viable gold mine.'

'Why?'

'Search me. I don't think Bernard Summers knows either.'

Suzie detached herself from Nick's arm and went to stand at the edge of the river. She was wrestling with the implications of what Nick had just told her.

'So, forget about domestic violence. Philip had another reason to murder her.' Her voice was hardly audible above the rushing of the water. 'Maybe *that's* what Frances Nosworthy found out. Maybe I was just imagining that there was somebody else standing over her, ordering her to make that call to me. Maybe she was just warning me off because she knew now that I couldn't help her clear Philip's name. That all the stuff about prospecting for minerals on Caseley land was actually pointing the other way. Because Philip really *is* guilty.'

She saw again the desperate look on the accused farmer's face as he took his place in the front pew, shackled to a prison warder, for his wife's funeral. His son sitting so pointedly on the opposite side of the nave.

Nick stood up too. 'Sorry. That rather knocks down a whole house of cards, doesn't it? It puts paid to the idea that there's some conspiracy to frame Philip and take him out of the equation, so that some evil mining magnate can get his hands on the loot.'

Suzie was still digesting the news.

Nick moved towards her comfortingly. 'It's good news in one way, isn't it? I know you saw yourself galloping to the rescue, saving Philip from being sent down when he was really innocent. But if there's no conspiracy, then we're off the hook. Nobody's been staring at you for sinister reasons. Clive Stroud is an ordinary, decent MP, going about his constituency business. Nobody's threatened Philip's solicitor. She's just discovered the truth. Case solved. We can go home.'

Suzie's thoughts were churning like the mill race, but she let him lead her back up the narrow lane towards the street. She had her head down, staring at the cobbles, when she felt Nick beside her check and stiffen. She looked up.

The top of the lane was blocked by half a dozen men, darkening the afternoon sunshine. There could be no doubt from their attitude that they were waiting for the Fewings.

TWENTY

Suzie looked them over with panicked questioning. They were all in their twenties or thirties. All dressed in tough country wear in varying shades of green and brown and khaki. She thought they were the same men who had been drinking in the pub. It occurred to her suddenly that the fresh-faced Young Farmers of the tractor pull might look like this in ten or twenty years.

One of them stepped forward, so close she could smell the beer on his breath. There was a high colour in his cheeks. He was a burly man, and he seemed to tower over her on the sloping path.

'You!' he said, stabbing a finger towards her. 'You're not welcome here. We've seen you, poking your nose in where you're not wanted.'

Nick started to protest, keeping his voice even. 'Steady on, now.'

The man swung round on him, 'And you can keep your big mouth shut, and all. Don't think we haven't seen you, taking off with Bernard Summers. He's bad news, he is. Folk in Moortown know better than to listen to him. But not you. Oh, no. There's some here that saw you making off to his house with him.' There was a growl of assent from the men behind him. 'What's he been telling you? If he's been blackening Philip's name, he'll have us to deal with.'

Nick held up his hands in a peaceable gesture. 'Look, guys, you're right. Eileen Caseley's death has got nothing to do with me and my wife. We happened to meet her a couple of days before, that's all.'

'Oh, yes? So what was your wife doing at her funeral?'

Suzie coloured. 'I just . . . felt sorry for her. I didn't mean to intrude.'

'And what were you doing talking to John Nosworthy just now?' cut in someone else. 'He's solicitor for the Caseleys. Well, Matthew now. It's none of your business.'

Suzie found a sharper edge to her voice. 'If you must know, I've been organizing this tractor tow for Age of Silver. John Nosworthy brought me some money from the stalls. I've never met him before in my life. It had nothing to do with Philip and Eileen Caseley.'

She was lying. There had been that strange exchange, when he had given her his mobile number and offered his help if she ever needed it.

Nick was still trying to keep the peace. 'Look, I can see why you might be upset. The Caseleys were obviously friends of yours. It must have been a shock. First Eileen being shot, then Philip accused of it. Of course you don't want strangers butting in. TV cameras. Reporters asking questions. I'd feel the same. But my wife's right. The reason we came here today has nothing to do with that. Just a charity fund-raiser. My wife works for Age of Silver. I just came along for the ride.'

'But Bernard Summers has been talking to you,' another voice put in from the knot of men behind their leader.

'About geology. I was rash enough to ask questions about the stuff on his stall.'

'Summers has got some crackbrained ideas. You stay clear of him.'

'I don't see any reason why I should ever meet him again.'

'Best for you if you don't.'

Suzie could sense the hostility subsiding somewhat. Had they really believed her? Nick hadn't told them the whole truth either. Both John Nosworthy and Bernard Summers, in their own way, had made a link between the Fewings and the Caseley murder. It had been none of Suzie and Nick's doing. They were being dragged into the whirlpool of emotions around this case, whether they wanted to be or not.

Only a few minutes ago, Nick had been reassuring her that many of the things she had been fearing had been the product of a too-lively imagination. That Philip Caseley was, after all, guilty of shooting his own wife because she stood in the way of opening up a gold mine on his farm . . . *Her* farm. Frances's phone call had not meant what she thought it did.

But here were a group of Philip's friends, fellow farmers by the look of it, willing to get aggressive with a stranger who might question Philip's innocence.

Nick was starting to walk her forward. It was intimidating to have to pass through this knot of muscular men still breathing dislike.

Maybe, she thought, they *didn't* think Philip was innocent. Perhaps that was what was fuelling their anger. A wound too painful to display to anyone from outside their small community.

She should leave it alone. Go now, and not come back to Moortown for a long time.

They were back in the street, with the square opening before them. Suzie felt physically shaken. Nick, too, was breathing fast. They said nothing to each other until they had crossed the square and found the car park where they had left their Mazda.

It was only as they started to drive away that Suzie remembered she had left a giant cardboard cheque for £2,200 propped against a pillar of the market hall.

'Well!' Nick let out an explosive breath. They had rescued the cheque and were driving along the country roads towards home. Cylinders of hay stood ready to be collected from the fields. It was the start of a peaceful summer evening. 'What was *that* all about?'

'I haven't the faintest,' Suzie said. 'We've hardly done

anything, and yet everyone seems to be singling us out. I'm losing count of the number of people who've warned us off now. And all we've done is go to a funeral and talk to some geology freak.'

'Which makes me think that, however much I try to tell myself otherwise, there *is* actually something quite a few people are afraid we'll find out.'

'They wouldn't know we'd found that survey nail at Saddlers Wood and told the police, would they? Or about what Bernard Summers found on Caseley land? You're sure he hasn't told anyone else?'

'He's got a very loose tongue, but he seemed genuinely scared when he realized he'd spilled the beans to me. It seems like gold's dangerous stuff.'

'Being scared seems to be the default value in Moortown. John Nosworthy was. He didn't say so, but I'm sure of it.'

'I thought he was just talking to you about the money from the stalls?'

Suzie looked at him blankly as he turned his eyes back to the road. Slowly the truth caught up with her. She had been so intent on telling him about her scary encounter with Clive Stroud that it had not occurred to her to mention that brief meeting with Frances's cousin afterwards.

'Yes. I forgot to say. He's Frances's cousin. He's got another solicitor's firm. Since he's dealing with Eileen's interests, they agreed that it would be better for her to represent Philip. I think that he's acting for Matthew, the son, too. It was nothing, really. He's been part of the team in Moortown organizing this event for me. Like I told those men, he came to bring me some money. But afterwards . . . well, I wasn't quite honest with them about it. He said I could ring him if I ever needed help. He gave me his phone number.'

'And what help did he think you might need?'

'He didn't say. But . . . well, it's just a hunch I had . . . the way he was looking around, as if to see who might be watching . . . I just had a feeling he might be scared of something, or someone.'

'Judging by what happened to us, he might have a reason to be. If he's representing Eileen's estate and the evidence is turning against Philip, then the heavy mob who tried to put the frighteners on us could have it in for him as well.'

'He's a solicitor! It's his job to safeguard her interests.'

'Try telling that to Philip's friends.'

TWENTY-ONE

Tom greeted Suzie's identification of the man in the photograph with incredulous laughter.

'I knew there was something familiar about that face! Of course. He's all over the local paper most weeks. Opening an agricultural show, supporting some campaign to keep the village pub open. Gets himself about.' He swung round to Nick, grinning broadly. 'Hey, the police are going to love us. Did you take the photo round there? I bet it's going all round the station. "Look, folks, it's those Fewings nutters again. Guess who they've pinned the murder on this time. Only the Moortown MP!"'

The probable truth of this mortified Suzie.

'*Did* you tell them?' She turned on Nick.

He nodded.

It was Millie who came to her rescue. 'Oh, and since when were MPs models of virtue? Just because he's a Member of Parliament doesn't mean he had nothing to do with Mrs Caseley's death.'

Suzie tried to turn the conversation to less embarrassing matters. She had been genuinely frightened in Clive Stroud's presence, but what happened afterwards had radically altered the picture.

'Nick's got something else to tell you.'

She looked round at him expectantly, and caught the sudden narrowing of his eyes. He reached into the pocket of his gilet and drew out a small paper bag. She watched in surprise as he extracted a little cardboard box and laid it on the kitchen table. He lifted the lid to reveal a piece of grey stone inset with a reddish layer curiously engraved with a network of lines.

Millie read the label. '*Icthyosaur coprolite. Fish scales visible.*

Found at Pormouth. Hey, prehistoric fish! Those scales are really pretty.'

Of course. If Nick had wanted to find out more about the geology of Saddlers Wood, he would have had to buy his way into the conversation, convince the geologist he was genuinely interested.

Millie turned a curious face to her father. 'What's coprolite?'

He grinned at her. 'Fossil poo.'

Millie dropped the stone and wiped her hands on her jeans, as though they could still be contaminated by the petrified remains.

'Ugh! That's gross! Why would you want to buy that?'

'It's from a prehistoric sort of dolphin, about one hundred and seventy million years ago.'

'Fantastic,' Tom said. His smile teased Suzie. 'Hey, Mum! This puts your thousand years of family history in the shade.'

'And, as Millie said, the scales of the fish it ate are really rather artistic, don't you think?' Nick suggested. 'There was this bloke in the square selling them. He did have complete fish, but I couldn't afford those. The great thing about it is, this didn't come from some place like South America. He picked it up on a beach not twenty miles from here.'

As the two teenagers bent over his find, Suzie lifted her face to Nick. He shook his head slightly and raised a finger to his lips.

So, she thought, he doesn't want to tell them what Bernard Summers found on Caseley land. Her mind flew back to something he had said in the car.

'Gold is dangerous stuff.'

It was true. Neither of them knew whether finding gold was really more valuable to Philip Caseley than any other mineral with commercial use might have been. But the very word carried a powerful, even fatal magic. She could tell herself that gold was just another metal, yet it was still undeniably beautiful. It had qualities of permanence and incorruptibility. You could dig up a two-thousand-year-old artefact and brush the soil away and immediately you would see the bright gleam of gold, unlike silver or iron. But it was something more than its beauty and permanence that made men go wild over it and fight each other to get hold of it. The Conquistadores had laid waste to large swathes of South America to get their hands on the fabled gold of El Dorado.

Nick had clearly judged that entrusting this secret even to Millie and Tom was too dangerous.

Suzie would have liked to share it with someone. They could have sworn the teenagers to secrecy. But now she must keep this dangerous truth to herself.

Did anyone else in Moortown know it, or guess?

'Oh,' Nick said triumphantly, 'and there's this.'

His long legs took him into the hall. He returned proudly bearing Suzie's giant cheque.

'Hey! Not bad!' Tom cried. 'Well done, Mum.'

'Well, I didn't exactly pull the tractor across the moor myself. And this is just the Young Farmers' sponsor money. There was a whole lot of other stuff going on around the square, like that stall where Nick bought his fossil poo. Someone gave me a big bag of money afterwards, but I've left them to count it and put it in the bank.'

'So,' Millie looked at Suzie thoughtfully, 'you've raised several thousand pounds. You've put a name to that sinister guy at the funeral, and found out he had a good reason to be there. Dad's obviously enjoyed himself. Sounds like a good afternoon.'

Can she pick up the vibes about how I'm feeling? Suzie wondered. We haven't said a word about that group of farmers hemming us in at the top of Mill Lane. Or John Nosworthy's eyes going anxiously around the square. Or Bernard Summers' explosive news of the real situation between Philip and Eileen. Does she guess? Or do I look like someone who's had a successful afternoon?

Back in their bedroom, she closed the door.

'We can't really keep this to ourselves, can we? I know Tom's right. We're probably a laughing stock at the police station. But what you found out is serious. If Philip really was sitting on a fortune, and Eileen wouldn't let him sell the rights . . .'

'Then it looks bad for him.'

'That's not a reason to keep quiet about it, is it? Nick, you have to tell the police.'

He ran a rueful hand through his wavy hair. 'I know that. Bernard Summers said he'd kill me if I told anyone else, but I'm hoping that was just a figure of speech.'

'We can trust him, can't we? I mean, he really does know what he's talking about with the gold? I don't think I could bear making a fool of ourselves in front of the police again.'

'It won't be you making a fool of yourself. Well, maybe over the photograph. But what happened with Bernard Summers is down to me. And he's not going to like it if I tell them. If no one else knows about his find, except Philip, then he's going to be a key witness for the prosecution when it comes to the trial.'

'There must obviously have been a rumour about finding something on his land. Philip fooled everyone into thinking he was against mining there. Nobody in Moortown seems to know what it was, or that it was really Eileen who was opposing it. Nobody knows except Bernard Summers. And now us.'

'I was thinking of leaving it until Monday. Now they've charged Philip, I guess a lot of the murder squad have been stood down. Back to office hours while they put the prosecution case together. But I'm beginning to feel I'd like to get this off my chest.'

Suzie put out her hand to touch his arm. 'You're not seriously worried, are you? About yourself? Those farmers didn't talk as though anyone in Moortown knows just what Bernard Summers told you.'

'That's what he said. But I told you, he has a loose tongue. I couldn't cross my heart and swear that he hasn't let slip a hint to someone else. And the farmers who threatened us know I was talking to him. That I went to his house.'

'That's small town life for you, isn't it? It's hard to keep anything secret.'

'I've had enough of secrets anyway. I think I'll slip round to the station this evening. I don't imagine DCI Brewer will be there, but I should find someone to take a statement.' He put his hand under her chin and turned her face up to his. 'Don't look so worried. I'm a big boy; I'll look after myself. Tell you what, I don't imagine you're feeling like cooking after a day like this. Why don't I take us all to that new Indian restaurant in town?'

Suzie accepted gratefully. It would be good to set a comfort zone between herself and the unsettling events of the day.

When she opened the bedroom door, Tom was waiting at the top of the stairs, excitement in his face.

'Result!' he crowed. 'I googled your man, and guess what? Clive Stroud is a director of Merlin Mines.'

After the meal, they left Tom in town and dropped Millie off at Tamara's house. In the driver's seat, Nick turned to Suzie with that boyish grin which told her he was nervous about what he was going to do, but would do it anyway.

'Shall we get this over with?'

'It's your call. You were the one he talked to.'

Nick drove past the avenue where they lived and turned into the police headquarters at the top of the hill.

'Stay here. There's no need for you to get involved.'

Suzie already had her hand on the door handle, but she let him get out and slam the driver's door behind him. She watched him walk across the car park to the steps of the police station and disappear inside.

There was some activity of police cars coming and going, but it was only mid-evening. As the Saturday night wore on, the police would have their hands full of drunk and violent offenders. Just now, this civilian part of the car park was rather quieter than she might have wished. She was not usually of a nervous disposition, but tonight she regretted not going inside with Nick. She found herself watching each new arrival cautiously.

What did she have to be frightened of? She was safely back in the cathedral city, miles from Moortown. That threatening group of farmers had no reason to menace her here. Her fears about the man in the photograph had been partially allayed. There now seemed to be a good reason for Frances to end their short-lived relationship so abruptly. Philip undoubtedly did have a motive to kill his wife.

Yet she found her hand straying back to the door handle. Was it too late to change her mind and go after Nick? He might still be sitting in the reception area, waiting his turn to speak to the duty officer at the desk.

Perhaps not. The very act of going to seek the comfort of

Nick's companionship would be an acknowledgement that she really did have something to be afraid of.

The minutes lengthened out before Nick reappeared.

He threw himself into the driver's seat. 'Just what you'd expect. He listened to me with a poker-straight face, like he's heard that kind of thing a hundred times before. "Thank you, sir. I'll pass on the information to DCI Brewer. If she thinks it's of importance, she'll be in touch with you."'

'He didn't say when?'

'Your guess is as good as mine. Now that Philip's safely in prison, I don't expect she's giving up her Sundays. Well, not on this case, anyway. Who knows what other crimes she's got on her plate.'

Suzie stared out at the leafy car park as he started the engine. 'That's a strange thought. The way it must look from her angle. We get marginally involved in a murder and it seems like the most important thing on the planet. I can't stop thinking about it, and everything that's happened since seems to tie into it. But for her, it's just a job. Arrest Philip Caseley, stack up a good case against him, and juggle half a dozen other serious crimes at the same time. It must be an odd way to spend your life. It has to take you over, like you're always seeing cops on the telly having to drop a night out with their wife or girlfriend because there's been another murder. And yet they can't afford to get too personally involved.'

They were turning into their avenue already. Nick turned to smile reassurance.

'Don't worry. We're not professionals, thank God. One murder at a time is quite enough for us.'

Suzie let the peace of the Sunday morning service at the Methodist church flow around her. When it was over, she was lapped about with the warm friendship of chat over coffee and biscuits. She walked back to the house with Nick, feeling happier.

The light was winking on the answerphone. Nick stopped to retrieve the message.

'Inspector Brewer,' he told Suzie. 'She'll see me tomorrow afternoon at the cop shop.'

'Did she sound interested?'

'You know what they're like. She wasn't giving anything away.'

Suzie had to wait impatiently for him to come home on Monday. He came breezing into the house with almost as much energy as Tom. She saw excitement in the flash of his blue eyes.

'There's something going on! I'm sure there is. I expected her to do the usual po-faced routine. "Thank you, sir. Just sign your statement. We'll be in touch if there's anything further." But it wasn't a bit like that. The moment I mentioned Bernard Summers' name, it was like I'd lit a fuse to a gunpowder keg. She practically exploded. Wanted to know every last thing I could remember. Exactly what he said. Where he took me. What he showed me. Everything I'd picked up about how he reacted.'

Suzie stiffened. Her hands were gripping the edge of the kitchen table. 'You don't think she knows something about him? Something you didn't get? Is it even possible,' the thoughts were racing through her head, 'that they think *he* could have done it? Killed Eileen?'

Nick dropped into an armchair. 'Search me. But something's going on, that's for sure.' He ran his hand through his black hair in that familiar gesture. 'That guy's a weirdo, I give them that. If I hadn't wanted to find out more about what's underneath Saddlers Wood, I'd have run a mile from someone as garrulous as that. But at least I thought he was harmless, just the local town bore. I was willing to put up with him, buy one of his fossils, just to get a glimpse of what might be behind all this. It's true, I got more than I bargained for. A pretty powerful reason for Philip to turn his gun on his wife. But I thought Bernard Summers was just the messenger. It never occurred to me that behind all this torrent of information he might actually be personally involved.'

'You said he threatened you if you told anyone else what he'd said.'

That rueful grin again. 'I did, didn't I? I took it for granted it was a figure of speech, though I have to admit that the guy did look scared that he'd said too much.'

'Whatever it was, it sounds as though it didn't need you to tell DCI Brewer about it. She obviously knew something about him already.'

'Yes, but she wasn't about to tell me what it was.'

Suzie frowned. 'But why would he be scared because he'd told you Philip and Eileen quarrelled over whether to allow mining for gold on their land? That doesn't incriminate him. Just the other way round.'

'Unless Philip promised him a percentage.'

'That would make sense, wouldn't it?' She stared at him with new alarm.

'Well, I've done it now, haven't I? Spilled the beans.'

'Then, if he really is guilty of something, I hope they get on and arrest him. I don't like to think of an emotionally precarious man like him walking around knowing you told them, when he swore you to secrecy.'

He stood up and fondled her hair. 'I'm a responsible adult. I can hack it. Are the kids in for supper?'

It was a fine evening. Nick laid the supper table out on the patio. There seemed no reason to switch on the local news indoors.

TWENTY-TWO

It was not until Wednesday, as Suzie was picking up some odds and ends in a small supermarket in town, that she passed a stand with the local newspaper. She did not buy it every week. It depended whether there was an interesting story. The banner headline this week was about the unexpected closure of one of the city's secondary schools. A quick glance assured Suzie that it was not Millie's. She turned the folded paper over to scan the lower half.

A smaller headline shouted out at her.

LOCAL GEOLOGIST FOUND DROWNED

Avidly she read on.

> *Bernard Summers, well-known geologist and fossil hunter of Moortown, was found dead in a stream on the moor yesterday . . .*

There was a photograph.

Suzie added the newspaper to her basket and headed for the till.

Outside, she found a circular bench around a tree on the pavement and sat down to read more. The name *Bernard Summers* was screaming in her head with the insistence of a smoke alarm.

> *. . . Neighbours became alarmed on Monday when he failed to open his stone and fossil shop. The police are believed to have entered the premises, where the geologist lived in a flat above the shop. Yesterday two walkers out on the moor discovered the body face down in one of the moorland streams. A police source would make no comment on how he met his death, but said that investigations are ongoing. Friends of the deceased said he frequently went out on the moor or the coast, prospecting for minerals and collecting specimens.*
>
> *Bernard Summers was well known to local people in Moortown. He was a respected geologist, who has several rare fossil finds to his credit, but also was a source of colourful stories.*

In other words, thought Suzie, he didn't know when to stop talking.

> *He was in the news recently advising a group of protesters about the risks of a proposal to open a tungsten mine just outside this delightful moorland town.*

There it was again, that link with mining and Moortown. It was her agricultural labourer forebears who had first drawn Suzie to Moortown, the Days who had once lived at Saddlers Wood. But delving further back, she had become deeply interested in her tinner ancestors in the town. It seemed that part of the story was not over yet.

She lifted the paper closer to study the photograph. Nick had not told her what Bernard Summers looked like. He had a shock of hair, which in the black-and-white photograph looked as if it might be turning from dark to grizzled grey. Horn-rimmed spectacles surmounted a broad, rather jowly face.

She stared down at it. It was a credible scenario. Geologist sets out alone on the open moor with his haversack and tools. Finds something of interest in a stream. Steps down on to a stone in the river to investigate more closely. Slips and bangs his head. If the fall itself did not kill him, he might have lain face down in the water, unconscious, and drowned.

Why did a cold shudder run through her for herself and her own family, as well as for the dead man?

Friends say they understood Mr Summers was a widower.
It is not known whether he had any children.

She sat, letting the news sink in. Two deaths in Moortown, in quick succession. Both soon after the deceased had talked to the Fewings. It couldn't be anything more than coincidence, could it?

She got out her mobile. There were two teenagers sitting beside her on the bench by the tree. Suzie moved around to position herself on the other side of the trunk.

She rang Nick. 'Listen. I've just picked up a copy of the local paper. There's something you ought to know. Bernard Summers is dead.'

'*What?*' There was no mistaking the shock in Nick's voice.

She read him the story, word for word. There was silence at the other end of the phone.

'Nick? Are you still there?'

'Sorry. Yes. I'm still thinking. It's hard to take in what it means, if anything.'

'It's possible, isn't it? I mean, it could be an accident. He goes out on to the moor on his own. Slips and falls in the river. It doesn't have to mean anything sinister.' It was herself she was trying to reassure.

'He said he'd kill me if I told anyone else about finding gold in Saddlers Wood. I assumed it was a figure of speech. But now he's the one who's dead.'

'You said the police were all over you when you reported the conversation you had with him. Do you think they knew then he was dead?'

'Hang on. Read that bit again. About when he was found.'

'A neighbour reported him missing on Monday, when the shop didn't open. I imagine they'd tried the flat and couldn't get an answer. The police broke in but couldn't find him. You talked to them on Monday afternoon. That must have been after they knew he was missing, but it was only yesterday that those walkers found the body in a stream.'

Another pause. 'I need time to get my head around this. As you say, it's perfectly plausible it was just an accidental death. But it does seem a very uncomfortable coincidence that it should happen so soon after he let slip his secret to me. I'm guessing it must have been Sunday he was out on the moor, if he has a shop to mind on weekdays. The next day after I talked to him.'

Suzie cast her mind back over that disturbing Saturday afternoon. 'You remember those farmers who stopped us? They knew you'd talked to him, that you'd gone to his house. You don't think they could have anything to do with this?'

'I'm as much in the dark as you are, but I shouldn't think so. I mean, it's hard to imagine them tracking him out across the moor and doing him in. Why would they? They just didn't want outsiders like us butting in and trampling all over Philip's reputation. I can't imagine they'd actually *do* anything violent.'

Suzie remembered the sense of fear she had felt in the narrow lane, confronted by half a dozen burly, hostile men.

'All the same, Nick. I think you should be careful.'

'Hang on. Bernard Summers was the one threatening to kill me – not that I imagine he meant it literally – and he's dead.'

'And, as far as we know, you're the only other person besides the Caseleys who knows what he knew.'

'Don't forget yourself. I told you too.' Was there a hint of laughter in his voice?

'Nick, I'm serious.'

'Sorry. You're right. It's not a joking matter. I'll be careful.'

'See you later then.'

'Take care.'

It was unsettling how that everyday phrase suddenly sounded so important.

*   *   *

Suzie felt more shaken than she knew she had any right to be. A man she had never met had slipped and fallen into one of the many rushing brooks on the high moor. It must be an occupational hazard for a geologist. He might just as easily have met his death hunting for fossils at the foot of unstable cliffs.

She should have gathered up her shopping bag and caught the next bus home.

Instead, she wandered in a partial daze beyond the High Street into the gardens that surrounded the remains of the city's Norman castle. She found a seat overlooking the dry moat, now grass-grown, facing the red sandstone tower of the keep.

Just supposing, for a scary moment, that Bernard Summers' death was not the unfortunate accident it appeared to be, what then? Something troubling was obviously going on in Moortown. It must have begun before Eileen Caseley's shooting. Suzie was becoming increasingly convinced that it must have something to do with the minerals on Caseley land, and not just domestic violence. Surely it couldn't be only her own tinner ancestry that was pushing her in that direction? If not, then how many other people were involved? Undoubtedly Bernard Summers had been. And now he was dead. Who else might have known?

The name Merlin Mines came back to her. Who else in Moortown might have had connections with it? Or was this the work of faceless people she had never met, who might strike again out of nowhere? The thought was even more frightening than the grip of Clive Stroud's hand and the penetrating look with which he had warned her that she had no further business in Moortown. Was it any better if you could put a name to your enemy?

Enemy? She, Suzie Fewings, was sitting here alone in the castle gardens. She glanced around her. Not truly alone. Men in shirtsleeves and women in summer dresses or casual tops and trousers were strolling along the path past the library behind her. Others, holidaymakers or locals, were sprawled on the grass a little distance away enjoying a picnic in the sunshine. It was ridiculous to think that she might be in danger.

More worryingly, though, was the thought of Nick. Too many people seemed to know that he had been talking to Bernard Summers on Saturday afternoon. It hadn't been just a casual chat at his stall in the square. Nick had gone with the geologist back to his home above the shop. If Bernard Summers had been killed because he knew too much, then what about Nick?

'Hi there, Mum!'

She was startled out of her blackest thoughts. A group of teenage girls had stopped on the path along the edge of the moat. Millie was standing over Suzie, her face alive with curiosity. Further along, the rest of her friends had paused and were looking back at her questioningly.

'What's wrong?' Millie asked. 'It's only me. You look as though I scared you out of your skin.'

Suzie was only then aware how violently she had jumped at the sound of Millie's voice. She tried to laugh it off.

'Sorry! I was miles away. You startled me, that's all. Are you out for an afternoon's shopping?'

Millie sat down on the bench beside her and waved the other girls on. 'Come off it, Mum. You're as white as a sheet. What's going on?'

Reluctantly, Suzie drew out the newspaper from her shopping bag. She laid it on the seat between them and pointed to the photograph.

'That's him. The geologist Dad talked to on Saturday. He's dead.'

Millie picked up the paper and read the story.

'Him? The guy who sold Dad that piece of fossil poo?' Then she lowered the paper and looked directly at her mother. 'So, the guy slips on a wet stone and drowns. Very sad. End of story. And you're sitting here looking like death warmed up and starting out of your skin because somebody speaks to you. You don't fool me, Mum. There's more going on here than you're telling me. Time to come clean. You haven't been telling us the whole story, have you? Split.'

Suzie struggled to give her a shamefaced smile. 'You're right. Your father didn't tell you everything on Saturday. Yes, he did meet this Summers man. He even went back with him to the shop where he lives. Bernard Summers told him something. Something he wished afterwards he hadn't. He seems to have let his tongue run away with him.'

'And you think . . .' Suddenly Millie stiffened as the implications of what Suzie had said struck her. 'You don't think this guy died of natural causes, do you? It wasn't an accident. You really think he was killed because he knew too much! Does this have anything to do with Eileen Caseley?'

'I'm afraid it might.'

'Then *what* did he tell Dad?'

Suzie was torn between the longing to share her fears with someone else and caution. 'It's probably better if I don't tell you. If someone did get killed because they knew too much, then the fewer other people who know it the better.'

'Look, Mum, I'm your daughter! *You* obviously know what it was. I bet Dad told you. Anybody who knows that can guess that Tom and I know about it too. So it won't make any difference whether you tell me or not. They'll *think* I know.'

Suzie looked away. The paths around the bench were clear again. A seagull circled around the flagstaff on the castle keep. The voices of children playing came from a distance.

'All right, then. But promise you won't tell another single soul. Not even Tamara.'

'Cross my heart.'

'Bernard Summers told Dad he'd found evidence of gold at Saddlers Wood.'

'Gold!' Millie's voice came louder than she intended. She clapped her hand over her mouth. 'Sorry. Go on.'

'Philip Caseley was keen to exploit it and sell the mining rights. But the land actually belonged to Eileen, and she said no.'

'Why, for heaven's sake? Their farm looked to be on its last legs. Surely they needed the money?'

'I've no idea. But it certainly gives a motive for murder. Either by Philip or somebody else.'

Millie ran her fingers through her short hair. 'You mean we've stumbled into something like a killer movie? And I can't *tell* anyone? Oops, sorry. This is for real, isn't it? Sometimes I lie in bed and think about that day we met her, and then what it must have been like for her seeing somebody else on the other end of the gun that shot her. Maybe her own husband. It doesn't bear thinking about, does it? Do you think Philip killed this Bernard Summers guy too? No, idiot. Of course he didn't. He's in prison, isn't he?'

She looked at Suzie with renewed concern. 'So somebody else is out there. Somebody who may have been the one who killed Eileen. And now he's killed this Bernard Summers. And you're thinking . . .' – Suzie watched the blood drain from her daughter's face – '. . . he might go after Dad, too, if he thinks he knows.'

Suzie stood up. 'I didn't mean to scare you. Anyway, Dad's already been to the police. It's too late for anyone to stop him telling Bernard Summers' secret. Killing him wouldn't help.' It seemed unreal to be using that word 'killing' in conversation, as though it was just part of everyday normality.

Millie stood too. 'Does Dad know?' She gestured at the newspaper in Suzie's hand. 'That he's dead?'

'Yes. I phoned him.'

'And?'

'He just said, "Take care".'

TWENTY-THREE

'You know what you said about it might be safer for me if you didn't tell me?' Millie and Suzie were walking down from the castle towards the High Street. 'Does that mean you really think we're in danger?'

Suzie glanced sideways at her daughter, alarmed that she might have frightened her. But Millie looked more thoughtfully curious than scared. Though she was not a tall girl, she carried herself with that unconscious confidence of a young woman who knows she is beautiful. It came as something of a shock to Suzie. She had grown used to seeing Millie as the gauche, scrawny younger child, in the shadow of her extrovert brother with his dashing black hair and vivid blue eyes. But last year, at fourteen, Millie had had her hair dyed ash blonde and cut in a gamine style that made her a head-turner. Shoelace straps on her lacy top and cut-off pink pants added to the glamour. A hand gripped Suzie's heart. Her beautiful daughter couldn't really be in danger, could she? She had spoken to Suzie more as if she was considering an intellectual question than one of personal risk.

'I really don't know,' Suzie said honestly. 'If I had any real idea of what was going on I might be able to give you an answer. Bernard Summers' death could perfectly well be an accident. But if it isn't, then the only logical reason is that someone wanted to silence him because he knew about the gold at Saddlers Wood.'

'Why? If somebody wants to mine it, it'll all come out in the open anyway, won't it?'

They turned into the busy High Street. Though Suzie was trying to speak calmly, she found her eyes darting anxiously through the crowds.

'Maybe whoever it is thinks they've got an edge on the competition, if they know about the gold and nobody else does. Didn't Tom say something about a company buying up the site as though it was just agricultural land, and only then putting in an application for a mine?'

'Mmm. But Philip knows, doesn't he? If what Bernard Summers told Dad is right. He'd want to make a packet if he sold it to anyone else.'

'Philip's in prison. And it's not his land. I don't know if Eileen left a will, but my guess is that the farm will go to the son, Matthew.'

'The hunk from Australia?'

A little thought lit like a spark in Suzie's mind. John Nosworthy was the solicitor acting for Eileen's estate and for Matthew. Surely the terms of the will, if there was one, must be have been through probate by now. The bequests would be public knowledge. John, more than anyone else, would know who inherited the farm. She was acutely conscious of the diary in her shoulder bag in which she had written the phone number he had dictated to her. Frances Nosworthy had warned her off, but John had invited her to phone him if she needed help.

And John had looked scared. She remembered his anxious eyes going round the square as he talked to her.

'You know,' Millie cut across her thoughts, 'it's all this damned secrecy. If there's so much panic about who knows and who doesn't, and you think somebody wants to stop it getting out, then wouldn't the best thing be to give the story to the press?

Splash it all over the papers and nobody's got a reason to try and keep it quiet any more.'

Suzie stopped dead on the pavement. She looked at her daughter with a new respect.

'I hadn't thought of it. But you're right. I've been hating this hole-and-corner thing, looking over my shoulder to see who might be watching or listening.'

'Well, then,' Millie demanded, 'who's going to tell them? You or me?'

It would be such a relief to have it out in the open. Then a new thought struck Suzie.

'The police already know about it. Dad went to them and told them about Bernard Summers finding gold. They obviously haven't mentioned it in a press release. Do you think they might be following it up? They could have someone in their sights. How do we know that, if we go public with this, we're not going to foul up their investigation before they can nail whoever is behind this?'

Millie made a face. 'Like you said, *we* could be the ones in danger if it's just us that know. I've been trying to keep cool about it, but a guy's dead. And you don't honestly think it's an accident, do you?'

DS Dudbridge. Her mind curled round his name, like a ship-wrecked passenger clutching at a rope. Was there a chance he might give his permission to go public on the news she no longer wanted to keep to herself?

'Leave it with me,' she told Millie.

'Are you sure?' The teenager's face looked disappointed. 'I was looking forward to landing a scoop on some lucky reporter's desk. It's too late for the local rag. They don't publish again until next week. But the nationals would go mad for a story like this. "Murder over a gold mine." You can just see the headlines, can't you? Mum, please, let's do it.'

'Not until I've squared it with the police. I feel the same as you do, but the last thing I want to do is get had up for fouling up a murder enquiry. I'll get on to the DS we talked to straight away. Promise.'

Millie still hovered, frustrated. 'OK. I'll be with the girls. Ring me. And don't take too long about it.'

'Will do.'

Suzie watched her elegant daughter stride off confidently into the busy crowds.

She got her phone out. Should she ring Nick first and tell him what she wanted to do? No, Nick would be busy at work. He had enough to worry about. She was convinced that what she was doing was the sensible thing. If she cleared it with the police first, there was no danger of making a terrible mistake.

Her thumb hovered over the keypad. Should she ring John Nosworthy before the detective sergeant? She felt an unexpected desire for the reassurance of his soft voice. Of course, there was little doubt about it. Matthew Caseley must be the heir to Saddlers Wood – could she risk letting his solicitor know just why it was of such importance? Was it possible that both Matthew and John knew already what lay beneath the soil of Saddlers Wood?

A little note of caution sounded in her mind. Trust nobody. Frances Nosworthy had changed her tone unexpectedly. So might her cousin John. She would have to be careful.

She made her decision, She had to find out more. She felt the tension in her throat as she dialled the number.

'John Nosworthy.'

A small feeling of relief. It still sounded like a friendly voice she could trust.

'This is Suzie Fewings. We met at the tractor pull in Moortown.'

'I remember.'

'Thanks for the extra cheque from the stalls, by the way. On top of the sponsor money that's a fantastic sum.'

'No problem. I take it that's not the only reason you're phoning me. You emailed me to say the cheque had arrived.'

'No, look, I know it's a bit of a cheek asking you, but I suppose the contents of Eileen Caseley's will are no longer private. I just wondered . . . who gets the farm?'

There was silence at the other end of the phone.

'Sorry,' she said. 'Have I stepped out of line?'

'No. It's not that. Anyone can get a copy from the Probate Office. Look, I'd rather not discuss this on the phone. Is there somewhere we can meet?'

She thought rapidly. 'It'll have to be somewhere in town. I don't have a car.'

'Right. Do you know the Fenwick Barton? It's a pub out on the edge of the city. You could get a bus there.'

'Next to the old priory? Yes.'

'About four?'

She glanced at her watch. 'Fine.'

'I'll see you there.' The call was cut off.

Suzie looked down at the phone in her own hand. She had wanted the reassurance of talking to a solicitor, someone who could tell her the legal facts. If Bernard Summers' death related to what lay under Caseley land, then it was important that she knew who owned that land now. Matthew? Philip? Who stood to gain by Eileen's death?

But surely the police would have looked into all of that.

Still the doubts nagged at her. Why had John Nosworthy cut off her question so abruptly, and why was it necessary to meet him in person? Was there something he was afraid of?

Or was it her question that had scared him? Was *she* what he was afraid of?

It was a disturbing thought.

With an effort, she pulled herself back to the task in hand. She had promised Millie that she would ask DS Dudbridge if there was any reason why the police would not want the Fewings to go to the press with the story of Bernard Summers finding gold at Saddlers Wood. She couldn't imagine he would be overjoyed at the idea. Well, it would do no harm to ask.

She did not have the detective sergeant's personal number, but when she told the operator who answered that she wanted to speak to him about Bernard Summers' death, she was put through.

'DS Dudbridge speaking. What can I do for you, Mrs Fewings?'

'Look, I know this may sound a rather odd request, but we've reported several times that people seem to be warning us off the Eileen Caseley case.'

'It's in police hands, Mrs Fewings. You can leave it to us.'

'I don't mean you, the police. Other people. Frances Nosworthy,

Philip's solicitor. Clive Stroud, the MP. Some farmers in Moortown. And my husband went to you with the information that Bernard Summers had found gold at Saddlers Wood. It's just that he might have been killed to keep that quiet. And *we* know. My family. It occurred to me and my daughter that the only way we can be sure something doesn't happen to us as well is to put the information out in the open. Tell the press. That way, it won't be a secret any longer. There would be nothing to be gained from anyone trying to silence us.'

A pause. 'Don't you think you're being a little melodramatic? We have no reason to believe that Bernard Summers' death was not an accident. We're looking into it, of course, as we would any other sudden death of this sort. I'm sorry if you feel threatened. But since your husband has told us the story, I think you can consider it in safe hands.'

'Are you saying I shouldn't tell the press, or that I can?'

'I would prefer it if you left the police to manage the release of information that could just possibly be related to a criminal case. Not that I'm saying it *is* relevant, you understand.'

'So is that a no?'

'I would advise you to leave everything concerning this case to us.'

Suzie was left with a feeling of dissatisfaction.

She rang Millie.

'Well? Is it on?' Millie demanded.

'He didn't exactly say no, but I think that's what he meant.'

'Bollocks! We can still do it, though, can't we? If he didn't come straight out and say we couldn't?'

'I wish I knew what was the right thing to do. Look, I'm meeting someone. John Nosworthy, Eileen Caseley's solicitor. I think he's going to tell me something about the will.'

'You mean something important? Something nobody else knows?'

'I've no idea. It can't exactly remain secret once the will is proved. He didn't want to discuss it over the phone. I'm meeting him at the Fenwick Barton at four o'clock.'

She was about to put away her phone when she noticed a text message she had missed. It was from Nick.

'*Working late. Don't wait supper. X.*'

She hesitated, then phoned him. When there was no answer, she decided not to leave a message on his voicemail.

TWENTY-FOUR

The ruins of Fenwick Priory stood on the very edge of town. The thatched pub beside it still had a rural air. There was a row of modern houses on the other side of the road, but beyond their back gardens the green fields began. The expanding city had only just caught them in its net.

Suzie walked along the road from the bus stop with questions tumbling through her mind. It had been her initiative to ask John Nosworthy about the dead woman's will, but why had the solicitor thought it sufficiently important for him to make this journey in from Moortown to speak to her? What was it that he had to tell her which could not be communicated over the phone?

Could she even trust him that this was not some sort of trap?

On an impulse, she stopped and got her phone out. She had told Millie where she was going, but it suddenly seemed important that Nick should know too. She dialled his number. His phone was still switched off. With a sag of disappointment, she left a message with the bare facts of whom she was meeting, where and when. At the last moment she added, 'It's something to do with Eileen's will.'

There was nothing more she could do to protect herself. She had been half-hoping that he would forbid her to go to the meeting alone, that he would insist on dropping whatever work he was expecting to keep him late and come rushing over to join her. She even considered phoning Tom. But he didn't have access to a car. He wouldn't make it, even by bike, in time for four o'clock.

She straightened her back and turned in at the gate of the Fenwick Barton.

The interior was dark after the sunlight. It was more sleekly modern than the thatched roof suggested. Chrome rails and green tiles gleamed at her. She looked around for the slight, fair-haired figure she remembered from the market square in Moortown. There was no one there she recognized.

'What can I get you?'

The soft voice behind her startled her. She turned. John Nosworthy was looking at her uneasily. Again she was struck by the neat formality of his dress, even on a heat-soaked summer afternoon. He wore dark trousers and a crisp blue-and-white shirt, the sleeves carefully folded to above his elbows.

'Just a lemonade, please.'

He brought the glasses from the bar. She noticed with some surprise that he had got a whisky and soda for himself. He motioned with a glass in each hand towards the side door.

'Shall we take these in the garden? It'll be quieter there.'

The pub was hardly crowded at this hour of the afternoon – Suzie could see only three tables occupied – but she followed him outside. Sunlight struck her eyes as they emerged into the pub garden. There were the usual wooden tables and benches, some with sunshades. A fountain played in a raised basin set in a circle of cobbles. A cartwheel leaned against a wall.

John Nosworthy led the way across the grass to where a table stood in the shadow of a tree overhanging from the priory next door. Suzie slipped gratefully on to a bench out of the sun. There was not much of the old priory left. The few ruined walls were the same red sandstone as the Norman castle in the city centre.

She sipped her drink, savouring the tang of Sicilian lemons, and wondered who should speak first. She was aware of John Nosworthy looking at her with a silent solemnity.

'Thank you for meeting me here,' she said, to break the ice. 'I really didn't mean to put you to a lot of trouble. It's just that we seem to have got ourselves involved in this case, whether we want to or not. At first sight, it looked as if it might just be another domestic murder. Husbands do kill their wives every week. And I know farmers are under a lot of strain. But the more we found out about it, the more it seemed as though it must have something to do with whatever has been found under Saddlers Wood.' She paused. She was struggling to remember whether she had spoken to John Nosworthy about Bernard Summers' discovery of gold. Perhaps he knew about it anyway. The serious face across the table gave nothing away. 'So,' she made herself go on, 'I felt we need to know just who inherits the farm. Is it Matthew?'

He set down his whisky glass. A cautious look around the garden. There was no one within earshot. Still he bent forward until his head almost met hers.

'Yes. That was the will as she first drew it up. Everything to Matthew, but Philip would have the right to stay on the farm for his lifetime.'

'But the son would hold the mineral rights?'

'Of course.' He frowned, questioningly. 'Why?' Again that quick look round. 'The will's gone through probate, so there shouldn't be any harm in telling you. There was a codicil. She made it the day she died.' A leaf from the tree drifted down on to the table. He twiddled it nervously in his fingers. Then his pale blue eyes looked straight at her. 'Matthew still gets the bulk of the farm, but there's a rough bit of land just on the far side of the wood, Puck's Acre. It looks like an outcrop of moorland, not much good for farming. She's left it to . . . Clive Stroud.'

'The MP?' Suzie was startled into speaking more loudly than she intended. She too looked behind her. A couple of men in green and khaki, the sort of army-style clothing farmers favoured, were drinking beer. She did not think they could have heard her, but she remembered the knot of farmers in Moortown and her stomach tightened.

'Why?' she asked more softly.

His voice was sober. 'The conclusion the police seem to have jumped to is that she was having an affair with him. She wanted to give him something, but she couldn't leave him the whole farm, of course. Philip was the obvious suspect from the beginning, and I'm afraid this strengthens the case against him. He could have found out about the affair.'

'Is that why your cousin Frances told me to drop the case? If she found out Eileen was being unfaithful, it would give her client a much stronger motive for shooting his wife.'

'It looks like it.'

'Did Philip know Eileen had drawn up this codicil?'

John stared down at his hands. 'Eileen didn't tell me. I doubt it. She swore me to secrecy. Not that I'd have disclosed her legal affairs anyway, even to her husband. What puzzles me is why

Puck's Acre? What good would that be to a man like Clive Stroud? She wouldn't tell me.'

'I know why.' It was Suzie's turn to lean closer. 'My son and I went back to Saddlers Wood two days after the murder. We found evidence that someone had been surveying there. And then, the day of the tractor pull, my husband went off with this eccentric geologist . . .'

'Bernard Summers?' John was sitting up, instantly alert. 'He's dead.'

'That's what scares me. That afternoon he told Nick what he'd discovered at this place you called Puck's Acre. There's gold in a stream running off it.'

John leaned back. His narrow face looked pale, even in the heat of the afternoon. 'A potential gold mine? And she's left it to Clive Stroud?'

'So, if what you say is true, Philip wasn't the only one with a motive to kill her.' The idea was still clarifying itself in Suzie's mind. 'But why would he? Clive Stroud, I mean. If she really loved him that much, all she had to do was divorce Philip and marry him. He'd have had the whole farm.'

'I'm not sure that Eileen would have done that. It's a very conservative community. Both she and Philip have their roots deep in the soil. Maybe she couldn't bring herself to throw him off the land. And then there was Matthew to consider. Not that he needs the property. He's done very well for himself in Australia, by all accounts. Still, she might not have wanted the scandal. Not until after she was dead.'

'I can't believe that. In this day and age? She wouldn't stay with Philip just because of that.'

'Or perhaps Clive Stroud had reasons for not wanting to marry her. Just a bit on the side.'

Suzie thought back to the harassed woman she had met in the farmyard. Those surprisingly smart clothes under the flowered overall. Could she really have appealed to the suave Clive Stroud?

'Divorcing your wife and marrying your mistress is hardly a career-wrecking scandal for MPs. These days, it seems to be par for the course. And to suggest that he'd take a short cut by killing her . . .'

John shrugged despondently. 'He might have tired of her, and wanted a quick way out before she changed her mind about the will.'

'Somehow, I don't buy that. It's a bit extreme.'

'That's what I thought, until you mentioned gold. It does strange things to men's minds.' He leaned towards her. 'I didn't tell you, but when Eileen came to my office that Monday I told her I'd have the codicil properly typed up and she could come in and sign it later in the week. But she insisted on doing it that same afternoon. I thought she seemed . . . frightened. And then, of course, she was shot that same day. It's occurred to me since that perhaps whoever did it knew she was going to change her will, and wanted her dead before she signed it. And Eileen must have been afraid of that. I fear that somebody has to be Philip and not Clive Stroud.'

'Why are you telling me all this?' A new thought struck Suzie. 'You didn't have to. It's not public knowledge yet, is it? It would have been all over the national newspapers, on TV. "MP inherits gold mine after lover's murder."'

John Nosworthy drained the last of his whisky and let out a long sigh. 'To be honest, there's something about this that scares me too. I can't discuss it with Frances. Things are a bit fraught between us at the moment. I don't know where you fit into all this, apart from stumbling across that find in Puck's Acre.'

'And the fact that Bernard Summers chose to tell Nick why it was so important.'

'Yes, there's that too now. I had no idea. No, it was something Clive Stroud's agent said to me the day of the tractor pull.'

'Gina Alford?' Suzie recalled the woman shepherding her MP like a protective dragon. Horned-rimmed spectacles, unruly hair dragged back into a ponytail.

'Yes. At one point she looked across at you and said, really vindictively, "That woman! She should learn not to poke her nose in where it's not wanted."'

Suzie was shocked. 'Clive Stroud's agent said that? Why? We've corresponded, but we'd never met before that day. What could I possibly have done to upset her?'

'I rather hoped you'd know. It gave me the feeling that we might have a common interest in this case. She was pretty edgy towards me too. I assumed it had something to do with Clive Stroud and Eileen Caseley, but why would she involve you in that?'

Suzie sat back, letting the thoughts mill around in her head. She hadn't liked Gina Alford. The agent had been too possessive of the MP, too scornful of Suzie's abilities to organize things properly without her checking up on everything. But she could think of nothing she had done to provoke the venom with which John Nosworthy had relayed her words.

It must be some protective instinct. She had clearly doted on Clive Stroud.

She shook her head. 'Right from the beginning, I've had this feeling that we've blundered into something over our heads. I don't understand what's going on.'

John made to rise. 'I'm sorry if I've alarmed you. You'll keep this to yourself, won't you? The police know, but it's not for public consumption yet. As you say, once it gets out, it's likely to cause a scandal. It won't look well, either for Clive Stroud or, I'm afraid, for Philip.'

They made their way out of the pub. John headed for the car park. He had his keys out and flashed on the lights of a blue BMW. At the same moment he hissed, 'What the blazes . . .?'

A second later, Suzie saw that all four tyres of the BMW had been slashed.

TWENTY-FIVE

John looked, if anything, even paler. He managed in a choked voice, 'At least it was my tyres and not my throat.'

Suzie turned to him in alarm. 'You think this has something to do with the Eileen Caseley business? You don't suppose it was a gang of local teenagers? There's a secondary school just down the road.'

It was the school holidays, but she told herself that some of the pupils must live nearby. Adolescent boys, bored, looking for a chance to wreak mischief and mayhem on an expensive car.

'There's something going on that I don't understand,' he said.

The words still came out strained. 'I'm only Eileen's solicitor. I can't change the terms of her will. But I've been feeling threatened.'

'By whom?'

'I wish I knew. Look, Suzie, this doesn't concern you. I should never have asked you to meet me here. Stay out of this. I just hope nobody saw you with me. Go home now and forget all about it.'

'You'll tell the police, won't you?'

'I said, leave it with me. Go.'

She felt unhappy leaving him in the car park, with whoever had slashed his tyres possibly still around, watching. But it was evident that her presence was adding to his strain.

'Keep me posted,' she said, 'if there's anything new.'

'Forget about it. Please.'

She left him alone, staring at his vandalized car.

Suzie sat on the bus as it made its way into town. John's words were still sounding in her ears. *'At least it was my tyres and not my throat.'* Was it really possible that the mild-mannered solicitor could be in real danger?

Was *she* in danger?

She recalled again that sharp crack of a dead branch in Saddlers Wood, her conviction that she was being watched. And all the Fewings had been doing then was innocently pursuing family history at the ruined cottage in the clearing.

She had a sudden vivid image of her great-great-grandparents, Richard and Charlotte Day, living in that cottage with their children. What pressure of poverty had driven them to make the momentous step and leave the limited rural area around Moortown, where their forebears had worked for so many centuries, and cross the county to find new work on the edge of the dockyard city? For generations, she had been able to trace Richard's line back, moving from parish to parish, or even from house to house, with annual hirings, but only ever within a few miles. And suddenly there was this one adventurous leap from country to city. The 1861 census had found Richard still as an agricultural labourer, but by 1871 he was labouring in the dockyard. It could only be the lure of better pay that drew him there.

And all that time, the stream from Puck's Acre must have been running with the sparkle of gold. The Days had never found it.

Would it have been better if they had? John was right. Gold did strange things to men's minds. For all Suzie knew, the find of a metal like tungsten might be more valuable. Who knew what things were worth in the modern industrial market? But gold had always been something special, something men – and women? – were prepared to kill for.

They were nearing the centre of town, where she would have to change to another bus. But she felt an urgent need to tell Nick what had happened. She got out her mobile. Still no response.

In town, she crossed the High Street and waited at the opposite bus stop. It had been a green choice to have only one family car. Nick was usually happy for her to take it on the few occasions when she needed one. On the rare occasions when that wasn't possible, she might hire a car from their friendly local garage. The bus service was adequate for most of her needs. But today she fretted at the wait. She wanted to get home and share this with somebody.

The bus drew up. She stepped aboard automatically and showed her ticket. She was wondering if she should tell Millie and Tom, or if there was some way to keep them out of this.

John Nosworthy had told her to forget about it. Before that, Frances had warned her off. The police had consistently said the same. She had an insistent vision of Clive Stroud subtly giving her the same warning as his hand pressed hers. At the time, it had seemed inexplicable, but she did not know then just how deeply he was involved. If the will and its codicil had cleared probate, the MP for Moortown would be the legal owner of Puck's Acre, and of the gold Bernard Summers had been so sure lay beneath its surface.

Bernard Summers was dead. It couldn't be a coincidence, could it?

The geologist had threatened Nick not to tell anyone. Now it seemed he must surely have been threatened himself.

She got off at her own stop and walked the short distance down the avenue. The shadows of the plane trees were lengthening. Ordinarily, by this time Nick would have been home before her, but he had said that he was working late. She felt a sharp disappointment. Now, more than ever, she needed the comfort of his presence, his sceptical common sense. Instead, she must either say nothing to the children, and leave the events of this afternoon churning in her mind, or face their wilder flights of speculation. She decided to play it down, in case it sent Tom haring off on some other ill-advised investigation.

The house was quiet. The gentlest beat of rhythm from Millie's room meant that she was probably listening to music on her headphones. There was no sign of Tom.

She wandered through the empty ground floor and stood at the edge of the garden. Nick's roses were in full glorious bloom. The flower beds glowed with carefully calculated gradations of colour: strong reds and yellows nearest the house, fading to misty blues, mauves and pinks in the middle distance.

She slumped down in a garden chair, realizing suddenly how exhausted she was. She felt as though she had run all the way from the Fenwick Barton.

Millie was suddenly at the conservatory door. 'Well? What's happening?'

'Nothing,' Suzie lied. 'At least . . . Well, I know now where Clive Stroud fits into all this. Eileen Caseley left him something in her will.'

'Money? Or a keepsake? You mean there really was something going on between them? He was her mystery lover? How romantic!'

Suzie refrained from saying that this keepsake was a gold mine.

'It could cause something of a scandal when it gets out that he was having an affair with a woman who was shot.'

'Over what? A locket, or something?'

Millie came eagerly across the patio and pulled out a chair beside Suzie's. Then she stopped and looked down in concern.

'Are you OK? You look white.'

'It's just the heat.'

'Can I get you something? A glass of lemonade with ice?'

'Make that a whisky and lemon.'

'That bad?'

Millie stood looking down at her, then went indoors. She came back with Suzie's drink and cranberry juice for herself. She sat down and looked at her mother reprovingly.

'You're not being straight with me. Something's happened, hasn't it?'

Suzie sighed. She took a sip from her glass. The whisky shocked her senses back into play, loosening her tongue.

'She left him Puck's Acre.'

Millie stared at her, baffled.

'It's that bit of rough ground just beyond Saddlers Wood. Where we found that survey nail.'

'But why would she . . .?' The realization dawned. She leaned forward, spluttering. Fruit juice sloshed from her glass. 'You mean that bit of land where the mad geologist said he'd found gold?'

'Shush!' Suzie looked around, fearful that neighbours might hear her. 'Look, I probably shouldn't have told you this. And don't pass it on to Tom. He'll only get some mad idea. But I needed to tell *someone*.'

'Well, that should set the cat among the pigeons when it gets out.' Millie narrowed her eyes. 'But it won't look good for him, will it? I mean, she was only . . . what? . . . in her forties? She could have lived for donkey's years. But now she's dead and he's got his hands on it.'

Suzie brushed her hair from her eyes. The whisky was making her feel more relaxed at last. 'Shall we just leave it to the police? It's not our business. There's nothing else we can do.'

She swirled the last of her drink round the bottom of her glass and thought of John Nosworthy as she had left him in the pub car park, pale and scared. He had told her urgently to forget all about it. He had been scared for her as well.

A door slammed in the hall. Suzie was halfway out of her seat in alarm before she stopped to think. Nick must be home only a little later than normal. She hadn't even started to prepare the evening meal. She looked a little shamefacedly at the whisky glass. It would be an admission that she had been upset. Was there time to rinse it out in the kitchen before Nick got there? Probably not.

Even as she turned towards the conservatory door, Tom came breezing through. Suzie was startled by her own reaction. Normally she would have been thrilled to see her handsome student son, savouring the precious days she had him home on vacation. Today she felt her spirits sag. It was not Nick, after all.

Recollecting their conversation, she made a face to Millie which said, 'Don't tell him'.

She was not entirely sure why this was important, but she knew Tom well enough to fear that he might dash off and do something unpredictable.

Millie nodded, with the small, secretive smile of a younger sister who believed herself wiser than her nineteen-year-old brother. This would be between the two of them. And Nick, when he came home.

'Dad not here?' Tom threw a cheerful look around.

'He's working late.'

That mischievous grin. 'Better watch yourself, Mum. That's what they always say when they're dating their secretaries, isn't it? Sorry. Only joking.' He dropped a light kiss on her forehead. 'Tea not ready? Do you mind if I grab myself something? I'm out tonight.'

'You've only just got in.'

'Yeah, that's the way it goes. Busy social calendar.'

'Who is she?' asked Millie.

'I beg your pardon?'

'Your date. The reason why you're in such a hurry.'

'I didn't say it was a girl,' he retorted, colouring.

'You have now.'

'There's cold chicken and salad in the fridge,' Suzie intervened. 'I was just going to start getting it ready.'

'Stay where you are. I'll make a sandwich.'

'Will you be late in?'

'Maybe. Maybe not. Depends how it goes.'

Suzie felt the wrench. What Tom did with his evenings, even who he spent the night with, was no longer under her control. Tom would not be so blunt as to tell her it was none of her business. He just acted as though it was not.

She heard the sounds from the kitchen as he got himself a hasty meal.

'Cold chicken and salad sounds perfect for a heatwave,' Millie said. 'Shall I bring ours out here?'

'Thanks,' Suzie smiled. 'Would you?'

Alone on the patio, she got out her phone again. No new messages. She read Nick's over again.

'*Working late. Don't wait supper. X*'

She sat looking at it dully. There was just that single kiss at the end. The rest was businesslike, abrupt. She remembered, shockingly, all those messages sent on 9/11, when couples pledged their undying love in a final call. If this was the last message she ever received from Nick, what would there be for her to cherish?

What an idiotic thought. It was a simple factual statement of why he wouldn't be back at the usual time. He hadn't even needed to include that kiss.

Nick hardly ever had to work late. He had said nothing to her when he left her this morning to indicate that he was meeting a client after office hours. Something must have cropped up.

'It's all right. You can eat it,' Millie announced.

Suzie had not noticed the two plates of food that Millie had set down on the table. She had even brought a jar of mango chutney and a bottle of white wine.

Suzie gave her an apologetic smile. 'Sorry. Miles away. This looks nice.'

She reached for the wine, then changed her mind. 'I think I'll stick to water.'

She went into the cool of the kitchen and held her glass under the tap. She ought to be relaxing by now. She had learned a lot more today about the possible reasons for Eileen Caseley's death, but it was none of her business. All the people who had tried to tell her that were right. It was John Nosworthy's tyres that had been slashed, not hers. There was not even anything she could tell the police that they wouldn't already know.

She heard the front door shut again, more quietly. Tom would be out for the evening.

The hours passed. There was nothing she wanted to watch on television. Millie had gone up to her room. Suzie switched on her

computer and got out her family history files. But for once the
idea of trawling through the newspaper archives looking for more
colourful stories didn't appeal to her. She tried a search for a
few names and drew a blank. What then? There was that line of
lords of the manor back in the middle ages. Should she take one
of the women who had married into that family and search the
internet to see if she could push the woman's own lineage back
a few more generations? There might be documents on the
National Archives website or information from someone else's
family tree.

She selected Beatrice Lamont.

But again she got no further than the information that Beatrice
was the daughter and co-heir of John Lamont of Combe Dennis,
and that she had married Amyas Doble. Suzie had already read
the history of the county's landed gentry which told her that.

It seemed that everything she tried brought her to a dead end.

Frustrated, she closed her laptop down and went to stand in
the garden. The evening sun had dropped below the houses. A
blackbird was singing its heart out. Nick's flower borders released
the scent of lavender and roses as she brushed past. If he never
came home, this garden would be his memorial.

What a strange thought to have.

She pulled herself up, shocked. What was she thinking? Nick
was seeing a client. No doubt a pleasantly profitable contract
hung on the result of this meeting. He might be wining and
dining the client somewhere.

But it was strange that he hadn't said so when he'd dropped
her off in town this morning.

Perhaps he wanted it to be a surprise. He might be planning
an unexpected holiday abroad on the proceeds. They would get
away from the unsatisfactory mystery which had dogged them
these last few weeks.

All the same, he might have told her more than he had. He
could have spoken to her, instead of texting. He should have
given her some idea when he would be home.

She peered at her watch in the twilight. Ten o'clock. She had
not realized she had been standing in the garden for so long.

Millie's voice came from the conservatory door. 'He's not back
yet?'

TWENTY-SIX

S uzie was startled out of the paralysis that seemed to have
gripped her. She moved swiftly back to the half-darkened
house. She couldn't remember where she had left her bag
and her mobile phone.

Millie followed her frantic searching. 'Here, use mine.' She
clicked on her father's name and handed the phone to Suzie.

The phone rang. Suzie's heart surged with joy. 'He's
switched on!'

The ringtone went on and on. Finally it died into silence.

'He didn't pick it up,' she said helplessly.

'You have to tell the police.'

Suzie sighed. 'We seem to have been back to them so many
times.' Yet she still held the phone in her hand, longing to do
what Millie said.

'If you don't, I will.'

Suzie moved to the phone book in the hall. Her mind was so
tired she couldn't remember the police enquiry number for everything but a 999 call. There was a notepad on the small table. A
name caught her eye, written in Nick's hand. *DS Dudbridge.* It
was a mobile number.

Alarm fluttered across her skin, tinged with indignation. DS
Dudbridge hadn't given them his personal number when he came
to the house. Nick must have been in touch with him since, but
he hadn't said anything.

She put down Millie's phone and dialled on the land line. The
detective sergeant's answer came reassuringly swiftly.

'Look, this is Suzie Fewings. I'm sorry to bother you so late,
but my husband went out this morning and he hasn't come back.
He texted me to say he was working late, but it's after ten. He's
not answering his mobile.'

'When did he text you?'

'This afternoon. I picked it up about . . . I don't know . . .
three o'clock? It wasn't there at lunchtime.'

'Does his work often keep him out all evening? I'm sorry, I don't remember what he does.'

'He's an architect. No, never. It's not often he's late home at all. And certainly not like this.'

'Have you tried his office number?'

'Yes. Just the usual out-of-hours voice message.'

'Did he have his car with him?'

'Yes. A Mazda Six. White.' She gave him the number.

'I'll put a call out to see if anyone's seen it. Do you have any idea where he might have gone?'

'No. I assumed at first he must have been meeting a client, and perhaps they went on to have a meal together. But I can't think why he wouldn't have phoned me to let me know. He must know I'd be scared, after everything that's happened. He talked to Bernard Summers on Saturday and now Bernard Summers is dead.'

'Steady on, Mrs Fewings. Let's not jump ahead of ourselves. We don't know yet that Mr Summers' death is suspicious. It could easily have been an accident.'

'You know it wasn't. Not after what he found at Saddlers Wood. I've talked to John Nosworthy, the solicitor. I know that Eileen Caseley left that bit of ground, Puck's Acre, to Clive Stroud. Don't tell me this hasn't got something to do with that. Very few people know about the gold, but Nick does.'

There was a cautious pause. 'Look, Mrs Fewings, I can understand why you're upset, but there's no reason to think that your husband has come to any harm. What would be gained by silencing him? The will is bound to be public knowledge soon. And since you know about the gold, I imagine other people do too.'

'We only know because Bernard Summers told Nick. And he regretted it immediately afterwards. He threatened Nick not to tell anyone.'

'Bernard Summers can't harm him now.'

'No, but whoever Bernard Summers was afraid of can.'

'I'll get someone checking speed cameras, to see if we can pick up where Mr Fewings went. Meanwhile, try not to worry. There's probably a perfectly simple explanation. I'll be in touch if we hear anything.'

The line went dead. It was several seconds before Suzie could bring herself to put it down.

At last she looked up at Millie. 'He's trying to be reassuring.'

Millie put an arm around her and led her back to the kitchen. 'Tea or coffee? Or would you like another whisky?'

Suzie was annoyed to find that her hands were shaking. 'Make that a strong coffee . . . How can you stay so cool?'

'I'm shaking inside,' Millie said, with her back turned as she filled the kettle. 'He's my dad.'

It was a long half hour later when the doorbell rang. Millie and Suzie were out of their seats instantly. They raced to the front door. Millie got there first.

Suzie's heart dropped sickeningly as she saw the two uniformed police officers on the doorstep. They showed her their IDs, but she was too alarmed to register the details.

'Yes?' she said, hoarsely.

'Is Mr Fewings here?'

'No! I've reported him missing.'

The two officers, one male, one female, looked at each other. Suzie could not read their expressions.

'Does he have a white Mazda Six?' The WPC read the number from her notepad.

'Yes . . . I told DS Dudbridge that.' Fear was growing in her. She must not allow herself to imagine what they had found.

She caught the flicker of surprise on the male constable's face before he spoke. 'I think we may have got our wires crossed here. A member of the public has reported finding your husband's car at Fullingford Castle. There was no sign of your husband, and the circumstances . . . looked suspicious. We thought it might have been stolen. The usual joyriders.'

Suzie stared at him blankly. 'Fullingford Castle? That's on the other side of the county.'

'It's not unusual,' the WPC put in. 'They drive it until the tank runs out. But in this case, judging by where the thieves abandoned it, they'll have a long walk home.'

Possibilities were swirling through Suzie's mind. 'You say Nick wasn't with the car? He hasn't had an accident?'

Again, the officers seemed to consult each other. 'No,' said the male PC. 'No, not an accident.'

A shiver ran through Suzie that she could not explain.

'Would you rather we talked inside?' the WPC asked.

'Sorry.' Belatedly Suzie ushered them into the sitting room. 'I'm afraid I didn't catch your names.'

'PC Ching and this is PC Gleaves. Mrs Fewings, you said you'd reported your husband missing to DS Dudbridge. Why the CID? Why not just to the missing persons department?'

Suzie wondered how much to tell them. She could feel the two uniformed constables' eyes on her, eager for something more than a routine car theft. Carefully she said, 'We'd given evidence previously in the Eileen Caseley murder case. DS Dudbridge came to interview us.'

'And you think your husband's disappearance may have something to do with that?' PC Gleaves was obviously excited now, his young face eager above his stab vest and fluorescent jacket.

'It seems the obvious reason, doesn't it?'

'Tea? Coffee?' Millie put in from the doorway.

'No thanks, love,' said PC Ching. 'We need to be on our way.'

'We'll radio in to CID,' promised her colleague. 'Don't worry. The car was reported empty. No blood. There's no reason to believe your husband has been hurt. We've got people over there now checking it out.'

They made their way back to their police car at the gate and drove off into the night.

TWENTY-SEVEN

'What's happened to him?'

Suzie turned to find Millie behind her, wide-eyed. She was no longer the competent young woman offering support, but a frightened child. Suzie moved to put her arms around her daughter and found her shivering.

'Ssh. Something's happened, but they weren't saying what. Something to do with the car. They said it wasn't an accident.

There's no evidence that Dad's been hurt. But he's not there. And there seems to be something wrong with the car.' She let Millie go with an outburst of anger. 'Why won't they *tell* us?'

'Where's Fullingford Castle?'

'It's the old stannary jail, where the tinners put their prisoners. It's about forty miles from here, on the western edge of the moor. You may not remember but we took you there when you were small. We were down in the dungeons when there was this thunderstorm.'

'Yikes! That place! I was scared out of my wits.' She sobered. 'And Dad's car is there? Something bad's happened to him, hasn't it?'

'The police are looking.'

Suzie paced across the sitting room to the window and stood looking out at the lamplit road. On a sudden decision she turned and made for the telephone. Her fingers seemed clumsy on the pages of the directory as she searched for the home number of Nick's office manager.

'Leila? I'm terribly sorry to call you at this hour. It's Suzie Fewings. Look, Nick texted me that he was working late, but he's still not home. The police have found his car at Fullingford Castle . . . Yes, I know. I haven't the faintest idea what he was doing there either, always supposing it was him who drove it there, not some teenage car thieves . . . No, what I wanted to ask you is what he was doing working late. Was he meeting a client?'

Leila's voice was thoughtful. 'He didn't say anything to me about a meeting. As far as I recall there was nothing in the diary for this evening.'

'Did anything out of the ordinary happen during the day? A visitor? Did somebody call him? Someone you wouldn't have expected?'

'Mmm. Let me think.'

'He sent the text message early afternoon. It would have been before that, but perhaps not much earlier.'

'No, I don't think so . . . Wait. He got a call from Clive Stroud. That would be soon after lunch.'

'Clive Stroud! The MP for Moortown?' Suzie felt the shock run through her.

'Well, I didn't speak to him personally. Just someone from his office. I put her through. Sorry, Suzie. I've no idea what it was about.'

Thoughts were pounding through Suzie's brain. Nick had tried to tell her that Clive Stroud was a perfectly innocent constituency MP, going about his business. But everything pointed to him being more than that. She now knew, as very few other people did, that Clive Stroud stood to gain from Eileen's will. And even John Nosworthy, who drew up the codicil, had not known then that the seemingly small and bizarre bequest was potentially worth a fortune. Enough to kill Eileen for?'

Nick knew only that Bernard Summers had found gold at Puck's Acre. He did not know yet that Clive Stroud stood to inherit it.

All the same, what possible gain could there be, she argued with herself, in causing harm to Nick, when the facts of the will were there in the lawyer's office and Nick had told the police about the find?

She was aware that Leila was waiting for some sort of answer. 'Sorry! That was a bit of a shock. Well, not really a surprise, but it was a name I didn't want to hear. Look, thank you. I wish I'd rung you hours ago. I've been sitting here worrying myself silly.'

'Are you sure you're all right? Is there anything I can do?'

'No, thanks all the same. The police are out looking for him. Now they've got the car, they should be able to find him.'

She hoped that was true. She had terrifying visions of Nick, bound and gagged, or worse, being tumbled out of the car in the dark, somewhere on the moor. How long would it be before anyone found him? And what *had* happened to the car?

Millie had been listening. 'Clive Stroud? That man in the photograph, the one you were scared of? He was meeting Dad?'

'It sounds like it.'

'Where?'

'Leila didn't know. She just put through the call.'

Suzie rang DS Dudbridge's number again. This time there was no reply. She left the information on his voicemail.

The hands of the clock were climbing towards eleven. Suddenly, Suzie could bear the waiting no longer. She hurried back to the

phone. This time the number she wanted was keyed into her
contact list. She tapped the name.

'Mike? You weren't in bed, I hope.'

'Nearly on my way. What can I do for you, Suzie, at this
hour?'

'I know it sounds mad, but I need to hire one of your cars.'

'Tomorrow morning?'

'No. Now. Look, I can't go into all the details, but Nick's got
stranded on the other side of the moor.'

'Can't the AA help? They'd run him home, surely?'

'It's more complicated than that. I need to go there myself.'

'Sounds mysterious. I don't like the thought of you setting out
on your own at this time of night. I'll drive you.'

'No, really, I'll be OK. I just need a car.'

She heard the silence as the garage owner thought over her
request. She knew Mike well. They went to the same church. He
serviced the Fewings' car and, on the rare occasions when Suzie
and Nick both needed one, he hired her one of his fleet. But
never at this hour.

'I'm not having you walking over to get it this late. I'll drive
it round to you.'

'No, don't worry. I'll come.'

'You stay where you are. Kay will bring our own car and drive
me home.'

It was a relief. It would have been a quarter of a mile through
the night streets. If she had qualms about that, then the craziness
of what she was envisioning was beginning to come home to
her. Perhaps Mike was right to be alarmed for her.

When she put down the phone, Millie had disappeared upstairs.

Suzie hurried up to her own bedroom and put on warmer
clothes: jeans, a sweater. She hesitated, then picked up her fleece.
The day had been hot in the city, but who knew what it would
be like at midnight on the moor?

When she came out on to the landing, she met Millie similarly
dressed.

'You're not coming too.'

'Oh yes, I am. You're not going haring off to that creepy castle
all by yourself. Besides, I don't fancy being left on my own.'

'I need you here to tell Tom what's happened.'

'Leave him a note. He can read.'

Millie pushed past her and made her way to the kitchen, where she started filling a thermos flask. She stuffed some chocolate biscuits into a haversack.

'Essential supplies.'

Suzie scribbled a note for Tom. It was hard to find a wording that would not alarm him.

'Dad's car's broken down. We've gone to fetch him in one of Mike's cars.'

She felt a twinge of guilt that she had not mentioned Clive Stroud. That really would have been explosive.

Her ears were alert for the sound of a car drawing up outside. When she heard it, she had the front door open before Mike was halfway up the path.

He was a small, greying man, nearing retirement. He was already cutting back on the garage work, but Nick and Suzie were friends as well as customers.

He held out the car keys. 'It's your usual, the Nissan. Don't bother about the paperwork. Pay me in the morning. I'm assuming this is just an overnight job?'

'Thanks, Mike. You're a star. Yes, we'll be back tomorrow.' She devoutly prayed this was true.

'I'm still not happy about this. Are you sure you don't want me to drive you? It's no trouble.'

'At half past eleven at night? No, you get your beauty sleep. I'll be fine.'

She hoped she was right, and that Mike would be sufficiently misled by the feigned optimism in her voice.

He lingered reluctantly on the path. 'OK, then. If you're sure.'

'I'm sure.'

'I'll give that husband of yours a flea in his ear when I see him, calling you out at this hour of night. Why can't he just find himself a bed and breakfast?'

'I told you. It's more complicated than that. I need to be there.'

She gripped the car keys hard in her hand, hoping her confidence would not drain away before she hit the road. Was she being incredibly foolish?

The pressure of the keys reminded her of the hard grip of
Clive Stroud's hand. She had a sinking sense that the threat she
had felt then had been all too real.

She raised her hand to Mike's wife Kay in the driver's seat
of the other car. Mike turned for a last farewell before he
climbed into the passenger seat. The two drove off, leaving
Suzie on the path, with the hired Nissan waiting for her at the
gate.

As Mike and his wife disappeared round the corner, Suzie had
a sinking feeling in her heart. She was sure that, if Nick knew
what she was doing, he would forbid it. She couldn't honestly
put her hand on her heart and say she knew it was the right thing.
It was just that she couldn't bear to sit at home all night waiting
and wondering. She was convinced that the police hadn't been
telling her the full truth of what had happened to Nick's car. She
had to see for herself.

She thought about Clive Stroud. As far as she knew, Nick had
never met him. Suzie had been the one who had, and who had
felt threatened by him. But why had Nick thought it unnecessary
to tell her where he was going and whom he was meeting?

He hadn't wanted to worry her. He must have known he was
taking a risk.

She had her hand on the driver's door of the hire car. She was
aware of Millie on the other side, opening the door and throwing
jackets, thermos and haversack on to the back seat.

'You're not coming,' Suzie said, with a sudden decision.
'There's no need for you to get involved.'

Millie slipped into the passenger seat. 'Stop fussing and get
in. You're not going by yourself.'

At that moment, Suzie almost changed her mind. She might
have persuaded herself that the dangers were imaginary if Bernard
Summers had not died. Now she knew that her fears for Nick
were more than just hysteria. She could not, with a good
conscience, leave Millie in the house alone, but she could have
stayed with her.

But when Millie told her to get in, she obeyed. Now she was
sitting in the driver's seat, turning the ignition key. The headlights sprang on. The car was starting to move away from the

kerb. She was committed, without being really sure what lay ahead.

A figure came round the corner under the street lamp. Tall, rangy, though perhaps without quite the usual swing in his stride.

'That's Tom!' cried Millie.

Suzie slowed the car to a halt and found the control to lower the window.

'What's up?' Millie leaned across and called. 'Bad evening? Nothing doing with the date?'

Tom stopped and scowled. 'I had a perfectly pleasant evening, thank you.' Then consternation took over. 'What's going on? Where are you going at this time of night? Where did you get the car? Where's Dad?'

'I've left you a note on the kitchen table,' Suzie told him. 'The police have found Dad's car over at Fullingford Castle.' Tom frowned. 'The old stannary jail on the other side of the moor. Dad wasn't with it. I'm going to see for myself. Mick hired me the car.'

Tom had his hand on her door handle. 'I'll drive.'

'No, you won't. There's no need for you to come as well.' Though she had to admit to a feeling of relief. Tom was so like a younger version of Nick. His very presence brought something of the comfort that Nick himself would have done. 'Oh, all right, then. You can come. But I'm driving.'

Tom went round to the other side and stood waiting, as if he expected Millie to relinquish the front passenger seat to him. She got out, folded the seat forward and kept her hand on it pointedly, forcing him to climb into the back seat.

'They didn't make these things for legs like mine,' he grumbled, as he folded himself into the rear of the small car.

Suzie drew out on to the main road and headed for the motorway that would take her around the city and on to the dual carriageway heading west.

The bright lights of the roundabout at the end of the motorway faded behind them. Suzie had briefed Tom on the evening's developments. Neither of the children said much now. There was hardly any traffic on the A road. They headed up the long incline towards the moor.

*   *   *

'Let's get this straight,' Tom said after a while. 'Dad gets this phone call from Clive Stroud.'

'From his office, yes.'

'He texts you to say he'll be working late. Well, that part could be true. He might be designing a house for this Clive Stroud bloke, couldn't he?'

'If you believe that, you'll believe in the tooth fairy,' put in Millie.

'I was just going to say, if you'd let me, that it wouldn't explain why he's still out at midnight, and why he hasn't phoned you. Have you tried recently?'

Millie got her own phone out and rang the number.

'Still nothing doing. He'll be all right, won't he? Nothing really bad's happened to him?'

'Well, at least we know nobody's tried to stage a car accident,' Suzie tried to reassure her. 'The police say there's no evidence that he was injured, and he wasn't with the car.'

'Concussed?' Tom suggested. 'Wandered off in the dark?'

'But what was he doing at Fullingford Castle, anyway? It's way across the moor.'

'Do we know where this MP lives?' Tom asked. 'Maybe Dad's gone to meet him there.'

'I didn't ask. When the police came to the house to say they'd found the car, I didn't know about the phone call. It was only after, when I rang Leila, the woman who runs Dad's office. She told me about the call. And even then, she didn't know for certain what it was about. We're only guessing that he's the one Dad was meeting. Leila said there was nothing in the office diary.'

'Do the police know about the phone call?' Tom demanded.

'I left a message on DS Dudbridge's voicemail. He hasn't rung me back.'

Should she have contacted DCI Brewer? Suzie wondered. But the Chief Inspector's demeanour towards the Fewings had never been encouraging. Correction. Nick said she had become genuinely interested when he told her about his talk with Bernard Summers. Was it too late to ring her now? She didn't have the chief inspector's number.

They reached the roundabout on the north-western corner of

the moor. Suzie swung off the dual carriageway and headed south. The digital clock on the dashboard had ticked its way long past midnight.

Would the police still be there when she arrived? They had no idea she was coming. They would certainly have told her to stay at home.

'Keep your eyes peeled,' she told Millie. 'Somewhere along here there should be a signpost for Fullingford pointing to the right.'

This narrower road was in total darkness. To their left, the moor climbed out of sight of the headlights. On the right there were hedges and stone walls marking the boundaries of fields. There were only rare clusters of houses or an isolated farm. Even then, lights rarely showed. They had not met a single vehicle since they left the dual carriageway.

Suzie was aware how tired she was and that she was doing a foolish thing. Should she ask Tom to take over the driving? She suspected he might not be covered by the insurance.

'There!' Millie cried. 'Damn. You've missed it.'

Suzie slowed to a halt.

'Sorry,' Millie said. 'The signpost was right on the junction. Couldn't warn you.'

Carefully Suzie reversed to the darkened turning and swung the car right.

The lane was barely wide enough for two cars. At times, the hedges brushed the side of the Nissan. The road was taking them gently downhill. Suzie found herself leaning forward, looking for the bends in the lane and any sign that they were approaching habitation.

The blank white wall of a cob barn glistened as they passed. There were more houses ahead. To her right she sensed a darkness more solid than the fields they had passed. The headlights picked out a sign at the entrance.

ENGLISH HERITAGE
FULLINGFORD CASTLE

There were lights beyond it. Police cars. A glimpse of something that could be Nick's white Mazda.

Suzie stopped the car. She gripped the steering wheel hard to stop her hands trembling.

'They're still here. I thought they might have taken the car away by now.'

Tom's hand grasped her shoulder from the back seat. 'Stay here. I'll talk to them.'

Suzie hardly heard him. Her eyes were fixed on the rear of Nick's white car, caught in the cone of her headlights. The bodywork appeared undamaged. The tyres had been slashed.

TWENTY-EIGHT

John Nosworthy's words sounded through her head. '*At least it was my tyres and not my throat.*' She clung to the desperate hope that that was true this time.

She cut the engine and the headlights, but the scene was still brightly lit. The police had rigged up lights to illuminate the car. Uniformed officers were coming towards her.

Millie was getting out of the car, pulling a fleece on over her thin jumper. Tom unfolded his longer legs and strode past her.

Suzie followed more slowly, as if sleepwalking. Words surrounded her, concerned faces under police caps and helmets. She had not taken in what they were saying to her.

'Where's Nick? Have you found him?'

'We've got a search out. But it'll be easier in daylight. You'd have done better to wait at home,' a burly sergeant was telling her.

There were more lights in a large house next to the castle. She saw white walls hung with ghostly cascades of wisteria. A man not in police uniform came walking down the path from the open front door. Too short to be Nick, who was the only figure she wanted to see.

'Mrs Fewings?' There was mild consternation in his voice.

Belatedly she recognized the goatee beard of DS Dudbridge.

'I'm sorry. I just couldn't sit at home doing nothing. I knew there was something your officers weren't telling me. It's the tyres, isn't it? Someone's slashed them.'

'If it hadn't been for your husband's involvement in the Caseley case, we'd have assumed it was the work of joyriders. Drive the car until the gas runs out, then vandalize it. As it is, well . . . maybe it's a warning?'

'It's the second time,' Suzie told him. 'I was with John Nosworthy today . . . sorry, yesterday. Eileen Caseley's solicitor. When we came out of the pub, his tyres had been slashed, just like this.'

A startled expression crossed the detective sergeant's face. 'You didn't report that? You left me a message about that phone call from Clive Stroud to your husband's office, but you didn't say anything about this other car.'

'I thought John Nosworthy would tell you himself. He told me to go home and stay out of it.'

A woman's voice called imperiously from the open front door of the house. 'How much longer are you going to invade our privacy? We know nothing about this unfortunate Mr Fewings and his car. I have no idea why he left it outside our house. If you don't mind, we should very much like to get to bed.'

Dudbridge made a wry grimace at Suzie. 'I suppose I'd better introduce you.'

He ushered her through the gate. Millie and Tom followed. In the light of the porch Suzie saw a tall woman with long dark hair caught at the nape of her neck. Her checked silk shirt and green trousers had a look of casual elegance.

'Mrs Stroud, may I introduce Suzie Fewings? It's her husband who's missing. Mrs Fewings, this is Elizabeth Stroud. Her husband is the MP for Moortown.'

'*Clive* Stroud?' The gasp escaped Suzie before she could check it. She stopped dead on the path.

She felt the detective sergeant's hand steadying her elbow. 'It's all right. Clive Stroud was in London today. He came down on the train this evening. It doesn't look as if he can have had anything to do with your husband's disappearance.'

'He's in there?'

'Yes. But as I said, there's nothing to be afraid of.'

The world was spinning slowly around Suzie. Nick was missing. Had been missing for hours on end. And here was his car, not outside Fullingford Castle, but outside the house of Clive Stroud, who had pressed her hand with such sinister significance as he told her she would have no more business in Moortown. DS Dudbridge's reassurances meant nothing to her. The lighted porch swam with shoals of dark fragments. She felt consciousness slipping away from her as she fell into oblivion.

She came to on a well-upholstered sofa. The large sitting room was full of the buzz of concerned voices. Tall Elizabeth Stroud was coming towards her with what looked like a brandy glass.

'Hot sugared tea be damned. Get this inside you.'

Suzie struggled to sit up. She registered Tom and Millie over by the window. Millie looked small and scared.

The room seemed to be full of people. Suzie recognized DCI Brewer, taller and thinner even than Elizabeth Stroud. She closed her eyes again, wanting to shut out what she was sure would be the Chief Inspector's disapproval. She was frighteningly conscious of another presence behind her. She had momentarily glimpsed him when she took the glass from his wife's hand. Clive Stroud. Despite what DS Dudbridge had said, she had an urge to jump off the sofa and run.

She felt trapped.

Detective Chief Inspector Brewer was leading him forward now, so that he stood in front of the sofa where she sat helpless. He leaned forward and fixed her with his gaze.

'My dear Mrs Fewings, I'm so sorry if we've given you a shock. Believe me, I've no more idea than you have why your husband's car is outside my house. I can assure you I haven't seen or spoken to him today. Or at any other time, come to that. It was only your delightful self I met in Moortown.'

'But the phone call?' she managed. 'You rang his office and asked to speak to him.'

'So the detective sergeant has informed me. But I've assured him I did no such thing.'

'But I asked Leila Mahfouz, his PA. She said someone from your office rang to put you through.'

Clive Stroud's eyes narrowed. 'My office? At the House of Commons, or my constituency office in Moortown?'

Suzie blinked and swallowed a gulp of brandy. 'She didn't say. I assumed it was the local one. Parliament's in recess, isn't it?'

'My dear lady, an MP's job is not confined to constituency matters, even in the summer. I frequently have work which takes me to London. Committees, boards of directors. No rest for the wicked.'

'What he means is any excuse to spend as little time at the marital home as he decently can. He just needs a decorative wife at his elbow for the photograph on his election leaflet,' Elizabeth Stroud said waspishly. 'He spends more time with his agent than he does with me.'

Suzie remembered the frizzy-haired woman who had been so possessive of her MP at the tractor pull. Surely the devotion she had shown him couldn't be mutual?

Elizabeth Stroud had said nothing about the far more serious affair between Eileen Caseley and her husband. Suzie glanced between the two of them. Would Elizabeth have known about that? Had they quarrelled? It occurred to her that here was a woman who might have had an obvious motive to wish Eileen Caseley dead.

And if she didn't know, how would she feel when she found the dead woman had left Clive Stroud a gold mine?

A mobile phone rang, shattering the tension in the room like broken glass.

'Excuse me,' Detective Sergeant Dudbridge said. 'I need to take this outside.'

'Oh, no you don't!' Tom's outraged cry brought all eyes to him. He erupted from the window seat, where he had been sitting with Millie, while the drama of Suzie's faint played itself out centre stage. Now he strode forward, his own mobile phone in his hand. 'I've just tried ringing Dad again. That's his phone you're holding, isn't it? You've had it all along. Every time we've tried to contact him, it's *you* we've been getting.'

Suzie sat bolt upright. 'When I tried to get him earlier, his phone was switched off. And then, this evening, it rang, only I still couldn't get an answer. I really thought, if he'd switched it on, he must be there. And all the time it was you, just checking to find out who's ringing him?'

Detective Sergeant Dudbridge coloured. 'We found his phone on the back seat of the car, yes. I switched it back on, in the hopes that he might get a call from someone who would lead us to where he is. I can assure you we want to find your husband as much as you do.'

'I doubt that,' Tom scoffed. 'But a nice try.'

'Look,' Clive Stroud put in. 'I really don't know what you're all doing here. I've answered your questions. I have not the faintest idea why Nicholas Fewings has left his car outside my house, but I can promise you it has nothing to do with me. You can search the house if you like. You won't find anything here.'

'It matters,' Suzie snapped back at him, 'because Eileen Caseley left you a piece of land in her will on which there is almost certainly gold. Very few people know about it. But Bernard Summers did, because he found it, and now he's dead. He told Nick, and now Nick is missing. So don't tell me you're not involved.'

The news dropped into the room like a grenade. DCI Brewer had taken a long-legged stride across the room in an effort to stop Suzie, as soon as she saw where this was going. There was fury in her face.

Clive Stroud's complexion turned a dull shade of purple. Elizabeth stood staring at him in outrage and horror.

Suzie caught Tom and Millie's eyes going rapidly from one player to another. Millie too had risen from the window seat where she had been sitting alongside Tom.

Clive Stroud looked round him somewhat wildly. 'I didn't know anything about this until John Nosworthy told me. About the legacy, I mean. I wondered then why. Why that particular piece of land, and why me? I assumed she thought I might find a use for it for one of my charities. But gold? No one said anything to me about that!'

Is it true? Suzie wondered, watching him carefully. Did Eileen really not tell him? Either about the codicil to her will or what lay under Puck's Acre? If not, then he's certainly a good actor.

But his wife could barely contain her anger. 'All this time! I've known for years you've been playing me along. The obligatory constituency wife. Opening bazaars, attending tea parties, sitting through hour after hour of excruciatingly boring speeches. And all to flatter your vanity and get you a safe seat. God knows why I've put up with it all these years.'

'Because you've done very well out of the proceeds,' Clive snarled back at her.

'But never in my wildest nightmares did I think you were mixed up in a murder case. That farmer's wife everyone thinks was shot by her husband? You and her? She left you a fortune in her will? For heaven's sake! Did she know she was going to die?'

Her husband was visibly shrinking back before her fury. He held up his hands placatingly.

'As God's my witness, Liz, I didn't know about this.'

'And what has this got to do with Mr Fewings?'

'Nothing! Poor Suzie's understandably upset, but to suggest I bumped off that geologist fellow because he knew about the gold . . . I didn't know myself before tonight. And what did I have to gain by removing him?'

He could be telling the truth, Suzie thought. I only told John Nosworthy this afternoon . . . no, yesterday afternoon. He might have rung Clive Stroud to tell him, but it seems unlikely.

DCI Brewer came between Clive and Elizabeth to take control. She scowled at Suzie, tight-lipped. 'I very much wish you had kept out of this, Mrs Fewings. You had no right to come here and interfere with a criminal investigation. What you've done could seriously prejudice police enquiries. I suggest you get back in your car right now and go home.'

'Are you fit to drive?' Dudbridge asked, more sympathetically.

'Yes,' said Suzie, swinging her feet to the ground.

'You've just had a stiff glass of brandy.'

Suzie said nothing about the whisky earlier.

'I'll do it,' said Tom, holding out his hand as if for the key.

'But what about Dad?' put in Millie. 'Where *is* he?'

A blank silence fell over the room.

'We'll get your father's car taken back to police HQ,' DS Dudbridge said. 'Do a real forensic job on it. Don't worry. If anyone's been in the car before abducting him they'll have left traces.'

'You think he's been kidnapped?' Millie was wide-eyed.

DCI Brewer cut in. 'We're not saying that. If he got a phone call and left a message for your mother, then he clearly had an assignation to meet someone. As far as we know, he did so of his own free will. There's no reason to suppose the worst.'

'Except that it's two o'clock in the morning and he still hasn't contacted us,' Tom objected.

'He left his phone in the car,' the detective sergeant pointed out.

'So what are you saying?' Millie demanded. 'That he went for a walk on the moor in the middle of the night?'

'We're doing everything we can to find him,' DCI Brewer told her more kindly. 'We'll set up a fuller search as soon as it's daylight.'

'Would somebody please tell me,' Clive Stroud pleaded, 'why whoever is at the bottom of this used my name to make that appointment and left Mr Fewings' car outside my house with the tyres slashed?'

There was no answer to that.

TWENTY-NINE

The lights of the police vehicles made the night around them seem darker. Nick's car had been covered with a green sheet. A recovery truck was getting ready to load it on board.

Suzie felt a pang of bereavement. As long as the car was there, where Nick had apparently left it with his mobile on the back seat, she could believe that he would come striding out of the darkness to reclaim it. There would be hugs and exclamations of joy. Nick would have a simple explanation for why he was here and why he had walked off without a word. She could not imagine what that harmless explanation would be. She had to believe that there was one.

Now there was an ominous finality about seeing the hook of the crane hovering over the car, the driver waiting to winch it on board. Soon it would be gone. Just the imprint of its tyres fading when daylight broke.

And Nick would have vanished without trace.

Tom's hand was on her arm, urging her forward to where the smaller hire car stood waiting.

'Key?' he asked.

She handed it over.

She was about to slip into the passenger seat, too numb to listen to what Tom was saying. Then her unfocussed eyes became aware that Millie was walking on past the car. For a puzzled moment she watched her daughter move out of the range of the lights, so that she was only a pale ghost of a figure approaching the wooden gate to Fullingford Castle. Millie tried the latch, but it was evidently locked.

Tom strode after her. 'Just what are you doing?'

His sister turned to face him. 'When the police came to our house, they said they'd found Dad's car outside Fullingford Castle. It was only when we got here that we found everybody was assuming it must really be outside Clive Stroud's house, because he lives next door. But what if it wasn't? What if he really *is* here?'

Wearily, Suzie joined them. Beyond the lights, the darkness was not as complete as she had thought. She looked up the grass-grown mound to where the square tower blocked out the stars.

'I'm sure the police will have thought of that first, before they knew about Clive Stroud. They'll have assumed Dad stopped here to visit the jail. Maybe slipped and had an accident. They'll have been to look.'

Millie, undeterred, was climbing the gate. Tom vaulted after her.

'Can't do any harm to check it out.'

Suzie sensed the need in them to be doing something positive, not just spectators to the drama which had played itself out in the Strouds' house.

The teenagers were already climbing the mound. Suzie followed them.

She caught them up at the base of the tower. Millie was struggling with the door.

'Told you,' Tom said. 'They're not going to leave it open, are they?'

'I keep remembering that horrible dungeon where we were when that thunderstorm struck. What if Dad's down there?'

Suzie put her hand on the stones beside her. They felt faintly damp and colder than she expected. Was it just the early morning dew, or was she remembering too vividly the history of this place? She thought of those ancestors of hers who might have sat in the stannary court and condemned wrongdoers to imprisonment here in the tinners' jail. It had been a strangely independent system of justice which had operated outside the normal courts of the country. The tinners' laws had been notoriously harsh. She remembered the punishment for adulterating tin: spoonfuls of molten tin being poured down the miscreant's throat. She shuddered.

What hidden forces of retribution had been at work here today? And how was Nick involved?

A muffled shout came from the other side of the tower.

'Result!'

Millie sprang away from the unyielding door and went rushing round the corner of the tower. Suzie followed the sound of their voices.

She made out the dark outline of Tom in the starlight.

'No glass in the windows. They're pretty narrow, though. Think you can squeeze through there?'

'I wish we had a torch,' Millie said. Her voice was more subdued now. The childhood memory of terror was still haunting her as she faced the blackness inside.

Suzie knew she should be telling them to go no further. They shouldn't be breaking into a scheduled monument. The police or the castle's custodian would surely have found Nick if he was there. Yet she could not fight down the faint hope that she was wrong, that Nick might be there, bound and helpless, waiting for her to rescue him.

'You don't have to come,' she told Millie.

'I'm not waiting here on my own.'

Tom was already inside, feeling his way through the darkness.

'Watch out for the steps,' Suzie called in sudden alarm.

'I'm not daft, Mum.' His voice came back hollowly.

She squeezed herself into the embrasure in the two-metre-thick walls. A narrow window, and then she was dropping to the stone floor.

She tried to remember that long-ago visit to this jail. She did not think there had been any furniture, just the stern stone shell. But who knew what might have changed in the intervening years?

She felt her way around the walls.

'Dad?' Tom's voice called, nearer now.

There was no answer. It was too much to hope that there might have been.

'He could be gagged,' Millie said behind her. 'Or drugged.'

'Steps here,' Tom called back. 'There's a rail.'

She felt the iron railing under her hand. There were metal treads underfoot. The darkness became even more oppressive as she descended. The railing led her in a spiral down to the lower level. No starlight penetrated here. The heat of the summer's day just gone seemed as though it had never entered this dark dungeon.

Suzie stopped at the foot of the metal staircase, unwilling to go further.

'Move yourself, Mum,' Millie said from the step above.

Suzie moved aside. She could hear the others shuffling around the darkened space.

'Ow!' Millie cried. Then, 'No, it's not him. It's something hard.'

The sound of something more ominous – the clank of chains. Suzie struggled to remember if there had been chains in the stannary jail – or perhaps they were a recent introduction, to satisfy the expectations of visitors to a dungeon, especially ghoulish children.

It was almost a relief when the two had made their circuit of the dungeon in the dark and came back with nothing to report. Her disappointment was less because she had never really believed Nick would be here.

But there was a tremor in Millie's voice as she said, 'I really hoped . . .'

Suzie put her arm round her daughter's shoulders. 'Let's go home.'

*   *   *

In spite of herself, her eyes were closing as Tom drove them north towards the dual carriageway. She felt exhausted.

Lights sprang out at them from the roundabout. The filling station must be open twenty-four hours. Beyond it lay the unlit café with a motel.

'Stop!' she said suddenly to Tom. 'Pull over here.'

'Why? Fuel's OK.'

'I'm just not happy about you driving. I'm sure the hire insurance on this car doesn't cover a nineteen-year-old boy.'

'Mum, you haven't signed any papers,' Millie reminded her from the back of the car. 'Remember? Mike said you could pay him in the morning.'

'All the same. We'll get a few hours' sleep here. They'll be searching for Dad at daybreak.'

'They won't want you,' Tom said, not unkindly. 'Honestly, are you sure about this? I can have us home in half an hour.'

'That's just what worries me. The last thing I want right now is to be had up for breaking the speed limit with an uninsured driver at the wheel. Yes, I'm sure.'

He turned the car off the road and drew up at the lighted shop. Suzie got out. She feared the door might be locked, with a night safe for motorists to pay for their fuel, but she walked in to a jangling bell.

'Have you got a room for the night? Three people,' she asked the young woman at the till.

'Bit late, isn't it?'

Suzie declined to offer an explanation. The cashier reached behind her and took down a key.

'One room or two?'

'A family room, if you've got one.'

'Number five.' She pointed round the side of the darkened café next door.

'No chance of a meal, I suppose?' Tom crinkled his blue eyes at her.

The cashier was impervious to his charm. 'Breakfast starts at six o'clock. There's coffee and tea in your room.'

Tom shrugged and scanned the shelves for food. He gathered up packets of sandwiches and chocolate and placed them on the table.

'Thanks, sunshine.'

'You're welcome.'

In the family room, Suzie nibbled at the chicken sandwich Tom handed to her, but it tasted like sawdust in her mouth. She swallowed more gratefully the coffee Millie poured for her.

She and Millie took the double bed, leaving Tom with the single.

'This is crazy,' he grumbled. 'We could have been home by now.'

'That's not the point,' Millie told him. 'It will start to get light in a couple of hours. Mum wants to be close when they start to search the moor.'

Is it true? Suzie wondered. Is that what I'm doing here?

She was too exhausted to know.

Once in bed, Millie and Tom fell instantly asleep, with the abandon of healthy teenagers. For all her weariness, Suzie found she could not sleep. Her mind kept playing over all the possible scenarios. Nick, pursuing some dangerous line of enquiry he had not wanted to tell her about. Nick, bound and imprisoned in something like the dungeon of Fullingford Castle. Nick, face down in a moorland stream in the dark, like Bernard Summers.

Nothing made sense. Why, out of all the people investigating Eileen Caseley's murder, should Nick Fewings be the one to be singled out as a victim?

She woke suddenly, with a stale taste in her mouth. Daylight was flooding the room. She must have slept at last, and far later than she had meant to.

Millie was wriggling into the jeans she had removed for the night. There were sounds from the bathroom which must be Tom. Suzie hurriedly got out of bed with a conviction of guilt.

'Don't panic,' Millie said. 'It's only seven o'clock.'

'I meant to be up at daybreak.'

'It's not going to help anyone if you run yourself into the ground.'

All the same, it was unlike Millie to be dressed and wide awake at this hour of the morning.

Tom came out of the bathroom rubbing his wet hair with a towel.

'All yours. Sleep well, Mum?'

'Not for ages. And now I've overslept.'

'Get yourself a shower,' Millie ordered. 'You'll feel better.'

Suzie would have gone straight to the car, but the children herded
her into the café.

'You're not going anywhere till you've got some food inside
you,' Tom ordered. 'And I'm certainly not.'

To her surprise, she was able to manage a poached egg on
toast, but she hardly noticed what she was eating. Her mind was
racing through the possibilities for the day ahead.

She checked her phone, in the vain hope that there would be
a message from Nick or the police. Nothing.

'We'll go back down the Fullingford road, just in case there's
something.'

'I don't think that's one of your better ideas,' Millie said over
her mug of hot chocolate. 'You weren't exactly flavour of the
month with the Strouds. What you told them sounded to me like
grounds for divorce.'

'Not them. I need to know what the police are doing.'

'Whatever it is, they won't want us in the way,' Tom said.

But in spite of their arguments, she drove back down the B
road from the roundabout. A thin morning haze was lifting off
the moor as the sun strengthened. It promised to be another
fine day.

At the turning to Fullingford, Suzie stopped the car. 'You're
right. There's no point in going back to the castle or the Strouds'
house. But if Nick left the car there, he can't be far away.'

'Unless someone else dropped him off before, and drove the
car on to Fullingford,' Millie said darkly.

Suzie did not want to think about that.

On the opposite side from the Fullingford lane, the moor
rose in its summer hues of golden gorse and purple heather.
She could make out the grey bulk of a granite tor on the
skyline.

'I'm going up there. I need to see what they're doing.'

She saw the look that passed between Tom and Millie, but she
ignored it.

The climb was longer than it had looked from the road. Every time they crested a rise, another one unrolled in front of them. At times, the tor itself was hidden by the folds of the land.

Once they plunged down into a deep, stony trough, overgrown with gorse and stunted rowan trees.

'What's this?' complained Millie. 'World War Two defences?'

'It's called a rake. The tinners gouged it out.'

'I thought a tin mine was a hole in the ground.'

'Not always.'

They struggled up out of the gulley. At last they were mounting the final grassy track through the heather.

The giant boulders of the tor rose like the walls of a fortress, with a narrow gap between them. It was the kind of place that the children had loved to play in when they were younger. The rocks could easily become a beleaguered castle, a Wild West fort, or the entrance to an underground kingdom through the shadowy crevices under the boulders.

Now Suzie had one objective. She hardly turned to survey the view before starting to clamber up the sloping faces of the rocks.

At last she stood on the highest slab. The moor sprang into view all around her. Nothing moved in the wilderness except the occasional moorland pony. But when she turned to look behind her, she caught her breath.

A line of figures in black uniforms or blue overalls was fanning out across the hillside. Others were combing the fields on the far side of the road. In that direction she could see the square bulk of the old stannary jail, and a glimpse of white beside it which must be Clive Stroud's house.

So DCI Brewer was taking seriously the probability that Nick was no longer in control of the chain of events since that phone call yesterday afternoon. There was a very real possibility he was lying somewhere helpless under a hedge or in the high wilderness that was the moor.

Suzie shivered, knowing what an immensity it would be to search.

Tom put a hand on her shoulder. 'Mum. Let them get on with it. They know what they're doing. Let's go home.'

Numbly, she let him steer her off the summit and help her down the pile of boulders to the base of the tor.

'It wasn't Clive Stroud,' she said, breaking the silence suddenly. 'He makes me shudder, but I can't see him slashing those car tyres. It's not his style.'

'Elizabeth?' Tom suggested. 'She was pretty mad with him. And it sounds as if he'd earned it.'

'But why *Nick's* tyres? It doesn't make sense. And it has to be the person who did the same thing to John Nosworthy's car.'

The words she had spoken on the morning air caught up with her.

'Of course! He said things had been fraught between them. It has to be her!'

'Who?' asked Millie and Tom together.

'Frances Nosworthy. His cousin. If anyone has a reason to keep quiet about anything which could damage Philip Caseley, it's her.'

'The solicitor?' Millie asked. 'The one you were so pally with over a cream tea?'

'She changed,' Suzie said. 'She choked me off. I thought she was doing it under duress, that Clive Stroud might be breathing down her neck. But what if she wasn't? What if she's falling over backwards to make sure the Fewings keep their mouths shut about just what Philip stood to lose from that new will? I'm going to see her!'

'Mum!' Millie protested.

Tom shrugged. 'If it makes her feel any better, why not? Either the police will find Dad, or we will.'

Suzie was already racing ahead of them, down the steep slope to the road.

THIRTY

Suzie drove through the hazy sunshine of the slowly unfolding morning. No one spoke much. She sensed that the reality of Nick's disappearance was slowly coming home to the teenagers. She thought of the forlorn lines of police officers, combing the ground either side of the road. She had a growing feeling that Nick would not be there, that whatever had happened to him had nothing to do with the Strouds. Someone could have left his car there, with the tyres slashed, to divert attention to the MP from himself – or herself.

Was she just trying to keep hope alive by persuading herself that the key lay in Moortown, perhaps with Frances Nosworthy?

This time, she took a smaller road that cut directly across the open moor. It was still too early for there to be much traffic. Sheep stirred reluctantly from their resting places on the sun-warmed tarmac. A herd of ponies with foals sauntered across the road ahead of her. It should have been idyllic.

When they passed the lone grey inn at the halfway point, she remembered the Young Farmers dragging their red tractor over this road. That was the day when the Fewings' involvement in the Caseley case had taken a new and more sinister turn.

They crested the last rise and the rest of the county lay spread before them. She picked out the tower of Moortown's church. Then they were heading down the long steep hill into farmland and the first houses.

Suzie fought back the coldly creeping doubt about what she was proposing to do.

As if he read her thoughts, Tom asked, 'How exactly are you planning to go about this? Do you just walk into her office and say, "Did you abduct my husband?"'

'I'm not sure,' Suzie said. 'I'll have to play it by ear.'

The little town was stirring with shoppers inspecting the local produce set out on the pavement in front of the shops. Walkers in hiking boots were getting ready to make the most of a fine day. Suzie parked the car at the roadside.

She found Frances's card in her shoulder bag and studied the address. Eleven Chapel Road. That should be easy enough to find.

'Stay here,' she told the children. 'It'll be better without a family deputation.'

'No way,' said Tom. 'OK, we don't come inside, but I'm going to be right out there on the pavement. Yell if you need help.'

Suzie tried to imagine the formally dressed solicitor attacking her physically. It seemed unlikely, but that was precisely what she was accusing Frances of having done to Nick. Though it would have to have been more subtle than that – a spiked drink, perhaps. But she would still have had to bundle his tall form into the car on her own. Or did she have an accomplice?

Was it possible that it was her gently spoken cousin John? Had they fallen out afterwards over just this?

She struggled to put together the sequence of events. No. Leila had said nothing about Nick leaving the office early. He would still have been at work yesterday afternoon, when John had met Suzie at the pub beside the priory.

The three of them threaded the streets and turned into Chapel Road. The granite Methodist church was prominent halfway along. Moortown had always been a hotbed of dissent. Religiously non-conformist; Parliamentarian in the Civil War, when all around them were Royalists.

Number Eleven was two houses before the Methodist church. A pewter and black plaque on the door read: *Frances Nosworthy, Solicitor.*

'Hey! Look at this!' Tom called from the house next door. 'A double act.'

Number Thirteen had a more old-fashioned look. Gold lettering in a cursive script on the downstairs window announced: *Thomas Nosworthy and son, solicitors.*

'That must be John's office.'

Thomas, Suzie guessed, must be either John's father, or the grandfather of both John and Frances. Hadn't Frances said something about the Nosworthys being the Caseleys' solicitors for generations?

She turned back to Number Eleven and drew a sharp breath. 'Wait here. I don't even know if she's in, or if she'll see me.'

A secretary sat in the front downstairs room behind a computer – a plump, middle-aged woman with greying hair. She looked too motherly to be the front woman for anything sinister.

'Excuse me. I need to talk to Frances Nosworthy. She gave me her card and told me to get in touch with her if I had any new information about a case she's interested in. Is she in?'

It was a half truth. That had been Frances's original request.

It was only later that she had made that phone call choking Suzie off.

'Your name?'

Suzie swallowed. 'Suzie Fewings.' What reaction would her name provoke when Frances heard it?

'There's nobody with her at the moment. I'll ask if she'll see you.'

The woman hurried away upstairs, her heels clattering on the bare polished boards. There was a telephone on the desk, but she had not chosen to ring through to Frances's office.

In a few moments she was back.

'Go up. It's the first on your left.' Suzie felt that the woman gave her a strange look before she resumed her seat.

The stairway was dimly lit. The offices had been adapted from a moderately sized private terraced house She wondered if Thomas Nosworthy had once lived 'over the shop' next door.

She was startled out of her thoughts by the realization that someone was standing on the landing above her. The shadowy figure was not directly at the top of the stairs, but looking down over the banisters at her side.

'What do you want?' Frances demanded. 'I thought I told you there was no need to contact me again.'

Suzie climbed the remaining stairs before answering. She did not want to feel at a disadvantage by standing below Frances.

'Something's happened. I'm sure you know about it . . .'

Before she could finish, Frances cut in. 'Not here, if you don't mind. We'll do this in my office.'

She led the way into a large room at the back of the house. It was furnished simply, with a large modern desk, a leather armchair and shelves of books and files which reached to the moulded plaster ceiling. A window gave on to the roofs of houses, and beyond that the moorland tors.

It occurred to Suzie for a panicked moment that Tom, on the pavement at the front of the house, would not be able to hear if she shouted.

Still, it was ridiculous to think that anything could happen to her here.

Frances settled herself behind her desk and motioned Suzie to the armchair. She was unsmiling. There was no hint of welcome or recognition in her face.

'You were saying?'

Some of the first impetus had gone out of Suzie. She wished she had not sat down. Should she stand up again and confront the seated Frances across her desk?

'Nick's missing. He went out to meet someone after work yesterday and hasn't come back. The police found his car on the other side of the moor. At Fullingford.'

'And?'

'This has to do with the Eileen Caseley murder. And probably with her will. Nick was warned off the case, the same way you did to me. You know something about this, don't you? Was it you he was meeting yesterday?'

'What a remarkable suggestion. As far as I can recall, I've never met your husband.'

'Where were you yesterday evening?'

'I don't think that's any business of yours.'

'Nick's missing. If that doesn't make it my business, I don't know what does. The tyres on his car were slashed. So were the ones on your cousin John's car yesterday.'

She saw the startled expression leap to Frances's face.

'I don't . . .'

'Suzie! What are you doing here?'

Suzie turned. John Nosworthy was standing in the doorway. His usually pleasant face was alarmed.

Frances rose. 'I could say the same of you, John. I would like to know what this is all about. Just what are you accusing me of?'

Suzie was on her feet too. Her voice was rising. 'I won't know that until I or the police find Nick and I know what's happened to him.'

'You think I kidnapped him? That's ridiculous!'

'You didn't want me to go on investigating the Caseley case, did you? You tried to stop me, to protect Philip. And then Nick found out something from Bernard Summers that would make things look very black for Philip indeed. A cast-iron motive to kill Eileen before she could change her will. Only he didn't know she'd already signed the codicil. Bernard Summers died because of what he knew, and now Nick has gone.'

Frances's face was blank.

'Suzie.' John came forward and stood between the two women. 'What you're suggesting is crazy. You can't really think Frances had anything to do with Bernard Summers' death? And as for Nick . . .'

'Thank you, John. I think I can defend myself,' Frances said, tight-lipped.

'Then why did you choke me off?' Suzie broke in. 'Before that, you left me your card and told me to contact you if I found out anything. What is it you were suddenly so afraid we'd discover? It was the gold, wasn't it?'

'Shall we just leave this whole investigation to the police? I'm sure they're looking for your husband, aren't they?'

'Yes, but at Fullingford. I think they're wrong. I think someone drove Nick's car there to throw them off the scent. I don't believe he's on that side of the moor at all. I'm sure he's here, and that you know where.'

'And just how was I supposed to get back from Fullingford after I'd done this dastardly deed? Walk?'

Suzie was left silenced.

'Suzie, you're barking up the wrong tree,' John tried to placate her. 'I'm sure whatever Frances did, she had a good reason for it. She's right. Let the police deal with it. Of course you're upset about your husband. I really hope he's all right. Can I get you something? A cup of tea?'

'I don't want tea. I want Nick.'

She pushed past him in frustration and hurried down the stairs. She should have known it was foolish to come, that Frances wouldn't tell her anything. The solicitor was too well schooled in the confidentiality of the legal system and the circumspection of law courts to give anything away. All she had done was perhaps to involve John in a fresh row with his cousin.

But something had made John afraid, from the first day she saw him.

She fled past the secretary in the downstairs office and tumbled out into the sunlit street.

Tom caught her. 'No joy? You didn't really think you'd get anything out of her, did you?'

'Leave her alone,' snapped Millie. 'At least she's trying to do *something.*'

THIRTY-ONE

'I 'll drop you off,' Suzie said, 'and then take the car round to Mike.'

'I'll come,' Tom offered.

'No need. The walk home might clear my head. At the moment, I feel as though I'm wading through porridge. Nothing I can think of makes sense.'

'You don't think it was her, then?' Millie asked. 'Frances Nosworthy? She didn't have anything to do with Dad?'

'I really don't know. She's changed her attitude since the first time I met her. But I think she may be right about one thing. If she was the one who left Dad's car at Fullingford, how did she get back to Moortown? There certainly wouldn't have been a bus that late.'

'And why?' Tom said gloomily. 'Nothing fits.'

Suzie left them at the end of their road and drove on up the hill to Mike's garage. She tried to put on a cheerful face as she handed the car over and belatedly signed the hire agreement. But Mike was too shrewd for her.

'Did you find Nick? Is he OK?'

This was the moment she had dreaded, when the Fewings' family catastrophe would escape beyond the small circle of those who already knew and become public knowledge. She couldn't bear the thought of the sympathetic curiosity of her friends.

'I didn't find him,' she said reluctantly. 'The police are looking for him.'

Mike gave her a measured look that was less shocked than she had expected.

'I thought there must be something going on. It's not like you to go tearing off in the middle of the night. A car crash, was it? And he's wandered off?'

'No, nothing like that . . . We think he's been abducted.'

Mike did whistle through his teeth then. 'Nick? Why ever would anyone do that?'

'It's a long story,' she sighed. 'Let's just say we got ourselves accidentally mixed up with something too big for us.'

'Look, Suzie, it's none of my business what this is all about, but if there's anything I can do to help . . .'

'No, thank you. You were a real angel last night, but at the moment we've just run into the sand. I can't think of anything else I can do.'

'Have you got your car back?'

'The tyres had been cut. The police have taken it away to check it for evidence.'

'Keep the Nissan, then. This is no time to be stranded without a car. On the house.'

'I couldn't.'

'Heavens above, woman. It's the least we can do. How are the kids taking it?'

'I sometimes think they're stronger than I am. But it's beginning to get through to Millie. As long as we were chasing around doing things, we could believe we'd find him. But now all we can do is sit at home and wait for the police to ring us. One way or another.'

'If it's any help, Kay and I will be praying for you and Nick.'

'Thanks, Mike. You're a friend. And I'd be glad if you'd keep this to yourself.'

'Trust me.'

She climbed back into the car. She had meant it when she said to Tom that the walk back from the garage would do her good. The rhythm of her feet on the pavement, the view out over the city, deep breaths of morning air. But Mike was right. She would feel less helpless with a set of wheels at her disposal. Even if she had no idea where she could go next.

Tom was waiting for her in the kitchen. He had made himself a mug of coffee and had the kettle ready to pour one for her.

'Millie's gone to lie down. She looks shattered.'

'It's the best thing. I need to do the same.' She took the steaming mug Tom offered her. 'Mike said to keep the car. I had to tell him about Dad. I swore him to secrecy, but I'm afraid a lot more people are going to know about it before long. I had to ring Leila to say he wouldn't be back to work.'

'We can hack it. And if it goes public, maybe somebody will come forward and say they've seen something. You never know.'

The words were meant to be comforting, but for once they lacked Tom's usually boundless optimism.

Suzie put the mug on the draining board. She suddenly felt overwhelmed with an enormous tiredness.

'I think I'll go to bed. It was a short night. I didn't get to sleep till about five.'

She was halfway across the kitchen when the urge to reach for a lifeline became too strong. She got out her phone and rang DS Dudbridge's number.

'Mrs Fewings? How can I help?'

'Is there any news of Nick?'

'We're searching. Don't worry, you'll be the first to know if we find him.'

'And you've no idea why his car was outside Clive Stroud's house?'

There was a hesitation. 'I probably shouldn't be telling you this, but we've taken Elizabeth Stroud in for questioning.'

'His wife? You think . . .' She thought of the tall, imperious woman handing her brandy. New scenarios chased through Suzie's head.

'We're just covering every possibility. We haven't arrested her.'

'Thank you.'

She put the phone away and turned to Tom. 'They've taken Elizabeth Stroud to the police station.'

Tom let out a whoop of laughter, which he cut short. 'She certainly did look as though she was about to kill someone. I guess Eileen Caseley was one infidelity too far.' He frowned again. 'But I'm blowed if I can see where Dad comes into that.'

'Maybe Elizabeth was the one who lured him to their house. What if it wasn't someone from Clive Stroud's office at all?'

'Yes, but why?'

'To incriminate Clive, if she really did have such a grudge against him.'

'Sounds a bit extreme, don't you think? Kidnap a perfectly respectable member of the population, just to get her own back on her cheating husband?'

'I've no idea how a jealous wife's mind works.'

'But why Dad? She didn't know him.' He put out a hand and touched her briefly. 'At least there's one thing. If Elizabeth Stroud did set this up to blacken Clive's name, she's hardly likely to have done him any real harm, is she? I mean, doing him in would be going a bit too far.'

The silence developed around them. All this time, Suzie had been trying to prevent herself from thinking the unthinkable, that Nick might not simply have been led into a trap, and be lying somewhere waiting to be found, but was actually dead.

She gave a choking cry and fled from the room.

Suzie lay awake on her bed, haunted by the horror that Tom's attempt at reassurance had conjured up in her. One part of her mind had known, of course, that if Bernard Summers was dead, so might Nick be. She had been filling the hours since his disappearance with frantic activity to stop herself from confronting that knowledge. Now she had run out of steam. She could do nothing but wait.

Now, in the stillness of the bedroom, her tired mind accepted the inevitable logic. Why should someone remove Nick from the scene, only to release him later safe and sound? What use would that serve? He would come back bursting with evidence against them. The only way they could be sure of his continued silence was through his death.

She gave an anguished cry of protest and turned over. She found herself confronting the empty side of the bed where Nick had lain only two nights ago. Where he might never lie again.

Mercifully, exhaustion claimed her mind. She slept.

She was awoken by the sound of the telephone downstairs. It took a startled moment before she leaped out of bed. It might be the police, ringing with news. It might even be Nick himself.

She went running downstairs, clumsy in her haste. She had not stopped to put on her shoes or comb her hair. She was part way down the flight when the ringing stopped. For a moment, she was terrified that the caller had rung off. But as she rounded the corner of the landing, she saw that Tom was answering the phone.

He held out the receiver. 'It's for you. They want to know why you weren't at work this morning. I passed the buck.'

She took the receiver from him. 'Hello? This is Suzie.'

'It's Margery, dear. From the charity shop. We were a bit concerned this morning when you didn't show up in the office. I rang to see if you were ill, but I couldn't get an answer. I don't have your mobile number, only the house one. Is everything all right?'

The question seemed to come from a long way away. Suzie wrestled to bring her thoughts back to everyday reality. It had not occurred to her for a moment that on any other weekday morning she would have been in the office of Age of Silver, behind the charity shop that helped to fund it. Dear, kind Margery, who managed the shop with her army of volunteers. Of course she would be concerned that Suzie was suddenly absent with no explanation or apology.

'Sorry,' she gasped. 'There's been, well, call it a domestic crisis. I'm sorry, I can't tell you more at the moment. I should have rung you.'

'Never mind me. It's you I'm worried about. Is there anything I can do to help?'

'No. No, thank you.' Suzie was trying to order her thoughts. What about tomorrow? It was unthinkable that she could go back to work while the likelihood of disaster lay over the family. Should she ring the national headquarters, tell them she would be unavailable for – who knew how long?

She lowered herself on to the chair in the hall and let the receiver fall back on to its cradle. The impossibility of a future without Nick stretched away in front of her. At some point they would find his body. There would be a funeral. Life would go on. It seemed impossible to imagine it.

The doorbell rang, startlingly. Tom was striding to answer it. Suzie was suddenly conscious that she was in crumpled clothes, her hair tousled, shoeless.

'Hi there, Tom. Can I come in? Is Suzie home?'

She heard the familiar warm voice of Alan Taylor, their Methodist minister. Next moment he was standing in the hall, in a sweatshirt that said 'Chaplaincy Team'. His round, and usually cheerful, face was lengthened in concern.

As she rose from her seat he moved forward and hugged her. 'Suzie! This is terrible news. Have there been any new developments?'

'No. Nothing. How did you know?'

'Mike told me. Don't worry. He said you didn't want it spread over the neighbourhood, but he thought I ought to know. I hope that's OK? Don't worry, I understand about confidentiality. It comes with the job. There are all sorts of people in the congregation who are hurting in ways the rest of you don't know about. The names we print on the prayer list are barely half of it. But what happened?'

Suzie led the way into the sitting room and ran her hand over her untidy hair. 'Nobody knows. He had a phone call yesterday afternoon, apparently setting up a meeting with Clive Stroud, the MP for Moortown. He told me not to wait tea. But he never came back. The police found his empty car outside Clive Stroud's house at Fullingford. There's been no sign of Nick since.'

'Do you know why he'd be meeting Clive Stroud?'

Suzie wondered how much she should tell him. 'It has to have something to do with the Eileen Caseley murder case. Do you remember that? A farmer's wife was shot, just outside Moortown. Her husband's been arrested for it. But it appears that she may have been having an affair with Clive Stroud. She left him – something – in her will.'

'And what has all that got to do with Nick?'

'It's complicated. Nick didn't know about the will, but he did know something important about the piece of land she left Clive Stroud. And the man who told him is dead.'

'That's scary. I can see why you're upset. But there's probably a simple explanation.'

'That's what I tried to tell myself yesterday. But today . . .'

'Have they arrested the MP? It doesn't look good for him, does it?'

'No. They've taken his wife in for questioning.'

'I see. Hell hath no fury, eh? The eternal triangle. But forgive me, I can see why she might kill the unfortunate Eileen Caseley, but why involve Nick?'

Suzie sighed. 'That's what none of us can understand. Nick had already told the police what he knew. It was too late to silence him.'

An expression of contrition came over Alan's face. 'I'm sorry, Suzie! I didn't come here to play detective. It's you I'm worried about. I was going to ask, "Are you all right?" But of course you're not. Nobody would be. Would it help if we prayed?'

'If you like.' Suzie was immediately sorry that sounded so cold. She had prayed so many wild, helpless prayers during the night.

She was aware of Millie hovering in the doorway. Tom, she suspected, would raise his eyebrows in tolerant amusement if she invited him to pray, but Millie stayed listening.

She let Alan's affirming words wash over her. The effect was more calming than she had expected.

He rose. 'If there's anything I can do . . . If there's any news, don't hesitate to ring. Any hour of the day or night.' He pressed her hand.

'I'm sorry. I should have offered you a cup of tea. Or a cold fruit juice?'

'No thanks. I get offered more tea and biscuits than is good for my waistline. I'll be off. Millie, look after your mother.' He smiled as he passed the pale, silent teenager. 'I'll be praying for you too.'

'That's it, then?' Tom reappeared as the front door closed. 'You've been signed off from work. We've been prayed over. There's nothing else we can do?'

'I've exhausted everything I can think of,' Suzie told him.

The rest of the day stretched out in front of her. And all the days after that. She tried not to think that the next time she contacted the minister it might be to arrange Nick's funeral.

THIRTY-TWO

T om was upstairs with Dave. There was no sound of music. Suzie had no idea what they were doing. She felt sure Tom must have told Dave about Nick – in confidence, of course. Millie would have rung Tamara.

How long would it be before the phone began to ring with friends giving her their sympathy and making well-meant but useless offers of help?

Suzie wandered through the house, unable to settle to anything. Her nerves were tensed, waiting for news from DS Dudbridge. She trusted him more than DCI Brewer. She both longed for and dreaded that call.

After a while, Millie came downstairs and went into the little-used dining room. She began laying things out on the teak table – a large Ordnance Survey map, a pad of paper.

'What are you doing?'

'Wait till Dave's gone.'

It was about five o'clock when the boys emerged from Tom's room. Dave came through to the kitchen, where Suzie was wondering helplessly what to do for a meal she did not feel like eating.

'Sorry about this, Suzie.'

So he did know.

The ginger-haired teenager hesitated. Normally, at this point, Suzie would have invited him to stay for a meal. But she was too preoccupied to be hospitable. And Millie was waiting silently in the dining room doorway.

'OK, then,' Dave said after a pause. 'I'll be on my way . . . See you, mate,' he said to Tom as he made his way to the front door. 'Chin up.'

The door closed behind him. The Fewings were alone.

Millie turned and walked back into the dining room. Suzie obeyed her unspoken command. Tom raised his eyebrows, then followed Suzie's beckoning gesture.

'Right,' Millie drew a deep breath. 'We've got to get to the bottom of this.'

'Do you think the police aren't trying?'

Millie ignored her. She gestured at the map. It covered the whole of the moor, with the towns and villages around it. 'This story is all over the place. Let's go right back to the beginning. It started *here*.' She laid her hand on Saddlers Wood, a mile or two outside Moortown. 'Two days before Eileen Caseley was shot, we were here. If we hadn't been, none of this would have happened. Mum wouldn't have gone to the funeral. Dad wouldn't have got Bernard Summers talking. You wouldn't have met either of those solicitors.'

'I would,' Suzie put in. 'John Nosworthy, at least. He had some money to give me after the tractor pull. That would have happened anyway.'

'And Clive Stroud,' Tom agreed. 'He and Mum were already set up to be there.'

'But it wouldn't have been the same,' Millie said impatiently. 'I'm sure it wouldn't. Right from the beginning, everybody thought Mum knew something. And then there's Dad. He meets Bernard Summers *here*.' She moved her hand to Moortown. 'And next day, as far as anyone knows, this geologist bloke meets his end in a stream somewhere *here*.' This time she indicated a wider area of open moor. 'Next thing we know, someone gets Dad to drive his car across the moor to *here*.' She pointed out Fullingford, far over to the west. 'He must have driven it himself, mustn't he? So why?'

'The police don't seem to know any more than we do,' Suzie said. 'Or if they do, they're not telling me. If they've taken Elizabeth Stroud in for questioning, that must mean they now think she's a prime suspect.'

Tom gave a short laugh. 'Perhaps it wasn't Philip who killed his wife, after all. If Stroud's wife found out Clive had been two-timing her with Eileen, she might have been the one who bumped her off.'

Suzie shook her head. 'Somehow, that doesn't fit. By the sound of it, he was a serial womanizer. Why should she suddenly take offence at Eileen? And what's it got to do with Nick?'

Millie was bending over, studying the map again, as if the

secret was hidden there amongst the contour lines, the marks of bridleways, the green enclosures of woodland. Her finger strayed eastward again.

'It comes back to the same thing. Whatever it is started that Saturday in Saddlers Wood. I'm sure it did. There must be something we've forgotten about. Maybe something we didn't even notice at the time.'

Tom blew out his breath and rumpled his hair. 'As I recall it, Dad drove us out to Moortown and we had lunch at a pub. I can't remember anything special that happened there.' He looked questioningly at the others. They stayed silent. 'Then Mum navigated us out to Saddlers Wood. There was this cart track going up to the farm. We parked at the bottom.'

'Were there any other cars there?' Millie asked suddenly.

A pause. 'Not that I remember. Wait. We did see a little green car driving away, but that was afterwards.'

'But if someone else was there, who had no business to be, they might have hidden theirs.'

'What are you getting at?'

'I don't know yet, do I? Go on.'

'Right. So we walk up this cart track. But before we get to the farm, we hear a gunshot. Then Philip Caseley comes charging out from the woods. He looks upset, but he rallies round when he sees us. Mum tells him about how she's chasing up the ancestry trail, and he tells us to go on up to the house.'

'And Eileen Caseley's there, and she looks upset too.'

'Oh, and I forgot to say, the last we saw of Philip he was heading off down a small path that we found out afterwards leads to that ruined cottage.'

'And on to Puck's Acre,' Suzie reminded him.

'Fair enough. Anyway, Eileen invites us in for tea. And the place is pretty run-down. Not like a couple who've been told someone has found gold on their land.'

'There'd been a quarrel between Philip and Eileen about that,' Suzie put in. 'And two days after we'd been there, she added that peculiar codicil to her will. And almost immediately after someone shot her.'

'Never mind about that,' Millie said impatiently. 'That happened later. Go back to Saturday.'

Tom frowned. 'Well . . . Eileen Caseley gave us directions to find the remains of the cottage. Mum's ancestral home.'

'And yours,' Suzie retorted.

'So we find these ruins in a clearing, beside a stream. And while we're poking around, and Dad's taking photographs, there's this sound of a branch breaking in the woods. Mum says she's sure someone's watching us.'

'That's what it felt like.'

'Dad thinks it's just an animal. A wild one, or maybe someone's taking their dog for a walk in the woods. We have a half-hearted sort of look, and Dad calls out to see if anyone's there, but there's no sign of anything odd.'

'I'm still convinced there was someone else there, besides us.'

'Philip?' suggested Millie. 'He went that way.'

Suzie shrugged. 'We'll never know.'

'But that's the point!' Millie exploded. 'Someone thinks we *do* know. Someone who doesn't want us to know they were there at all.'

'Clive Stroud!' Light was breaking in Tom's face. 'If he was on some secret assignation with Eileen . . . If Philip found them . . .'

'That's what she was all dressed up for!' Millie exclaimed. 'I thought she looked remarkably smart for someone out in the back of beyond.'

'Maybe that's what that gunshot was about. Philip was trying to scare him off. Literally firing a warning shot across Eileen's bows.'

Suzie shivered. 'That could explain why Clive Stroud was so sinister that day of the tractor pull. Why he warned me off coming back to Moortown. Infidelity is one thing. But with a murdered woman . . .'

'Terrible PR for an MP,' Tom said.

'Except that Eileen was already dead by then,' Millie said sceptically. 'If you'd known he was there, you'd have reported it to the police, wouldn't you? It would be too late to stop you.'

'And you really think that day in the woods has got anything to do with someone carting Dad off?' Tom asked.

There was a painful silence. To Suzie it seemed as much of a dead end as it had been before.

Then Millie gave a great yelp and leaped up from the map she had been studying.

'What was that you said just now?' she asked Tom eagerly.

'Which bit?'

'While we're poking around, and Dad's taking photographs.'

Tom and Suzie stared at her.

'Got it!' Tom cried. 'Did he show you those photographs, Mum?'

Suzie struggled to remember. The search for her ancestors seemed far away and unimportant, compared with all that had happened since. 'He copied two of the best ones across to me for my files. I didn't see the rest.'

'Where's his camera? He didn't take it with him yesterday, did he?'

'On a work day? I shouldn't think so.'

Millie flew next door to the study. As Tom and Suzie crowded after her, she dragged open the drawer where Nick kept his camera equipment. She pulled out the Canon and waved it triumphantly.

'Turn on the computer, Mum. We've got to see this. I'll swear the answer's here.'

Tom rummaged in the drawer for the right cable to connect the camera to the computer's USB port. Suzie found that she was holding her breath. Would there be any more photographs left on Nick's camera from that day, besides the two she already had? Nick had selected for her a close-up of the cottage ruins and a longer shot of the clearing in which it stood, looking down over the pink spires of fireweed towards the stream with the ruins in the foreground. She had noticed nothing unusual about either of them.

'Got it!' Tom took over the desk chair. He brought up on the screen an array of thumbnail images. He scanned the dates. 'Result! Trust Dad to take forty photos where half a dozen would do.'

'So he didn't delete the rest.' Millie craned forward in excitement.

One by one, Tom began to bring each of the photographs from that Saturday up to full screen. Some were similar to the ones

Suzie had added to her files. There were more of the old cottage, taken from different angles, the shapeless walls of cob, disintegrating once they had lost their roof. There were artistic close-ups of weeds springing out of the crevices, a wall split by a young ash tree. Nick had picked out the wild flowers that carpeted the clearing. Even the word 'clearing' was losing its meaning as the trees began to take back what had once been a large open space. Charlotte Day's kitchen garden, no doubt. The place where she hung her washing. Where her children played. Nick had peopled some of these photographs with his own family, sometimes not. Suzie's imagination supplied other figures from a century and a half ago.

She snatched back her wandering thoughts. What should she really be looking for?

Tom leaned closer to the screen. 'Not sure what he's trying to get here.'

Nick had turned his camera away from the cottage, to focus on the woods beyond the stream. Through his lens, Suzie saw more gradations of colour among the foliage than she would have thought possible. Her less artistic eye would have dismissed these leaves as simply green, but Nick had found a variety of shades of gold in the oak, the blue-green needles of fir, the glossy darkness of holly.

'There!' cried Tom and Millie simultaneously.

Suzie's attention snapped back to the new image which had suddenly appeared on the screen. The stream still ran sparkling in the foreground. Beyond, there was that same wall of trees. Except . . .

'What is it?' asked Millie. 'It looks like a very small car's headlights or a very big owl's eyes.'

'Somebody's glasses,' said Tom. Suzie could hear his breath coming fast.

Her own eyes had fastened on what they were staring at. To the right of centre, among the leaves, Nick's camera had caught the flashes of light from two small circles.

'There *was* someone there in the woods,' Tom breathed. 'Well done, Mum! I assumed it must be a deer or something. But deer don't wear spectacles. Someone really was watching us.'

Suzie leaned further over his shoulder, craning to see more closely. Was that all there was? Just the reflection of light on a pair of glasses from – what? – thirty metres away? Nick had not used his most powerful lens.

'Can you enlarge it?' she urged.

Tom homed in on that detail. A bigger, more blurred image replaced the whole. It was just possible to make out a pale oval surrounded by a darker smudge which merged into the leaves.

Suzie scrabbled through her memories, trying to think of any of the players in this story who wore glasses. Philip? She thought not. Eileen? Possibly. Frances Nosworthy? No, and she was almost certain John Nosworthy did not. She couldn't be sure about Clive Stroud. It was strange, but when you thought about almost any of your acquaintances it was possible to imagine them wearing spectacles, and less easy to remember which ones actually did.

'Try the next picture,' Millie ordered.

The image on the screen changed again. Nick had shifted the angle, so that he was looking further up the stream. The screen of foliage was still there on the left, but more of the foreground was now the sunlit flower-strewn grass on the nearer side of the brook. There was no sign of a flash of light among the leaves.

'Must have scared her off. She never realized she'd be photographed,' Millie said.

'She?' asked Suzie and Tom together.

'Of course it's a woman. Didn't you see her hair?'

Tom clicked back. Those twin flashes of light reappeared. He enlarged the detail again. Suzie frowned. She felt that if she stared at it long enough, she could believe that Millie was right, that there was a cloud of darkness surrounding that indistinct face. Something more crinkled than the texture of the leaves it melded into.

'Do you suppose Dad noticed it?' Millie asked.

'I doubt it. He would have said so, wouldn't he? We only saw it because we were looking for something out of the ordinary. Something whoever was there that day didn't expect us to see.'

Suzie was still staring at that blur of a face with what must be quite a large pair of glasses. Horn-rimmed. Where had she seen a pair like that?

Suddenly she jumped, so violently that she knocked Tom sideways on his swivel chair.

'Yes! I'm almost sure it's her! Those glasses!'

'Who?' Tom and Millie demanded.

'Oh, what was her name? . . . Gina Alford! Clive Stroud's agent.'

THIRTY-THREE

'**A**re you sure? You can't really recognize her from this blurry photo, can you?' Millie asked.

'Of course I'm not sure. How can I be? I corresponded with her, but I only met her once, at the tractor pull. But she does have big horn-rimmed glasses like that.'

'I bet the police have got the kit to enhance this better than we can,' Tom said.

Suzie's mobile was already in her hand. She dialled DS Dudbridge's number, her thumb clumsy with haste. To her relief, she got through.

'Mrs Fewings? Still no joy, I'm afraid. We're not giving up, though.'

'We've found something. On Nick's camera. This could be the person he was meeting.'

She poured out their discovery, and their attempts to distinguish the face.

'I can't be a hundred per cent sure it's Gina Alford, but it fits.'

'I'm coming over.'

'No. Don't waste time. If she knows where Nick is . . . if she's got him, you have to find her.'

'Point taken. I'll send someone round to pick up the camera. We can probably get a better identification than you could.'

Suzie put down the mobile. Her brain was working overtime,

trying to disentangle all the implications if what she guessed was right.

'But what would Clive Stroud's agent be doing in Saddlers Wood?'

'Spying on him?' Millie suggested. 'We said that he might have had an assignation with Eileen that day, and Philip found out. They had a row, Philip fired his gun, and then came storming out when we met him.'

'What's that got to do with this Stroud guy's constituency agent?' Tom asked. 'What he does in his spare time is his own affair.'

Suzie thought back to that sunlit afternoon in Moortown square. Gina Alford, possessively aggressive. Scorning Suzie's ability to have set up everything right for her MP. Even then, Suzie had sensed that the frizzy-haired, bespectacled agent's demeanour was more than professional jealousy.

'I think she's in love with him.'

'You mean . . .?' Millie was rapidly working out the consequences. 'It might not have been Philip who shot Eileen because she was having an affair with Clive? It could have been this Alford woman taking out a rival who looked as if she was getting too serious.'

'If she overheard an almighty row, and knew that Clive really was thinking of divorcing his wife, and Eileen was going to leave Philip, she might have felt driven to stop her, yes.'

'So,' Tom said slowly, 'she goes back on Monday, gets hold of Philip's gun and does the deed. But she's worried because she remembers there was this family in the clearing on Saturday taking photographs, while she was on her way back to wherever she'd hidden her car. She knows there's a chance that this guy with the camera might have caught her in one of them.'

'But she wouldn't know who we were,' Millie objected.

'I went to the funeral,' Suzie said. 'Clive saw me watching the burial. He obviously suspected me of something. Maybe he thought I knew more about his affair with Eileen than I did.' She frowned, trying to remember what happened next. 'He might not have known about her will then. John Nosworthy would have been in touch with him after the funeral to tell him about the codicil. I think he was genuinely shocked last night when we told him about the gold. But I was so busy being scared of him, it never occurred to me that Gina Alford might have recognized me too.'

'So it could have been then that she found out who the photographer was,' Tom said, realization dawning in his face. 'And since nobody had questioned her, she figured Dad hadn't yet spotted what he'd got and gone to the police. But any day now he might look back over his pictures and find her. It might not be too late for her to stop the only guy who could link her to Saddlers Wood.'

'Yes, but where does Bernard Summers fit into all of this? Why would she kill *him*?'

A pause. 'We don't know that she did,' Suzie said. 'It could have been a genuine accident. Those moorland streams run fast. People do slip on the stones. It begins to make sense.' She straightened up from the computer with a renewed sense of dread. 'Idiot! That phone call came from Clive Stroud's *office*, not from him. Why didn't I think that it had to be her? I was so sure it was Clive behind it. She lured Dad out on to the moor. Somehow, she got him to go to the Strouds' house, so that Clive would get the blame. She must have been waiting to meet Nick outside. Unless the Strouds know more about this than I think they do.'

'And then what?' Millie snapped. 'The only thing that matters is where is Dad now? What did she do to him?'

The worst possibility of all was waiting at the bottom of Suzie's mind for someone to voice it.

It was Millie who answered her own question in a small, scared voice. 'If she killed Eileen Caseley, could she be mad enough to kill Dad too, to stop him from finding that photograph?'

Suzie turned and walked out of the study, trying to shut Millie's words out of her head. Wouldn't she know in her heart if Nick was dead? She felt a terrible fear, but it was not certainty. It was still possible, wasn't it, that DCI Brewer might arrest Gina Alford in Moortown and force her to confess what she had done with Nick? It might still not be too late to save him. She had to believe that.

She found herself standing in front of the conservatory windows, looking out at the pageant of summer colour that was Nick's flower garden. A cascade of yellow roses tumbled over trelliswork at the side of the house. The rich dark red of Bishop of Llandaff dahlias glowed from across the lawn. This was what would remain of him. His creation.

No! She must not let herself think like that. She should be praying. For Nick, for the police. Even for a softening of Gina Alford's heart.

Was it too late for that?

Sooner than she expected, the doorbell rang. She wondered if it was a well-meaning friend, come to offer sympathy, or Alan, the minister, again.

'Mum,' announced Millie, 'it's the police. They want Dad's camera.'

By the time she got to the study, Tom had already disconnected the leads and was handing the Canon over to a fresh-faced constable. Suzie was given a receipt to sign.

'This is what you need to be looking at.' Tom wrote the number of the image on a slip of paper. The constable left.

'All the way from the police HQ to pick it up,' Tom said scornfully. 'Have these guys not heard of email?'

'Maybe they need to have the camera to prove the source,' Millie suggested.

Suzie knew in her heart that, however the police laboratory enhanced Nick's photo, it was unlikely that it would be good enough to get a positive identification that would stand up in a criminal trial. And even if it did, what would it prove? That Clive Stroud's agent was in Saddlers Wood two days before Eileen Caseley's murder. That would hardly make her guilty beyond reasonable doubt. She felt the heaviness of despair threatening to overwhelm her.

'What do you suppose they're doing now?' she asked out loud. 'DCI Brewer and co.'

'It sounds as though they're taking you seriously,' Millie tried to comfort her. 'That has to be good, doesn't it? Your police sergeant latched on to the idea that they've got to get to Moortown and find this Gina Alford. If only they can make her tell them what she's done with Dad!'

Suzie turned away. Though she tried to control it, her voice came muffled. 'They wasted all that time searching around Fullingford. Of course she wouldn't have left him there. It was too obvious. He won't be in Moortown either. He could be anywhere.'

'Our only hope is that they can scare her into believing they know for certain she did it. She might confess then.' Tom's fists were clenched. He was as tense as she was.

Suzie wandered back to the computer. Tom had saved Nick's photographs on the hard disk. The screen was showing that idyllic scene: cob walls, hung with ivy, drifts of fireweed, pink in the sunlight, the wall of trees across the brook. Suddenly, with piercing clarity, she knew.

'That's it! It's got to be! Where it all started. Where she found them together. The reason all of this happened.'

'What are you talking about?' Millie asked. 'Are you all right?'

'I know where Dad is. He has to be. She took him back to Saddlers Wood.'

She was already in the hall, grabbing her shoulder bag and the borrowed car keys.

'Mum,' Tom was saying, 'it's just a guess. You can't be sure.'

'Have you got a better one?'

He shook his head.

She was running towards the drive. 'Thank you, Mike!' she murmured as she unlocked the Nissan.

Millie and Tom were behind her. She tried to ignore the looks they were giving each other.

'At least tell DS Dudbridge what you're doing,' Tom pleaded.

She passed him her phone. 'I've keyed in his number. You do it.'

She didn't protest when Millie climbed into the back and Tom took the passenger seat beside her.

It took all her concentration to steer them safely through the city and up the long hill that would take them out to Moortown and Saddlers Wood.

At the roadside below Saddlers Wood stood a new placard. GRAZING TO LET.

So Matthew had taken possession.

This time Suzie did not park the car on the grass verge, but drove on up the rutted track towards the farm.

'Do you really think she's here?' asked Millie in a low voice, as though someone in the woods around them could overhear her.

'I shouldn't think so. She'll be back at work today, acting the part of Clive Stroud's faceless assistant. Just as she did when she made that phone call to Dad's office.'

They parked in the empty farmyard.

'I wonder what happened to the dog,' said Millie, climbing out.

'What now?' Tom asked. He was watching Suzie closely. She felt that he did not completely trust her, but would come with her anyway.

'I don't know,' she said slowly, looking around.

Images from the past were all about her. This would be the same farmhouse where Richard Day's employer had lived, back in the 1850s. Richard must have crossed this yard thousands of times in the course of his work. He would have mucked out these byres, fed and harnessed the horses in these stables, drawn water from that well in the corner. But none of it gave any clue to where Nick – or Nick's body, a cold voice said – might be now.

'We were in the clearing by the cottage when Nick accidentally snapped her,' she said at last. 'Maybe that's where she took him.'

They began to walk back down that path.

The clearing opened up before them. The woods cast longer shadows now in the early evening sun. The yellowish cob of crumbling walls glowed between the smothering creepers.

But now Suzie could not waste time on memories of the past. She plunged into the deepening shadows of the ruined walls. With her bare hands she was tugging away the brambles and ivy that shrouded its corners, in the vain hope that there might be a body, bound and unconscious, hidden under them. This small hope was overshadowed by the dread of what she might really find.

Outside, Millie was down by the brook, peering into the water.

Tom was combing the ground more widely. 'No sign of any recent disturbance in the ground here,' he called.

Was that what they were looking for? Suzie wondered. Not a prison, but a grave?

'We're wasting our time,' said Millie, suddenly appearing behind her. 'She couldn't have carried him here by herself, could she? And there were no marks of car tracks.'

Tom and Suzie turned to her.

Before Suzie could answer, there came the blare of police sirens. Not one but several vehicles were approaching fast along the road. They turned in at the cart track. The noise was mounting towards the farm, deafening now.

The Fewings broke into a run.

THIRTY-FOUR

The farmyard was crowded with vehicles and police. Suzie's eyes, swiftly searching, came to rest on one group that made her heart constrict. Handcuffed to a uniformed officer was a woman, undistinguished-looking except for the frizzy brown hair that bushed around her bespectacled face, in spite of her efforts to tie it back. Suzie fought to break through to her to demand answers, but another policeman blocked her way with arms outspread. Others were setting up yellow tape around the yard.

'Why aren't you searching the place?' she said angrily to the officer in front of her.

'They are,' Tom told her quietly. He nodded to a corner of the yard.

This was not the widespread search she had envisaged, with police spread out in lines, combing the yard for clues, entering the farmhouse and the outbuildings to examine every hiding place.

Instead, a knot of figures, some in uniform, some not, were clustered around that single place in the yard which Tom had gestured to. Even from the back she recognized the tall figure of DCI Brewer.

Slowly the knowledge took shape in her mind of what it was they were surrounding. She had stood in this yard not half an hour ago, imagining her great-great-grandfather at work here. Drawing water for the horses from that same well.

'No!' she whispered. '*No!*'

She made to rush forward, to break through the tape. This time it was Tom who held her back. She could not see what they were doing. She thought she glimpsed an officer in overalls clambering over the low brick wall that surrounded the well. She imagined all too vividly the rope around his waist, the dark shaft into which he must be descending. The cold water at the bottom. She could not bear to think what he might find there.

Tom was standing in front of her, his hands firm on her shoulders.

Beyond him, there was more activity now. The surrounding officers were not just onlookers. They must be hoisting that other officer out. Or raising something else. She strained against Tom's restraining hands, but he stood his ground, blocking her view.

Another siren screamed into the hush that had fallen over the yard. This time it was an ambulance that came rocking into sight to stop on the concrete farmyard. Two paramedics jumped out and went running towards the well. Suzie's fingernails were digging into her palms as she prayed in desperation. She knew it must be too late, but her mind would not accept it.

She turned her head and saw Millie, white-faced, beside her. Suzie reached out and took her daughter's icy hand.

It seemed an age that the group around the well remained largely hidden from her by Tom's shoulders. There were murmurs of unease and sympathy from the rest of the officers spread around the yard. To one side, Gina Alford stood defiantly still, handcuffed. Suzie tried to shut out from her mind all the vengeful things she would like to do to her. Nothing was more important now than the overwhelming grief she felt for the wounded body of her husband which they must now be hauling out of the depths.

Millie gripped her hand tighter.

There was new movement across the yard. The ambulance was creeping forward towards the well, turning, stopping again. Its back doors were open. A little party was carrying a stretcher towards it. Too far away to see the details of the dark burden it bore. Past Tom's arm she saw them loading it into the ambulance. The paramedics boarded their vehicle again. The ambulance moved off, through the quiet ranks of watching police officers. Past a silent Gina Alford.

'That was Dad, wasn't it?' Millie said softly as the chequered vehicle disappeared down the track.

Suzie hugged her wordlessly.

Someone was coming towards them. The beanpole figure of DCI Brewer. Suzie tensed, waiting for the reprimand which would tell her she should not be here.

The Chief Inspector's grim face unbent slightly.

'He's alive,' she said. 'Just.'

THIRTY-FIVE

S uzie's heart leaped with a mixture of joy and panic when she saw Nick next morning. All night she had sat in the hospital waiting room, while he was treated for hypothermia, X-rayed, plastered. They had allowed her a brief glimpse of him in the intensive care ward, sedated and asleep.

Even now, only his head showed, propped up on pillows in a hospital bed. A white bandage swathed his black hair. His face beneath was deathly pale. There was a mound beneath the covers near the foot of the bed. She came hesitantly forward and touched him tentatively, as if she was afraid he might break.

He managed a ghost of a smile, though there were creases of pain and weariness around his darkened eyes.

'Not too long,' the charge nurse warned. 'It's been touch and go.'

Suzie bent to kiss him lightly, then drew up a chair beside him. 'How are you?'

It sounded a trite thing to say, but it was all she could think of. She took his hand, and was alarmed at the slightness of pressure with which he responded.

'Tired,' he said. 'My head aches.'

'I'm not surprised.'

She touched his face tenderly, marvelling that she could still do this. That she was listening to the voice she had thought she would never hear again.

'I was an idiot. Going to meet her like that. Thinking I'd arranged to see Clive Stroud.'

She pressed his hand in sympathy.

'You couldn't know.'

'I was going to give him a piece of my mind for frightening you. That's why I rang him, or tried to. Instead I got her, and walked right into a trap.'

'You phoned *him*?' Suzie exclaimed. 'Not the other way round?'

'No.' He closed his eyes and lay back. 'I was going to tell him that you knew nothing about the murder, or about him and Eileen. That he should stop scaring you. She rang me back to say she'd fixed up a meeting.'

'And you didn't tell me? Just said you wouldn't be home for tea?'

'Well, I wasn't, was I?' His pale face creased in a half smile.

'And you didn't realize it was her you'd got when you were taking photos in the wood?'

'Photos? What's that got to do with anything?'

'You don't know? Of course you don't. It was Millie's idea. We went through the photos on your camera you'd taken that Saturday in Saddlers Wood. And there was a flash of light through the leaves on one of them. Tom enlarged it. And there she was. Just the blur of her face and those horn-rimmed glasses. But it was enough. I knew she must be the one we'd heard in the wood. And she had to have been there for a reason. The only thing that made sense was that she was spying on Clive and Eileen. And if it meant that much to her, then it could have been her, not Philip, who shot Eileen. And used his gun to do it.'

Nick's eyelids closed again. 'Sarah Lund has got nothing on you lot.'

'The police were searching for you around Fullingford, after they found your car. You drove there, didn't you?'

Nick's forehead creased again. 'I don't really remember what happened. But they tell me someone cracked my skull. After that . . .' A long shudder shook him. 'I came round up to my neck in cold water, with the grandmother of a headache and a broken leg. Apparently I've cracked a vertebra as well. It was as black as hell. And cold like you wouldn't believe. I thought no one would ever find me . . .'

'I know. They told me.' Her hands squeezed his, trying to put warmth into it.

'It was a miracle I landed the right way up. And that there wasn't room for me to fall flat. As it was, my face was only inches from the water.'

'Thank God it hasn't rained and the groundwater's low.'

They sat in silence, holding each other.

'I thought I was going to die there. They only found me because you told them it was Gina Alford.'

'I take back everything I've said about DCI Brewer. She conned Gina into thinking they had more proof than they did. Just one fuzzy detail in a single photo.'

'My photography's not as bad as that. I'd have used a zoom lens if I'd known.'

'It was a bluff. But it worked. Brewer convinced her it could help her if she told them where you were.'

'Time's up,' said the charge nurse, returning. 'You can come back this afternoon.'

'Can I bring Tom and Millie?'

'Give it till tomorrow. He needs to rest.'

Suzie leaned over and kissed his face.

There would be another morning for them. Nick had a fractured skull, broken bones from the fall, hypothermia. But he was alive.

Tears of joy were running down her face as she left the ward.

'I never thought I'd see this day.'

Nick looked round at Tom and Millie. He was sitting in a chair in a sunny courtyard outside his ward. His leg was in plaster, his head still bandaged. But Suzie's heart warmed to see that colour had returned to his face.

In a low-walled ornamental pond, goldfish flickered in the

sunshine or hid under lily leaves, showing only their quivering tails.

'So it had nothing to do with the gold?' Tom asked. 'After all that!'

'Apparently not,' Suzie told them. 'It's doubtful whether Gina Alford even knew about it. Of course, if she had, it might have made the idea of marrying Clive Stroud even more attractive.'

'When she found he wasn't going to fall into her arms once Eileen was dead, I'm surprised she didn't kill *him*,' Millie said.

'It must have been a terrible shock for her,' mused Suzie. 'To find she'd done something so awful for nothing.'

'Perhaps she still hoped he'd change his mind.'

'But she'd be terrified that someone would find out.'

'Us,' Tom said. 'Dad's photo. She must have known he'd caught her.'

'Let's not talk about that,' said Nick.

Suzie took his hand. He had less obvious wounds that would take a long time to heal.

'What happens to the farm now?' Millie asked. 'Presumably they've let Philip out of jail.'

'It's not as simple as that,' Suzie sighed. 'After the funeral, Matthew put the farm up to let and went back to Australia. I think they sold the sheep off immediately.'

'That's terrible!' Millie exclaimed. 'The poor guy's innocent, and he's lost his wife, his home, his job. Everything.'

'He'll get the farm back. Eileen's will said he could stay there for life. But it's worse than that. It was heartbreaking to see them both at her funeral – Matthew on one side of the aisle, Philip on the other. Not speaking. Matthew wouldn't even look at his father.'

'I guess if your son thinks you're a murderer, when you're not, that takes a long time to get over,' Tom said more soberly than usual.

'Gina Alford has a lot to answer for.'

'But she couldn't separate us.' Millie jumped up and ran to hug her father. 'I wouldn't have believed that of you, whatever anyone else said.'

'Steady on,' Nick laughed. 'I'm breakable, remember.'

'And Clive Stroud has got Puck's Acre,' Suzie mused. 'I wonder if he'll do anything about the gold? He might want to keep it quiet, adultery with a murder victim.'

'He's a director of Merlin Mines, remember?' Tom said.

Suzie watched the goldfish darting in and out of the sunlight. She had Nick back. That was all the gold she wanted.

AUTHOR'S NOTE

The people, places and institutions in this book are fictitious. However, I am indebted to the many real-life people and organizations who have done so much to help my own family history research in ways that have inspired this book, or have given me other advice. They include the following:

Devon Record Office and the Westcountry Studies Library, now combined as the Devon Heritage Centre: www.devon.gov.uk/about_the_devon_heritage_centre.

British Newspaper Archive: www.britishnewspaperarchive.co.uk and through subscription websites such as www.findmypast. co.uk and www.ancestry.co.uk.

National Archives, Access to Archives: www.nationalarchives. gov.uk/a2a.

Genuki genealogical website: www.genuki.org.uk.

Census returns, 1841–1911: www.ukcensusonline.com, www. freecen.org.uk, or subscription genealogy sites.

Parish registers: Devon Record Office and Devon Family History Society at Tree House.

While I have given free rein to my imagination here, many details owe their inspiration to people and places in my own family history research:

Richard and Charlotte Day's tombstone on which Charlotte is recorded with her first married surname, though she had remarried after Richard's death – The tombstone of Richard and Charlotte Lee in Higher St Budeaux churchyard. Charlotte had married Thomas Cross before she died.

Richard and Charlotte's move from a Moortown farm to the dockyard – Richard and Charlotte Lee moved in the 1850s from agricultural work at Moortown, outside Moretonhampstead, to St Budeaux, where Richard got work in Devonport dockyard.

The farmer fined for overgrown hedges – Robert Harris of

Mariansleigh, reported in the *South Molton Gazette*, 24.12.1887.

The murder in the house next door to the Days – An unconfirmed memory of being told that a murder had taken place in a house my parents later moved into.

Advertisement of farm sale – Sale of the stock and implements of Trittencott, Mariansleigh, Devon, 1901, *South Molton Gazette.*

The church of St Michael the Archangel in Moortown – St Andrews church, Moretonhampstead.

The find of gold in the Leigh Valley and at Puck's Acre – In 1997 gold was found in potentially commercial quantities in the Crediton Trough in Devon. The first indication was minute particles of gold in local streams.

The Young Farmers' sponsored tractor pull across the moor – In August 2012 Chagford Young Farmers hauled a tractor across Dartmoor from Princeton to Moretonhampstead in aid of Macmillan Cancer Relief.

The Avery family who ran a tannery in Moortown – The Nosworthy family of Moretonhampstead.

Suzie's tinner ancestor Barnabas Avery – Matthias Nosworthy Gent of Moretonhampstead appears in 1691 in a List of Tynners for the stannary of Chagford. Devon Record Office: Moretonhampstead 2961/PM 4.

The stannary jail at Fullingford – Lydford Castle, Devon.

The tinners' parliament – In Devon, the tinners' parliament met at Crockern Tor on Dartmoor.

Moortown as a centre of Dissent – Moretonhampstead.

The market hall in Moortown square – The Yarn Market at Dunster.